D1096729

NO GOOD ABOUT GOODBYE

CT Liotta

ROT GUT PULP

Philadelphia - Ha Long Bay
London

Rot Gut Pulp: An Imprint of St. Ire & Sons Publishing, St. Petersburg, FL

No Good About Goodbye
Copyright © 2021 by CT Liotta

All rights reserved. No portion of this book may be reproduced in any form without permission from the publisher, except as permitted by U.S. copyright law. For permissions contact: StIrePress@gmail.com

All characters and corporations or establishments appearing in this work are fictitious. Any resemblance to real persons, living or dead, is purely coincidental.

Library of Congress Control Number: 2021915947
ISBN: 978-1-955394-02-4
Cover Illustration & Design by Malinda Dekker
Typography by Corliss Wilborne

Rot Gut Pulp. *Entertainment, Not Genius.* ™
Twitter: @rotgutpulp

21 22 23 24 25 GN/DN 10 9 8 7 6 5 4 3 2 1

First Edition

For my parents, Jim & Ellen,
who were never authoritarian.

No Good About Goodbye is a work of fiction. It is not intended to be an authentic depiction of lived experiences, and may contain difficult subjects and questionable characterizations, tropes, themes, and language.

Not everybody will see themselves or their communities reflected, and it may be a poor fit for readers seeking solicitous representation.

Sensitivities vary from person to person, and neither the author nor the publisher offer further advisories.

—

A snippet or two of dialogue in this text hint at the stories of my youth. Out of respect for the authors and copyright law, I'd like to acknowledge Ian Fleming's *Live and Let Die* (Macmillan, 1954), *Diamonds are Forever* (Macmillan, 1956), *From Russia With Love* (Macmillan, 1957), and John LeCarre's *The Tailor of Panama* (Knopf, 1996).

1: ALGIERS

On a Tuesday night in late August—four hours and fifty-eight minutes after the sun fell beneath Raïs Hamidou and Pointe Pascade in Algiers, Algeria—a battered, white SUV swerved from an access road and tore through an otherwise quiet olive grove near Houari Boumediene Airport. Branches snapped and scraped against dented fenders and fell under tires that upended the earth. Cracks of gunfire followed. The driver, a fifteen-year-old boy, wore a black Pittsburgh Pirates baseball cap, and a weathered pair of Adidas Sambas.

He shifted into fourth gear and stomped the accelerator. His brother had been teaching him to drive, and he did not have a feel for the clutch. At five-foot-three, he was short for his age and had difficulty reaching the pedals.

He calculated the likelihood of a calamitous encounter with a tractor or irrigation wheel and turned his lights off. With luck, the ordered rows of trees would continue to the horizon. The suspension protested against the uneven terrain.

Beside the boy sat his mother, unconscious, unmistakable in resemblance. The night air caught her hair, and with it, lingering notes of Shalimar and vodka. In the cup holder between them was a SIG Sauer P226. The boy eyed it and pressed the de-cocker, fearful it might discharge in the shaking vehicle.

The rear bumper fell off. "*Cosa facciamo ora, Deena?*" asked the boy, filled with uncertainty. "What now?" He liked to call her by her first name because it irritated her.

The rearview mirror reflected the pinpoint headlamps of a pursuing Jeep. There were three rapid flashes of gunfire. "Flash-to-bang," he muttered, remembering what his brother had said. He counted the seconds until the distant report of the guns sounded over the engine. Three seconds. Three seconds times 330 meters per second put the Jeep a kilometer away. Given wind direction and velocity, terrain, elevation, circular error probable, and handicap while firing from a moving vehicle, he knew he was beyond range.

A bullet ripped through the back window with a startling crack. The glass fell from its frame and the remains of the rearview mirror spun onto the dashboard. Air rushed in.

"This was a terrible idea," said the boy.

The grove ended near a traffic cloverleaf. He steered onto National Highway 5 and pointed the vehicle toward the city. The engine light flickered. He shifted into fifth gear.

Explosions lit the sky over El Biar *daïra*, which blazed orange and black and shimmered with haze. Tanks and troops moved through the streets. A cyclone of spark and ash blew through the roof of the United States Embassy. The boy crashed through a security gate and into a concrete barrier. Guards hung dead from the window of a booth.

Inside the building, alarm strobes flashed. Bodies of embassy personnel lay dead on the mosaic tile floor. Blood covered the walls. A lifeless hand held a wet bandana. The boy seized it and used it to shield his nose and mouth. Helicopters flew low. The ground shook, and scorching heat changed direction without warning.

He made his way through dense smoke. Near a room containing the embassy's central computer server, he moved to avoid collision with a half-dozen men. They held machine guns and wore *shalmar kameez* and red balaclavas. The boy hid behind an ornamental Ficus.

One man's hair fixative stank under his hood. A coil of wire hung from his right hand, and he used his left to eat dates from his pocket—an odd time for hunger.

The group's commander, a brace on his wrist, twisted and capped wires on a duct-taped bomb made from a rusted oil drum. He shouted for a detonator.

The man with the dates searched his pockets without success. By the time he turned to see if the detonator had fallen out near the Ficus, the boy had escaped through the smoke.

A gunship fired into the far end of the building, answered by distant screaming. A section of the roof collapsed and a cloud of dust and embers rose.

The boy stopped at a door in the corridor. On a plate outside was his brother's name: *Erik Racalmuto, Public Diplomacy.* His brother, ten years older at age 25, had followed Deena into a career with the State Department. Their offices were two doors apart.

He tested the doorknob for heat. It was cold. Somebody stopped him from turning it and pinned his opposite wrist to his back. When he twisted his head, his dark eyes met those of his brother.

"Hello, Erik," said the boy, relaxing.

"Ian," his brother nodded.

Erik Racalmuto, dressed in impeccable high-end casuals and a summer blazer, rotated the knob. The door swung forward under its own weight and stopped. He pointed to a gossamer string and cut it with a pocket knife. Had Ian forced the door, an improvised explosive would have taken his legs.

A blast of air met them. Explosives had torn away the exterior walls and ceilings of the offices aligning the corridor. The rooms stood like Roman ruins, intact but for their open view of the courtyard and the night sky.

"Where's Natalie?" asked Ian.

"Disabling the central computer," replied Erik. "We're cooked if outside actors gain access. She's overdue by three minutes. Is mom here?"

"In the car. East courtyard. We have to get her to a hospital, but she sent me here for her phone, first. It's on her desk."

Erik's face drained of color.

Ian continued, "She thought it would be secure in the embassy! Is her office locked?"

Erik raised an eyebrow and nudged his head toward her office, two rooms away. Through twisted steel and gaps in concrete, the phone glowed on Deena's desk. Ian shrugged.

"The six guys in the hallway aren't Islamic State," said Erik, helping Ian move rubble.

"Private military contractors with Nightwater," replied Ian. "They're playing dress-up with their *shalmars* and hoods. Speaking English. I recognize two—Winter and Kitteridge. Winter always smells like Murray's Pomade, and Kitteridge forgot to remove his carpal tunnel glove. Winter was using his left hand to eat. No Arab would do that. Anyway, their bomb won't work. I picked Winter's pocket and stole his detonator." He held the blasting cap.

Erik smiled. "I picked *Kitteridge's* pocket and stole his trigger." He withdrew a small remote control—a stick with a red plunger that would signal the detonator to explode.

"They're idiots," said Ian. "I was outside Winter's office last week. He doesn't know how to calibrate the laser on his Beretta. It has a 38-degree offset at ten yards. He only scares me if he's aiming somewhere else. You should have heard what his commander said when he found out."

Erik laughed. "Everyone in the embassy knows by now."

Footsteps drew near. The brothers hid behind a door as a pair of men passed, their hands filled with dynamite and curly wire.

Erik rotated the bezel on a Breitling watch, took the blasting cap, and handed Ian the remote control. "Get the phone. I'll find Natalie. In six minutes, get outside, grab your balls and hit the remote." Erik took off into the smoke-filled corridor. "Meet at the car."

"Fallback?" asked Ian.

"Security keeps a pair of motorcycles in the basement. Do you remember how to ride?"

"Do *you*?"

Erik smiled. "Don't let that phone fall into anybody else's hands. No dilly-dallying. *Veloci! Andiamo!*"

"You sound like mom."

"We have to hurry. This shirt is Fendi, and the ash is ruining it."

2: SORGHUM

Ian squeezed through bent rebar and entered Deena's office. He unplugged her phone and tucked it away. On a mouse pad at her desk, a curious Zippo lighter with a letter *R* engraved in mother-of-pearl reflected a flare in the sky. He held it between his finger and his thumb and pocketed it, too. Atop a cabinet behind him—next to a bowling trophy, an old Dictaphone, and a soda siphon—a stately metal cremation urn the size of a cookie jar stood upright.

"Those ashes are your great-aunt Judy's," Deena once told him. "Nobody in the family wants them. She was a profound alcoholic. Legend has it that when it came time to cremate her, the funeral director touched the glowing end of a matchstick to her remains and they went up like a tinderbox."

Ian smirked.

The office door broke open, jarring his thoughts. The men with red hoods pointed machine guns at him.

He raised his hands.

A tall, serpentine man with a white Borsalino hat, long blond hair, and a crimson necktie pushed to the front of the gunmen. His shoes clicked as he walked. Richard Fenzel was the deputy chief of mission at the embassy—the ambassador's second in command. He spoke as though someone had wired his jaw, and he refused to chew gum. His administrative assistant spread rumors he slept with a mouth guard at night to prevent bruxism.

"Ian Racalmuto," said Fenzel. "Running errands for mother?"

"Hullo, Richard," said Ian. "What's this about?"

Fenzel took Deena's phone from Ian's pocket and plugged a small device into the bottom. It flashed from red to blue and the phone unlocked.

"Sorghum," said Fenzel.

"Sorghum?"

"The fifth most precious cereal grain in the world. American farmers sell a billion dollars of sorghum to China every year—or did until the Chinese government levied tariffs. Now, our sorghum rots in bins in the heartland as our farmers go bankrupt. The Chinese have our farmers' *balls* clenched in their *fists* and they're *squeezing them gray!*" He crushed his fingers together and shook his fist.

Ian bent forward and shifted in place. "Sorghum," he mumbled.

Fenzel returned his attention to Deena's phone and thumbed through its contents. "Weak leadership, Ian. Weak leadership is why America depends on China. Our State Department discards my advice—sound advice based on a consummate understanding of geopolitics—to appease Peking. It's but a matter of time before the Chinese People's Liberation Army grows strong enough to overcome our borders and pillage our sorghum. Mark my words, they will."

Ian raised an eyebrow. "Peking?"

Fenzel fixated on the phone. "Mmm."

"So you'll defend American sorghum from Chinese invaders by raiding the embassy in Algeria?" asked Ian. "How?"

Droplets of spit jumped from Fenzel's mouth when he answered. "I will launch a cyberattack using the security codes on your mother's smartphone and bring down the great firewall of China from this embassy's computer server. All of China will have uncensored, open internet. The Chinese Ministry of State Security will see the cyberattack coming from a U.S. interest, interpret it as an act of aggression, and bombard our fleet in the South China Sea. It will start the inevitable, cathartic war between our countries that will shape the world order for the next hundred years. We must fight while we can win."

"Why would my mom have codes on her phone?" asked Ian. "She's a consular. She fixes passports and visas."

"Is that what she tells you?" replied Fenzel. He scanned Deena's desk. "You didn't perchance see a cigarette lighter here, did you? A Zippo? Mother of pearl? Letter R?"

Ian grew quiet. "Diplomatic Security will hang you by the neck."

"Diplomatic Security will never know it was me," said Fenzel. "When I finish, I intend to destroy this embassy with a bomb."

"You're using a political uprising in Algeria to raid your own embassy, launch a cyberattack using my mom's phone and the computer server, start a war with China, and wipe your tracks clean with a bomb?" asked Ian.

Fenzel smiled.

"I hope you have a contingency plan. Natalie McLauren is

here. The embassy computer server may be less operational than you think."

"Natalie McLauren?" asked Fenzel. He motioned toward a man in the back. He rolled Natalie McLauren's decapitated head, and it stopped at Ian's feet. Her face wore a look of surprise. Blood leaked from the neck.

Ian turned away, sickened.

Fenzel looked at the man with the carpal tunnel glove. "Signal my superior. Let him know we have the device." He turned to Ian. "Who else is here?"

"I'm alone," said Ian.

Fenzel dropped Deena's phone in an outer suit pocket, walked to Ian, and studied his face. He slapped the boy with a sharp backhand.

"Liar," he said. "For you, honesty has always been malleable when the truth is unsuitable." He removed his necktie, wrapped it around Ian's neck, and drew it tight. "Again, I ask who is with you?"

"Erik." Ian flailed.

"Where is he now?"

Ian gagged. "Destroying the computer mainframe before you can start your war."

"How?" asked Fenzel.

Ian gasped and squirmed and could not speak.

"How?!" Fenzel repeated. He loosened the tie.

"With your bomb," Ian said, sucking in air as stars flashed.

"Another lie," Fenzel grunted. "He has no trigger. Anyway, it would cause a delay at most. I can use your mother's phone to implement my plan from Main State in Washington, same as here."

"Then you're screwed from both ends," Ian croaked. "I

have the trigger. I also picked your pocket and recovered mom's phone."

Fenzel searched his pocket. It was empty. His eyes moved to Ian's hand, which gripped the trigger.

"Do I press the red thing with my thumb?" asked Ian.

Fenzel's eyes grew wide in horror. He shouted as Ian depressed the plunger. The walls disintegrated, and a terrific roar knocked them to the ground.

3: BAGGAGE CLAIM

TUESDAY.

An alarm blasted through baggage claim B at Philadelphia International Airport, and a nearby carousel rattled to life.

Ian had arrived ten minutes earlier, and the sudden noise triggered a rush of adrenaline. He gripped a woman next to him to keep his balance. The woman shook him off.

"Sorry," he said, releasing her.

She grunted.

He had arrived forty-five minutes earlier on a flight that made a clumsy landing through drizzle and fog. Four weeks in a German hospital subtracted ten pounds from his already-thin frame. Faded bruises dotted his face, and twenty-five stitches itched under his Pirates cap. His backpack rested at his feet.

A parade of luggage surfaced from the basement on an ancient conveyor and spun on an oval track. He lifted suitcases and packages belonging to absent family. His mother, according to a grief counselor who visited his bed in Landstuhl, did not survive the coup. They cremated her like

Aunt Judy, but lost the ashes. Erik had disappeared—consumed, they said, by the fire.

Ian's father, Cardiff—a dentist who did charity work in developing countries—stayed in Algeria to speak with attorneys and authorities. He placed Ian in charge of transporting a prized Louisville Slugger signed by Willie Stargell. Ian reached for it on the belt, but missed and waited for it to come back around. Most of their goods would arrive by sea in an intermodal crate.

A garish Louis Vuitton garment bag passed six times before a middle-aged Indian man recovered it. As the man turned to leave, he focused past Ian and grinned. "Mario!"

Ian closed his eyes and exhaled. His grandfather's shadow crossed his shoulder.

"Doc!" the old man's voice boomed from behind. "You were right! It *was* my prostate! I'm not bothering with the pills, though." He reduced his voice to a whisper. "I have leather shoes."

Ian gritted his teeth and stared forward. The men cackled. They spoke a moment longer, then parted ways. Ian would never look at a walnut the same way again.

"How long have you been in my wake?" Ian said, at last.

"Long enough to have killed you with a garrote," said Mario.

Ian rubbed his neck. "It takes longer than you might think."

"I've been calling for an hour," said Mario. "*Nessuna risposta.* Where's your phone?"

Ian threw his hands toward the conveyor as it spit luggage. "Security made me put my phone in my coat and my coat in my valise. This airline always loses my bags." He turned at last.

Mario Racalmuto's father had been Sicilian, and his mother, Kenyan, so he was—as far as America cared—an old, black man. Mario's late wife was a pale *Trentina* from Vallagarina. Their son married Deena Ricciotti, a Calabrese. By the time Ian was born, he looked nothing like Mario. Nobody had to counsel him about how to behave if stopped by law enforcement, though Deena once suggested he run for his life from the *politsiya* in Moscow.

Mario's remaining hair grayed under a gentleman's cap. His mustache remained ageless. A bowling shirt tucked into tweed pants clung to a soft midsection that hung over his waistline. He smelled of *Il Frutotto* citron soap. In his younger days, he walked with Ian's distinct gait before injury caused a limp.

The two embraced. Mario tipped into sentiment and dried his eyes with a cloth handkerchief. "Let me look at you. You're too thin. *Andiamo al ristorante per i cavatelli stasera.* You've grown. How tall are you? Five-five?"

"Five-three. Don't overestimate my height."

"Short men cause all the trouble in the world. Are you still picking pockets?" he chattered. "Lift your cap. How's your head? Did the trauma turn your hair white?"

"I'm fine, Grandpop. *Ora basta.* My hair's still black." Ian produced Mario's billfold. "And yes. I'm still picking pockets."

"Open it," said Mario. The wallet contained shredded newspaper and expired video store cards. A fake driver's license with Mario's picture identified him as Lando Raab.

"You carry a decoy?"

"Back in the day, I'd stuff it with pocket litter and

dezinformatsiya. There's no better disguise than what another person thinks they've discovered about you."

"You did this when you were a secret agent?" asked Ian.

"Secret agents don't exist. I sell suits at Wanamakers," replied Mario. "Besides, I would have been a spy runner, not an agent."

Ian lifted his hands. "Come on!"

He was certain Mario had once been a spy. For over a decade, his grandfather alluded to an adventurous past and then said nothing more of it. "Anyway, how good could you have been if your career ended when an orange fell on your head in Sorrento?"

"It's always the little things," said Mario. He tugged at a red-and-white-striped *unaccompanied minor* sticker on Ian's shirt. It fell to the floor with no resistance. "You removed this already. Did you imbibe on the flight?"

"Lufthansa had Chinon. France under-cropped Cabernet Franc grapes two years ago. Everyone knows it was an outstanding vintage. I couldn't pass it up." Mario opened his mouth to reply, but Ian extended a finger. "I can't be a sommelier someday if I have to wear a kid-sticker. Only a fool ignores opportunity."

"No flight attendant would serve you, sticker or not."

"I nicked it from the beverage cart." He withdrew a fresh bottle from his pocket and gifted it to Mario.

The old man examined it. "They vinify Cabernet Franc for blends. You hate blends."

"They vinify Chinon alone in the Loire Valley."

Mario stood in silence a moment longer. "What kid wants to be a wine steward? Can't you follow basketball?" He waved Ian off. "Your nose is too small to be a sommelier."

The conveyor spun for twenty minutes while Ian and Mario caught up. Ian's voice differed from his grandfather's. His Italian was perfect, but his English fused accents learned around the world. He merged British and American dialects, rolled an occasional r, and mispronounced words. He hated his patois. Worse was that, like Mario, he flailed his hands when he spoke. Deena would sometimes say that to silence the two, she might cut off their arms.

"Sorghum?" asked Mario.

"It's the fifth most popular cereal grain in the world," replied Ian. "It could start a war with Peking."

"Peking?" Mario raised an eyebrow. "Where is Fenzel now?"

"Dead."

"They recovered his body?" asked Mario.

"No, they found three of his teeth."

"Teeth aren't vital," said Mario.

"Of course they are," said Ian. "He won't be able to chew things, and he'll die." He tilted his head. "Even if he survived and still wanted to start his war, he'd have to find mom's phone and fly to D.C. to activate it. I hid the phone inside Aunt Judy's funeral urn. Diplomatic security recovered it while I was in hospital. It's out of my hands."

"You're certain they have it?" asked Mario.

"They said they would handle it," said Ian.

"Shit," Mario groaned under his breath. A blue suitcase appeared. "*Ecco qua!*" he said.

"No," said Ian. "Mine has a Pan Am logo on it."

Mario wheeled a cart toward them and stacked the bags Ian had pulled. A glittery tag on a steamer chest revealed

Deena's address in her script, and Mario's eyes saddened. "You shouldn't be the one to do this."

"Someone has to," replied Ian, "though I'd rather be with dad."

"Algiers is too dangerous."

"Algiers has always been too dangerous!" Ian erupted, throwing his hands up. Mario stepped back, surprised by the outburst. Ian lowered his voice. "*Non voglio pensarci.* Erik's missing and dad's sitting alone in a hotel room with a stuffed shirt convincing him he's dead. I can hear the conversation now. *Erik is gone. It's a recovery, Cardiff, not a rescue. Little Ian has an undeveloped frontal cortex and uses denial to cope with grief.*" He dug his hands in his pockets and settled back.

"Are you in denial?" asked Mario.

"I would deny it if I were," said Ian. "I've developed the good sense to shut my mouth when adults think one way and I think another. *Let's discuss it*, they say. Discussion only ever means debate. I'm sick of debating. I'll say whatever people want me to say in public if it makes it easier to be who I am in private."

"No man can wear one face to himself and another to the multitude without finally getting bewildered as to which may be the true." Mario winked. "That's Nathaniel Hawthorne. Bet you didn't know that. In spycraft they call it *the wilderness of mirrors.*"

Ian raised an eyebrow. "Erik's out there. I have, at best, seven days to locate him before the trail turns to ice. It's not just about finding him—living with him abroad is the only way to get my life back on track. Philly is perdition. No offense, but I shouldn't be here."

The bag carousel stopped. Mario pointed to a stuffy office

for lost bags, and Ian gathered his backpack. They approached an elderly black woman with enormous glasses. Ian pushed past Mario, a claim check wedged in his passport. A television on the wall played cable news.

The woman stopped him. "The gentleman with the cart was ahead of you."

Such situations were an irritating mainstay of his childhood.

"This is my grandson," said Mario. "I have a comparative MRI of our brains at home, if you don't believe me. The similarities are striking." He ended with a brisk wink.

Ian stared at him and shook his head.

The woman softened, ensorcelled by the old man's tone. "Where are you coming from?"

"Frankfurt," said Ian, directing his attention to her, "though I cleared customs in Atlanta. I'm missing a blue leather case with a white Pan Am logo."

She thrust a laminated card toward him, had him point to a picture of a suitcase that looked like his, and tapped numbers into an ancient computer. "China's still cleaning up from the wet market virus and baggage is slow. The whole system has been on the fritz." She dialed a phone beside her.

The television droned. The bombastic American president, Andreas Espinoza, gave a press conference about the Algerian embassy and blamed "radical, anti-American Islamists." Questions turned to the embassy's ambassador, Caleb Reid.

"He's resting in D.C.," said the president. "Beekeeping, if you call that relaxing. With the gloves and the hat." Espinoza drew a circle around his head. The press corps laughed.

Mario tapped Ian and pointed to the television. "Do you

know the ambassador?"

"He didn't keep bees in Algiers. He stunk of cologne and cigarettes and had a voice that sounded like phlegm," said Ian. "Reid fancied himself a cowboy and carried a LeMat revolver—an old Confederate pistol from the Civil War. Mom hated him."

Espinoza continued to deliver extemporaneous remarks from the dais, calling China a third-world pigsty. "It's a petri dish for diseases like the one that melted people's lungs. Did they create the disease in a lab to kill Americans? I don't know. We're looking into it. My message to the people of China remains the same: don't come here until you've cleaned yourselves up. Don't make people sick. It may not be politically correct to say that, but is it unreasonable?"

The news went to commercial.

The woman at the desk dropped her phone back in its cradle. "Your suitcase blew up."

Ian stood at attention. "It blew up?"

The woman handed him a complimentary toiletry bag and a $25 Visa gift card. "I don't know what else to tell you."

4: NEW NORMALS

"Bags blow up all the time," said Ian. "It's not like someone's out to kill me."

Mario Racalmuto drove a black Lincoln Continental over the Platt Bridge into South Philadelphia. He adjusted the speed of the windshield wipers and cleared his throat.

Ian said, "I need a new coat and a working phone." He played with the Zippo he found on Deena's desk. Why had Fenzel asked for it? He clicked the lid. "Did mom smoke without my knowing? I can't imagine it. She didn't have an ashtray in sight, so she would have had to flick into Aunt Judy's urn or something."

"Never," said Mario. "She would say smoking is for the lower classes. We haven't talked about Deena. I'm sorry about what happened. I can't imagine what you must feel."

"I don't feel anything. *È così.*" Ian traced the engraved letter R with his thumb. "Maybe numb is the new normal. Is that wrong?" He struck the lighter. It was out of fluid, and the flint was deficient.

"New normals take time to unfold. Grief visits in disguise. Let me know if you need me." He turned the radio down.

"You got into a fight with your best friend at school in Algeria. Cardiff wanted me to ask about it."

"It was a misunderstanding."

"You knocked out his tooth."

"It makes no difference. I'll never see him again."

"He won't be able to chew things and he'll die," said Mario.

Ian shifted in his seat. After a few moments of listening to the water under the tires, he said, "When you talk to people, they fall in love. When I talk to people, things fall apart."

"Do you want to discuss it?" asked Mario.

"You mean debate it?" Ian replied.

Mario stared at the road ahead. "I set up your bedroom."

"Dad's old room, in the back of the house?"

"The middle room. We need Cardiff's bedroom for storage. Your family's stuff arrives at the shipyard on Saturday, and everything the moving company doesn't warehouse will go there."

"The middle room is tiny. Where will I put my fermenter?" asked Ian.

"In the basement," said Mario.

"It will draw gnats," said Ian.

"The carbon monoxide from the furnace will kill them," Mario replied.

Ian removed a map of Algeria from his backpack and drew a crude 50-kilometer radius around Algiers in red ink. He wrote *7 days* beside it.

At 4 PM, the drizzle became a steady rain. It grew dark enough for street lamps to illuminate.

Ian and Mario arrived in Lower Moyamensing, a

neighborhood where Italian laborers had constructed long rows of connected two-story houses a century ago. No gap existed between them, and each had unique brickwork and trim. Statues of the Virgin Mary and St. Francis decorated the windows.

Mario parked on Tree Street. He cut his motor, rushed into the rain, and limped under a yellow fiberglass awning. "Get the bags," he shouted before climbing a small flight of stairs and disappearing inside his house. After a few seconds, his hand reappeared. His thumb stabbed at a button on a fob, and the lights on his car flashed. The horn chirped, and the trunk popped open.

Ian grumbled. The rain soaked his clothing. He heaved the bags out and shoved them under the awning. Deena's steamer chest refused to budge. A teenage girl riding a skateboard along the opposite sidewalk slowed her roll as he struggled. She was tall and black and unbothered by the downpour, her hair wrapped in a plastic shopping bag.

"You need a hand," she shouted over the rain. It wasn't a question, and she didn't wait for a reply. She upended her board, crossed the street, grabbed the chest, and helped Ian hoist it atop the steps.

"Thank you, girl with the plastic bag on her head!" said Ian.

She grinned. "I love the rain, but it took me by surprise. The pH of Philly rain turns my hair to dryer lint. What else do you have?"

"Just my backpack." He held it up. "I had a valise, but it blew up."

"Weird," she said.

"Right? How does a valise blow up?"

"I mean, who says *valise* in the twenty-first century?" she asked.

He turned red.

"What's your name?"

"Stephen."

"You're Ian Racalmuto, of Frankfurt am Main," said the girl.

Ian's brow furrowed. He looked down at an airline tag on his backpack and removed it with a sharp yank.

"Too late," said the girl. "Stephen. Sounds like Ian. Smart sobriquet. You'd turn around if somebody called it out in a room. But why lie?" she asked.

"I try to be cautious. What's your name?"

She smiled, backed up, and made a peace sign. "I am cautious. I'll see you again soon, Stephen." She dropped her board and skated away.

Rain fell from Ian's hair and he waved thanks.

5: A DUTY TO BE RED

Ian closed the heavy front door behind him and looked around Mario's tiny house. He spent many holidays there with his family. Plastic covered the furniture. Faucets dripped, and water entered the basement through a crack in the roof. The stairs were narrow and steep. The room was still.

"This is the first time I've experienced silence since leaving Algeria," said Ian, pushing his luggage into the living room. "Did you notice the girl that helped me with mom's trunk?"

"In this weather? What did she look like?"

"Tall. black. a little older than me. Bag on her head."

"Did you get her name?"

"She got mine."

"The lady next door has a doorbell camera, but she's away on business," said Mario. "We can watch the feed this weekend when she gets back into town. For now, take your stuff to your room. I just put a new bed up there."

Ian walked upstairs. His bedroom was an architectural afterthought, squeezed between the master bedroom in the front and a bathroom in the middle of the hallway. A queen bed, accessible only from the foot, touched three of the four walls. Two feet of floor separated the foot of the bed from a dresser and a closet. Atop the dresser sat a new television, an ancient Xbox, and a hardbound copy of Victoria James's *Wine Girl*—a gift from Mario.

Ian unpacked his father's Louisville Slugger, held it to his shoulder, and turned in a circle. There was no room to swing.

Mario had placed the catalog of classes for Boy's Preparatory School atop a folded blanket in the dresser. The rigid curriculum held students to Herculean standards, and Ian was already a month behind. His stomach churned looking at the pictures of boys with neckties reading Latin and building robots in the science lab. *Forging a new generation of leaders,* it touted. Many of Deena's colleagues went to fancy preparatory schools like this one. They were idiots, drunk on the idea that schools like Boy's Prep made them smart.

The bell schedule divided the day into eight periods and lunch. He inked lines above and below it with a fine-tip pen. If class started at 8 AM, he'd wake at 6 and leave home at 7:15; If class ended at 3, he'd be home at 4, barring extracurriculars. Homework would last from 6 to 9. That gave him an hour to drink wine and search for Erik before bed.

He looked again at the science lab picture, unsure where the robots stopped and the humans began. Barely a year ago, he had been in Berlin and Mumbai, dodging bullets and bombs with Erik and Deena. Now, his father said, he could have a safe, normal life.

He placed the baseball bat in his closet and tacked his Algeria map to the wall. He stuck a pin through the town of Tablat. "*Dove sei, Erico?*" he whispered. "Here's the deal. I'll get you out of there if you get me out of here. I can't be in a place I'm expected to be normal. It won't work."

What was Erik doing now? Moving between towns? Bloating in the Sahara? He'd likely gone silent—crushed his phone, abandoned his computer, and moved to a safe house. "If a killer thinks you're dead," he once instructed, "don't argue with her."

By age ten—fueled by Mario's nonsense, according to Deena—Erik Racalmuto had gained a voluminous knowledge of espionage, tradecraft, and analog spy methods lost to a digital world of computers and drones. When Ian was born, Erik made his brother his agent.

Ian enjoyed the difficult aspects of cold war-era intelligence gathering. He had patience to wait, listen and communicate at essential times. By the time he was eight, he had developed an instinct for details and his talent for picking pockets and making small objects disappear. It made him precocious and unbearable. Cardiff reminded him to play with other kids instead of listening to grown-ups having grown-up conversations. Ian liked the grown-up conversations better.

Ian walked past the bathroom, into Cardiff's old bedroom. His dad's high school yearbooks had blurry photos taken with cheap cameras in a time before digital photography. Basketball trophies decorated a nightstand beside a picture of Cardiff with Deena. Cardiff looked like Erik. Deena looked like him. They were Ian's age in the photo. Cardiff was bent at the waist with his arms outstretched like an airplane. Deena clung to his back, laughing. She wore a class ring he had never seen.

He made a mental note to ask her what became of it, then caught himself.

"So life just goes on, huh?"

He returned to his bedroom and placed the picture beside the television. Could some ethereal piece of Deena hear or see him? He closed his eyes and listened. Rain drummed against the window. He could remember her laugh and the cadence of her speech. Might it fade in time, leaving him with less than he had already?

He sat on his bed. Without a phone, he could not text friends. Without *friends,* he could not text friends. He had lost dozens of numbers and hundreds of pictures when his phone exploded. Of those numbers and pictures, though, who truly knew him? Only one—and that person hated him.

Mario had been correct. The best disguises are peoples' assumptions. What happens, though, when people see through a disguise? When a cover's blown and nobody likes the person beneath it?

The refrigerator hummed in the kitchen. Mario shuffled to the base of the steps. "*Allora,*" he said. "There's a soccer game tomorrow night at the high school around the corner. I thought we'd walk over."

"The forecast calls for heavy rain tomorrow, same as today," Ian shouted from his room.

"The games draw a crowd, even in the rain," said Mario. "We can wear ponchos."

"I'm not wearing a poncho," Ian replied.

"The school has a beautiful new stadium with a snack bar," said Mario.

Ian groaned. "That school is like a prison yard, only without barking dogs and concertina wire. How did they get a new stadium?"

"They got a grant."

"And they spent it on sports?"

"Not entirely," said Mario. "The principal got a new Mercedes Benz, as well. Anyway, the snack bar is great. The cheesesteak is excellent."

"Cheesesteak is a mess," said Ian. "The beef will fall from the back of the roll and ruin my shirt. Besides, Erik needs me. Every day without finding him is another lost."

Mario cleared his throat. "Come downstairs. Have a glass of pinot and consider my offer."

A long pause.

"Noir or Grigio?" Ian asked at last.

"A wine's first duty is to be red," said Mario. "It's Shatterhand. Fruit-forward and full-bodied, with notes of currant and plum."

"You win, old man." Ian walked downstairs. He uncorked the bottle with the deftness of a professional steward, poured a glass, and let it rest. "I hate soccer. I don't want to deal with people, and I don't want to wear a poncho."

"Humor me? You can forgo the poncho."

Ian drummed his fingers. "What time's the game?"

"Six," said Mario. "In the meantime, we'll get you some new threads at the thrift and you can get to know The Professor."

"The Professor?"

An ancient, fat tuxedo cat with an opaque right eye peered around the corner and screeched a meow.

6: WILL XIANG

WEDNESDAY.

"Will sucks, coach! Why is he on the pitch during a regular season game?" Craig Brooks screamed at Coach Sylvester Osbourne, a graying man in his late 40s. He pointed at fifteen-year-old William Xiang, who sat on the bench as rain pooled on the soccer field at Southeastern Philadelphia High School. Mud streaked a vinyl banner that read *Home of the Marauders.*

The old coach closed his eyes, nodded, and gestured downward with his hands. "Everybody gets game time at least once a season, Craig."

"Substitutions are for the end of the game, when it doesn't matter! He fucked up the first half!"

"Language, Craig!"

"He has no skill! He stands on the grass like a pottery soldier!" He drew close and spoke through gritted teeth. "You expect him to think fast? He's Asian. He can't make decisions without his parents' permission."

"Let it go, Craig," said the coach.

Craig turned to Will and gnawed at a mouth guard.

"You're in America. Think for yourself."

Over three horrifying minutes, Will lost control of the ball twice. He fell. The crowd groaned. He recovered, only to pass to an opposing player.

Will bit the inside of his cheek. "I'll make up for it—"

"You'll sit your short ass down the rest of the season and not open your mouth!" shouted Craig. "If you want to do some good, cough on their forward and melt his lungs."

"Enough, Craig!" replied Osbourne.

"Or what?" asked Craig.

Craig—a 16-year-old junior with sandy blond hair, an attractive grin, and a statuesque German-Irish build—was a rising star in U.S. Boy's National Soccer. His parents had enrolled him in private training at age four and spent thousands making him competitive.

The school slipped money to Craig's short-tempered dad, Paul, who pretended Coach Osbourne discovered and trained him. The fabricated rags-to-riches story kept the grant money flowing, though Osbourne was now under pressure to deliver a winning season as part of a five-year renewal.

"This is the last time Will will be on the field, right?" asked Craig.

"He's starting Saturday," said Osbourne. "Zeke Diakite's sister passed away—"

"Scouts are grading my performance on Saturday!" Craig shouted. He punched a water cooler hard enough to tip it, then stuck his finger in Osbourne's face. "I look weak if *I* can't solve the problems *that* faggot creates. I have too much to think about on Saturday. Do *not* play him."

Osbourne returned the cooler upright, and Craig walked away.

Will's eyes welled. He sorted through a deck of playing cards from his backpack and performed a series of flawless trick shuffles.

How many people had witnessed Craig calling him a faggot and telling him to cough on people? He glanced up, then down at his cards again. Twenty-two. Twenty-three, counting his parents' landlord, who stood at the fence and flapped a prosthetic left hand, trying to catch Will's attention.

Will took a breath and turned to Craig's best friend, Daequon Griggs. Daequon was 16 but looked 20—lean, muscular, and a foot taller than Will. He had a voice like a bassoon and wiry facial hair. His athletic skill was beneath Craig's, but good enough to attract notice from local colleges.

"I'm not gay," Will said to him. "I'm Christian. Ask Rebekkah Batiste. She's been giving me advice about homecoming—"

"I don't care, shorty," Daequon interrupted. He spat on the ground, slid down the bench, pushed short dreadlocks back with both hands, and wiped the rain from a pair of plastic glasses.

Rebekkah Batiste, a junior with long auburn hair and gold earrings, had dated Craig since eighth grade. They were going to homecoming together. She was on the court and had been a nominee for queen. She took pictures from the sideline with a camera that looked like a battleship cannon and posted them on the school's social media accounts. 25,000 people followed her. Parents loved her close, shallow-focused images of Craig leading the team to victory. In private, she AirDropped humiliating photos of Will to anybody with an open connection.

Craig's phone blew up with pictures. "Jesus Christ!" he

howled at Will from several yards away. "Are you crying? How do you think it makes us look?"

Will held his breath and twisted his face to appear angry.

"You look retarded! Stop!"

When the interval ended, Craig and Daequon stood. The old coach pointed Will to the bench.

"Go back to China, anchor baby," Craig said. "Do America a solid and screw things up there."

The soccer team loved Craig's virulent nickname for Will. They pinned a sketch of a jersey with the name *anchor baby* to his locker. He laughed and pretended it was affectionate, though it made his stomach bubble with nerves.

Will had been born in Shenzhen. When he was six months old, he moved to Philadelphia with his father, Eddie, and stepmother, Li. They had overstayed their tourist visas for a decade and a half. With no legal path to citizenship, he anchored nobody to the United States—least of all himself. He wouldn't know how to go back to China. He spoke neither Cantonese like both his parents nor Mandarin like his father. His English carried a thick South Philly accent. What would he eat? He loved peanut butter and hated ginger and craved cheese with hard, crusty bread. He wanted to see the National Parks and dreamed of camping and hiking and sandwiching marshmallows between graham crackers. Chinese immigrants at the school found him unrelatable. The American-born Chinese kids called him Will *Xiāngjiāo*—Will Banana. Yellow skin. White inside.

His landlord flapped his rubber hand again. Will made a jack of hearts disappear from the top of his deck and imagined dispensing with the man likewise.

The rain turned to drizzle. On the field, Craig latched on

to a clever throw-in, stormed down the right flank, and slotted the ball to tie the game. The crowd leaped to its feet. Play continued. The clock wound down. With seconds to go, Daequon stood open in scoring position. He picked his underwear free from his crotch. Osbourne signaled for Craig to pass, but Craig, winded from running, instead made a clumsy toe kick. It slow-rolled past the stretch of the goalkeeper and tapped the back of the net.

The team rushed the field and held Craig on their shoulders. He peeled off his shirt, flexed his abs to balance himself, and wiped his nose on his forearm.

Will shrunk and drank from an aluminum water bottle.

Craig found him behind the crowd. "Anchor baby!" he shouted, the team carrying him away. "Suck a dick!"

Two girls sheltering under the roof of a nearby snack bar held up their phones. "Hey!" one called.

Will pointed at himself, unsure whether she was speaking to him.

The girl nodded in the affirmative. "Can you move?" She waved her hand to the left.

Will stumbled sideways and swallowed hard. People brushed past him on either side.

The girls took pictures of Craig, who pointed to God in the sky and cheered.

A startling crash returned Will's attention to the snack bar, where a boy he did not know had collided with a wire garbage can and knocked it on its side. The boy balanced a cheesesteak in one hand and scrubbed a stain on his shirt with the other. A stream of water from an overflowing gutter fell into the sandwich, tipping it from his grasp.

"Watch it!" shouted the girls with the phones, jumping

away from the splattering beef and ketchup.

The boy screamed curses in Italian, struggled to return the can upright, threw the cheesesteak inside, and kicked a support column in frustration. His wet, black hair fell over half his face. He blew a jet of air upward to move it, caught Will observing him, and stared.

Will stumbled back, dropping his water bottle. He glanced away and retreated to the locker room.

Over the noise of a rattling industrial fan, Craig Brooks's veneration ceremony continued outside Southeastern's empty changing room. Craig had made the varsity soccer team his freshman year and loved showing off a letter jacket that now hung on a wooden peg. Will pulled the sleeve to examine the captain patch sewn to the breast.

Beside the varsity jacket, a teammate had taped a photograph of Craig flexing. He wore only tight briefs that emphasized imposing genitals.

Will stared at the photo and turned red. He would die if someone took a picture of him half-naked, even as a joke. Unlike Craig, he had almost no body hair and didn't work out at a gym. His muscle accumulated in his legs, which looked fat and exaggerated when he stretched his socks to his knees.

He sat on a low bench and removed his cleats, then tossed his lucky deck of cards in his backpack and withdrew a rolled tee shirt. He unfurled it, catching a pink, rhinestone-bedazzled flip phone hidden in the middle. It was a hand-me-down from his stepmother, who had called him three times during the game.

The outside door opened, filling the room with shouts and cheers of teammates. He stuffed the phone deep into one of his shoes, returned his shirt to his backpack, and rushed to the showers.

Nobody but him showered at school.

Steam filled the air. Against Will's chest was a small silver cross on a thin necklace. It had arrived in the mail with a postcard from a nun requesting a donation. He hoped it would shield him from evil like a talisman, but it never worked. Perhaps the nun needed the donation to activate it.

He scrubbed the peaks and troughs of acne, wishing it would clear. When he finished, somebody had stolen his towel. He waited until the bellowing and cursing and sounds of packing ended before emerging from the stall.

His backpack was open on the floor and a stream of warm piss crept from it toward a drain. His clean clothes dripped, and his deck of cards had disappeared. He tugged his dirty soccer uniform back over his wet skin and stepped outside to collect the water bottle he had dropped. Rain poured again.

The water bottle stood upright on a table under the snack bar where the boy with the cheesesteak had been standing.

His phone screeched like a hawk—his voicemail tone. Wednesday evenings were for church, and Li was likely reminding him to go. The news was more dire. "Come home immediately after the game," she said. "Something is wrong with daddy."

7: THE WILDERNESS OF MIRRORS

Mario Racalmuto joined Ian under the snack bar. "Had you worn your poncho, you wouldn't have cheesesteak all over your shirt," he said. "You're soaked through."

Ian nodded toward Craig, who continued to ride around on his teammates' shoulders in the distance. "Maybe I should have taken my shirt off, like that asshole."

They walked to the exit. Rowdy students collided with them on every side. "That game was a travesty," said Ian. "The team is like *Lord of the Flies*. If you brought me to this school so I can better appreciate my privilege, it worked. It's slum tourism."

Mario adjusted his plastic hood. "Your parents and I went to this school."

"It was different back then, I'm sure," said Ian. A football crashed next to him, and a boy with a neck tattoo who stunk of dried sweat shoved him out of the way, collected it, and ran off. Ian continued, "I saw the Boy's Prep catalog in my room. Do my credits transfer from Algiers? I don't want to repeat Latin."

Mario opened his mouth to respond, but a gruff middle-aged woman interrupted from across the crowd. "Lando!" she croaked.

"Lando?" Ian mouthed.

"Christ," Mario muttered through his teeth, "That's Carol. I helped her jump a car battery in a casino parking garage. I didn't want her to know my name." He grinned and waved, then pointed at Ian and yelled back. "My grandson. He starts school here tomorrow."

"Here in Philly," Ian elaborated as the woman nodded. "At Prep."

Mario continued grinning. "He's prepping to go to Southeastern." He whispered to Ian, "we can discuss this later."

"Got it, Lando." Ian winked and smiled. "I'll maintain cover." He yelled, "Go Marauders!"

Mario cleared his throat.

Ian's face went flat. "Wait—"

"I'll explain at home," said Mario.

"*Porco Dio!*" Ian screamed, throwing his hands to the sky. "You're serious?"

"Don't blow cover!" said Mario, waving him back. "Your Latin credits transfer."

"Latin? Students here can't read or write English! Who am I going to be friends with? The kid with the neck tattoo? The half-naked soccer captain with the reckless mouth?"

"A lot of pretty girls go to Southeastern," said Mario

"Jesus take the wheel!" screamed Ian. "Mom would shit!"

They walked home without a word between them. The rain became steady again, and they dove under Mario's yellow awning. Ian broke the silence. "I'm prepping to go to Southeastern? Is that like going to the state pen instead of

Penn State?"

Mario chuckled.

"It isn't funny! They'll tear me apart at Southeastern. You have to fix this."

"Prep didn't admit you," Mario said.

Ian's mouth hung open. He sat on the steps leading to the house. "You eat breakfast with the dean on Saturdays at the diner. He's your friend. You have *no* pull with him?"

"He heard you knocked out someone's tooth."

"How did he hear that?"

Mario fell silent.

"*Mi fa cagare!*" said Ian. "You told him?"

"It was a good story! We were laughing about it over flapjacks."

"It was a misunderstanding!" Ian slammed the palm of his hand into the wall beside him. His eyes shifted sideways into the street. "That diner's gross. I can't believe you still go."

"I steal the Sweet 'N Low packets off the table when nobody's looking. It's expensive."

Ian slouched and bit his knuckle.

Mario collected his mail and sat. "I'm normally grateful when you're quiet, but you're biting your knuckle. You're scheming."

"Finding Erik will require minimal adult supervision and a good amount of deception. Prep would never grant me the freedom. Will anybody at Southeastern know if I skip class?"

"I'll know."

"The adults at schools like Southeastern spend every minute of instruction time breaking up fights and putting out fires. It isn't like anyone will hold me to account as long as I'm quiet. It may be a perfect front," he said.

Mario uttered a soft hum. "Be mindful. Using the broken conditions at an underprivileged urban school as a backstop for personal goals isn't right."

"Who cares what's right?" Ian countered. "Subterfuge is about what's effective. Vulnerable people have been collateral damage since before Christ."

"Who taught you that?" asked Mario.

"Lando Raab."

Mario cleared his throat. "Your brother and your mother always tried to do what was right."

"Look where it got them."

Mario paused. "Young men like you seek to learn what they're capable of doing. Old men like me try to forget. What's good, what's true, what's fair and what's right are four unique questions that don't always share the same answer. The soccer team played fair. It was a true win and a good result. Did they do it right and did it matter?"

Ian could not purge from memory the Chinese kid on the field after the game, standing like someone had shot his horse from under him—nor could he forget the team captain calling the boy a fag.

Mario handed Ian an issue of *The Economist* and an envelope addressed to him. "Welcome to the wilderness of mirrors."

8: FAITH LIKE THE MUSTARD SEEDS

Throughout Philadelphia, the rain cleared the sidewalks of debris. Near Will's home at 7th and Winton, it glued discarded paper to the ground and waterlogged loose shopping bags. Runoff collected in an old tire on the corner of the street and bred mosquitoes. The murky effluvium soaked through a pair of denim Chuck Taylor low-tops he had worn since early freshman year and dirtied white laces he had recently replaced. His shoes would stink until they dried.

Neighbors cracked their screen doors and shouted to one another. An elderly woman called Will over. Her eight-year-old grandson stood next to her. She spoke to the young boy in Cantonese.

"She says your landlord was looking for your parents," said the boy. The old woman's song-like dialect hummed in the background. The boy continued, "your parents owe two months of rent, and if you don't pay in the next three days, he'll lock you out."

Will nodded, unsurprised. "*Doh je,*" he said to the woman in thanks.

"*M goi,*" the boy repeated to his grandmother, correcting

Will's error. "Why don't you speak Cantonese right?" he asked. "My mom says you're *gwailou.*"

Will shrugged.

News of the rent was unsurprising. The gas company had already suspended service to Will's house. It hadn't mattered over the summer, but now the weather was cold, his house was chilly, and he had to bathe with water from a kettle when he didn't shower at school.

He placed his shoes on a rack and his water bottle beside them, then dried himself with a thin towel from the kitchen.

His father and stepmother sat in an open dining area. Li smoked a cigarette and stamped the lipstick-coated butt next to two others in a rusted coffee can. Papers and prescriptions and medical instructions covered a chipped Formica table next to an enormous orange pill bottle.

"What's all this?" asked Will.

"Daddy fell from his delivery bike and cut his leg," said Li. "The injuries weren't bad, but the doctors found other problems."

They spent the evening hours deciphering and interpreting what a nurse told Eddie—cancer was spreading through him, and he needed chemotherapy and surgery. It would be expensive.

Li took $250 she had reserved for rent and instructed Will to wire it to China from the Quick Cash across from his school. It was to go to a traditional healer who worked beneath a neon sign in Shenzhen. The healer would send a licorice tincture good for the liver.

"You can't take from the rent," said Will. "The landlord will kick us to the street. He was stalking me at the game, today."

Li lit another cigarette. "Don't argue. Do as I say and the Lord will provide. We must pray with sincerity tonight."

Will leaned forward. "But licorice—"

Li pounded the table. "Faith! Grains of the mustard seeds! I'm asking little of you!" She muttered to Eddie in Cantonese and blew smoke from her nostrils.

"Listen to mommy," said Eddie. "You will understand when you are grown."

Will settled back and crossed his arms.

"Uncross your arms!" said Li. She inhaled, and the end of her cigarette burned down. "Say nothing to cousin Ruthie about your father's illness," she added.

Li and her cousin Ruthie grew up in the same house in Guangdong Province. Ruthie now lived three blocks away in a beautiful rowhome. She had received citizenship through marriage. Her son, Benson—only five years older than Will—would soon marry a girl of good lineage. Ruthie credited her prosperity with devotion to Jesus Christ.

Li contemplated for hours why such blessings did not flow upon her family. Mrs. Nguyen, who owned the beauty shop where Li shampooed hair part time, had promised her a styling station. A year and a half on, Vietnamese migrants replaced one another in front of the bright mirrors as Li's fingers pruned and peeled and turned white. She attributed her family's misfortunes to weakened faith and insisted they attend church with ever greater frequency.

Eddie moved to a worn sofa to sleep on his side. He gritted his teeth, no longer afraid to express the pain he'd hidden for weeks. Will took a kerosene heater from his room, placed it nearby, and tucked a blanket around his father.

"How was soccer?" asked Eddie.

"Coach wants me to start on Saturday," said Will.

"I would like to see you play, if I'm well enough," said Eddie. "I can't work until my leg heals."

Will didn't know what to say. "I'm not very good."

Eddie smiled and touched Will's forearm. "Mommy worries sport will interfere with your studies and doesn't want you to play. Work hard, however, and you will be famous like Sun Jihai. Save tickets." He coughed. "You won the game tonight?"

"Craig did. Like always," said Will

"Every day is the same," said Li from the kitchen. "Nothing changes but the frustrations."

Li stared at the pill bottle. Will stared at his water bottle. She handed him a carbon-copy remittance form she had filled out, and he squeezed back into his wet shoes.

Will walked past Southeastern High on his way to the Quick Cash. The rain blew sideways, and his cheap umbrella turned inside-out. The school's computer lab was open late on Wednesday nights, so he ran inside for cover. A lazy volunteer sitting in the hallway granted him access.

A cluster of mixed Asian students in the back of the room watched K-Pop videos and gaming tutorials. They nodded to Will, but talked among themselves and did not invite him over.

Molly Yang, a quiet girl with black hair to her waist, gave a brief smile. Molly went to Will's church. She played three instruments, won calligraphy competitions, and served as president of the school's math club. Her mother was Li's most hated friend. Once, at a church luncheon, Li intimated Molly and Will would pair well. Mrs. Yang responded by calling Will a *jook-sing* and blamed Li and Eddie for teaching him only English. She later insisted the comments came from a place of concern—that Will lived with no connection to Chinese culture, deserved sympathy, and needed friends—but it turned him into a piteous cautionary tale.

Neither Li nor Mrs. Yang knew Molly was dating Daequon Griggs and had accepted a homecoming proposal from him a week ago.

Will sat at a computer in the front of the room and scrolled through social media pages filled with embarrassing pictures and blistering comments from the soccer game. *Lost dog*, Rebekkah had posted with a portrait of him on the field. *Obedient, but clueless without instruction.* Over 200 people had liked it, including Molly. She commented, *you are what you eat.*

Will glanced over his shoulder. Molly buried her head in a monitor. He continued scrolling.

A picture of him sitting in the mud. A picture of him trying not to cry.

He could feel his pulse in his neck. The mouse he used became slick with sweat and slipped from his grasp. He fumbled to catch it but failed, and it clattered on the tile floor. The volunteer looked in from the hallway.

"Easy!" said Molly. Then, in a mumble, "You're going to screw it up, like everything else."

Will flushed. He retrieved the mouse from the floor and slammed it onto the desk. "Do you like it when people say your family eats dog meat?"

"It's a joke," she replied. "Calm down. People know you don't eat dog." She scooted forward in her seat. "You aren't Chinese."

Someone snorted.

Will moved to a far corner, withdrew the envelope from his pocket, and counted the wet bills he was to send for licorice. Faith like the mustard seeds. Three days to eviction. What then? Cousin Ruthie had offered them a room if ever there was trouble, but the proposal insulted Li's pride. She'd sooner live on the street.

His stomach gurgled. He read the carbon-copy remittance, pictured his father clutching his side on their sofa, crumpled the paper, and called his parents' landlord.

The man's voice was trenchant. "Two months of rent by Saturday or you go!" he said.

"I have $250," said Will. "Can you give us three weeks more?"

"No!"

"It's an emergency. Three weeks. Or, kick us out and get nothing."

The man paused. "Two weeks," he said at last. "Money by Saturday."

Will paused. The rain had stopped outside. "Don't tell my parents we spoke. I'm on my way."

9: HE'LL SCREW IT ALL UP

Paul Brooks leaned against Coach Osbourne's desk in a cramped office on the first floor at Southeastern High. He balanced an iPad on a bandaged left hand and reviewed Craig's game-winning kick. "What is this shit?" he asked. "If their goalie were awake, you'd have gone into overtime. This is what you do after years of training? Toe kicks? Like a ballerina?"

Craig sat in a chair facing his father and Coach Osbourne and stared sideways at a dusty trophy buried in the corner of a bookshelf. Mud dried on his uniform.

Daequon Griggs worked through trigonometry problems in the back of the room and waited for a ride home. He ignored Paul. The man's behavior frightened him and always worsened before an audience.

"I won the game," Craig mumbled. "Look where we stood at the interval."

"You didn't win the game! Nancy Netkicker won the game! You panted and puffed like a fat girl battling a staircase!" huffed Paul. He rewound the video on his iPad and displayed it. "If anybody saw this, do you think you'd have any chance on a real team?"

Osbourne nodded in agreement. "It's inappropriate for your level of play. You could have broken a toe. Griggs was open."

"Shut up, Osbourne," said Paul. "He didn't have to assist. He should have kicked the goddamn ball like I trained him to do. And what was with you substituting the Oriental in the first half? That kid is worthless."

Osbourne sputtered.

"That's what I said!" Craig interjected. "Coach is starting him Saturday."

Paul gritted his teeth. "Scouts are coming to watch Craig Saturday."

"The roster's thin," said Osbourne. "The scouts are watching Craig, not the team."

"Craig *is* the team!" Paul roared. He stood upright. His iPad fell from his hand. He kicked a metal garbage can, and it sailed to the back of the room. Daequon shot upright, and the air fell silent but for the blowing rain outside and the can rolling on the floor. "Play shorthanded! Having nobody is a better alternative!" Paul turned to Craig. "Get your shit from your locker."

Craig nodded and removed his varsity jacket from the back of his chair.

"Go with him," Paul said to Daequon. "I'll be in my car at the Jackson Street exit by the southeast stairwell. Speed Craig along. He's huffing and puffing today."

Craig opened his locker on the second floor of the school and added books to his backpack. "Did you see Osbourne shit his pants when my dad kicked the trash can?" he laughed.

"That was amazing," said Daequon. "Don't let him get to you. Everyone on the team would trade for your skill."

"He only wants what's best," said Craig. "He's been having trouble at work since your old man left the factory for Florida. Mama-san moved him to nights and weekends, and he isn't sleeping."

Daequon's father, Leon, had been Paul Brooks's manager at an aerosol can factory where they had worked for over a decade. When a Wuhan conglomerate purchased the plant, they busted the union, imported managers from China to improve efficiency, increased automation, lowered wages, and demanded longer hours and longer shifts. Leon moved to Orlando. His replacement was a Chinese woman with thick glasses who spoke broken English and demanded Paul return to work hours after a hand injury on the factory floor required medical attention. Paul coined her nickname.

Craig said, "A Chinese dude came to work sick the other day, coughing all over the place. Mama-san didn't send him home. Those people hack and spit everywhere and never take days off. Dad's worried about getting the virus."

"Did he get the vaccine?"

"No. He heard the side effects are worse than the disease. Besides, it will only mutate and it won't matter," said Craig. "Don't *you* cross the street if you see an Asian coming the other way?"

"If I did that, I'd never see my girlfriend," Daequon snickered.

Craig elaborated, "I mean Chinese people from China. Not, like, Molly."

"Molly crosses the street if she sees a foreign-born Chinese coming the other way," said Daequon. "But come on—didn't your dad ever go to work with a cough?"

"My dad never had a disease that melted peoples' lungs," replied Craig. "Anyway, he wishes Leon was still around. Dad never had a problem with the blacks like he does Chinese."

Daequon gave Craig a sideways glance. "Your dad never called them *the blacks*."

Craig shrugged and gave a guilty smirk. "Yeah, well. He never meant you or your dad. Black dudes would leave the line to smoke weed or whatever, but nothing like what's going on now with the Chinese. You guys aren't really black, anyway."

Daequon laughed out loud. "Shut *up*."

"I'm serious. How many black friends do you have who aren't relatives?" Craig asked.

"Not my fault. My mom always said, 'When you surround yourself with successful people, you don't get to pick who's in the room with you.' Still, it's not like she picks my friends."

"She would shit if you gave up soccer and got tight with the guys who play basketball on your neighborhood court."

"And your dad would shit if you sucked my dick, which you will through bloody gums if you keep talking," replied Daequon.

Craig grinned and reset the lock on his locker. They walked down the hallway toward the southeast stairwell connecting to Jackson Street. "Anyway, something's gotta change, D. Dad says half of the Chinese at the plant aren't legal and none of them ever apply for citizenship. They work for nothing, pack five and six to a room in cheap houses, and wire all their money back to China. They only talk to each other and they don't even try to make friends with Americans. They all talk like they have shit in their mouth. Nobody can understand them, so they push their kids to get smart and speak English and translate for them."

"Too bad they don't teach them soccer," said Daequon.

Craig didn't laugh. "Someone needs to stop anchor baby before he screws up everything Saturday. He'll make me look like a fool. I could lose everything."

"You aren't the only one," said Daequon. "Some guys from Lincoln University are coming to watch me. I have a full scholarship riding on this game. Tell him to call out."

"It would have to come from Osbourne. Asians submit to authority," said Craig.

They approached a connecting hallway near the southeast stairwell. Will Xiang rounded the corner.

Daequon stopped and slapped Craig with the back of his hand. "You've gotta be kidding. Did we conjure him?"

Craig glowered, and his nostrils flared.

10: KICK HIM AND MAKE IT COUNT.

Will walked from the computer lab through a dark, humid corridor to the second-floor exit. Tightness gripped his chest, and his forearms tensed. He drew a deep breath. He'd never be good at soccer and Molly Yang would always be a bitch, but at least he'd have a few weeks to live under his own roof. Perhaps his father would be back at work by then. He did not notice Craig and Daequon turning the corner until Craig called out, "Anchor Baby!"

Will shook himself to attention. "Hey," he replied. "Why are you guys still around?"

"We had a meeting with Osbourne about Saturday's game," said Daequon.

"We thought it would be best if you didn't play," said Craig.

"My dad wants to come to see the game," said Will. "I promise I can help. Run some plays with me. We can both get better."

"*You'll* help *me* get better?" asked Craig.

Daequon looked to the floor and shook his head.

"I need a little advice, is all," said Will.

"I'm giving you advice," said Craig. "Quit."

"Come on," said Will. "You know what I mean. Help me out."

"Get it through your skull," Craig replied. "I will never help you. Or like you. Stop trying to be friends. Go home to your incense and your ancestors or wherever you belong, but not here. Not on this team."

Will turned away. "Whatever," he said.

"That's the spirit," said Craig. "Fortune cookie say you make right decision."

Will became lightheaded and looked away. "Kiss my ass." He wasn't sure where the words came from, or if he intended them for Craig or Molly, Li or God almighty.

"Say what?" asked Craig.

"Who cares?" asked Will. "It's a stupid game."

Craig grabbed Will's arm and pulled him forward. "It's my life!" he shouted. "That's what you don't get! And I won't be told to kiss your ass!"

Will locked his eyes on Craig. "See you Saturday."

Daequon gave an exaggerated gasp.

Craig's eyes widened. He sunk his weight into his left foot and threw a haymaker from his midriff. Will's nose crunched under his knuckles.

Blood drained onto the floor, and Will collapsed.

Daequon recoiled. Craig shook out his hand and threw down his backpack.

"Get his feet," Craig shouted to Daequon. He grabbed Will's armpits.

They lifted him up, and he screamed for help.

"What are we doing with him?" asked Daequon, scanning the empty hallway.

"I don't know," said Craig.

"You've lost your mind!" said Daequon.

Will kicked and squirmed and leaked blood over his shirt. They carried him through a heavy set of double doors into the southeast stairwell. A vast, uninterrupted run of 35 steps covered a 20-foot drop between the second floor and street level.

"Let go!" Will thrashed and screamed, his voice bouncing from the cold walls. Craig moved to the top of the stairs and rocked Will over them. Daequon, off-balance and struggling to find his footing, followed Craig's lead.

"Don't swing him too high," said Daequon. "We'll all end up at the bottom."

"Stop moving," Craig shouted to Will, "I'm losing my grip."

Will wept as Craig and Daequon swung him ever higher over the stairwell. His phone and his envelope of cash fell from his pocket onto the landing.

"That's your phone? With jewels and shit?" laughed Daequon.

Will spat blood from his mouth. His eyes filled with tears. "Stop!" he sobbed.

"When you cry, it makes me want to swing harder," Craig yelled. He swung higher.

Will screamed again.

"Stop screaming!" said Craig. "You pathetic queer!"

Daequon, struggling to hang on to Will's ankles, slowed.

"Keep going!" said Craig. "Don't be a pussy!"

"I don't have a grip!"

Craig again looked at Will. "Promise you won't show up on Saturday."

"I promise!" shouted Will.

"Or ever again," said Craig.

"I'll do whatever you say!" Will cried.

"Swear you won't ever talk to me again."

"On my mom's grave, I won't!"

"Damn right you won't," said Craig. He let go. Daequon lost his grip. Will flew out over the steps, dropped twelve feet onto his side, and rolled 25 feet to the bottom, where he came to a rest.

"Jesus Christ!" screamed Daequon.

"Weren't you holding him?" asked Craig.

"I told you I didn't have a grip!"

Will moaned.

"Fuck him," said Craig. "He's alive." He kicked the pink phone to the base of the steps, where it shattered. He opened the envelope on the floor and held up the money. "If he's so poor and can't pay any of his bills, what's he doing with all this?" He gathered his backpack from the hallway and stuffed the envelope in Daequon's coat pocket. They made their way down the steps. "Free food stamps, free heat, free electric, free water, and a fistful of cash. He probably has lobster in his freezer at home and a new flat-screen. That's how it goes."

They walked past Will. His body heaved.

Daequon looked back. A security camera stared at them from the top of the steps. "We should call an ambulance," he said. "We'll be screwed if we get caught."

"Stop with the worry," said Craig. "This school needs me. Nobody cares about his worthless ass." He waved to the camera. "Kick him."

"What?"

"In the ribs. Hurry. Dad's waiting outside."

"No!"

"Are we in this together, or do you want to handle things on your own if there's trouble? Because you damn well won't go to Lincoln or anywhere else, and you know it."

Daequon took two steps back.

"Make it count," said Craig.

Daequon planted a foot and kicked Will hard in the torso. Will howled.

"Stop screaming!" shouted Craig. "It isn't like you'll ever have to pay for an ambulance, so stop crying." He examined his sleeves. "I didn't get blood on my jacket, did I?"

They left through the door.

Will faded. He took quick breaths. Everything hurt. His hands shook as he reassembled his phone, smearing blood. Once it worked, he didn't know who to call. His parents would admonish him for losing the money and creating trouble. He called his church, but there was no answer.

His silver chain was loose around his neck. The cross had fallen off. Through most of his childhood, Will feared an angry God who punished him for misdeeds. He had been wrong. God did not know he existed.

He closed his eyes. His teeth chattered. Was he to spend the rest of life begging for Craig's mercy and coming up with scraps of money for his parents to survive? He was a burden to everybody. He could do nothing right. Maybe if he fell asleep on the floor, he would never wake.

He dragged himself to the Jackson Street door and leaned against it. It swung out into a dark, shallow alcove where homeless people retreated to shit on the concrete. Wind stung his face. Spots floated in front of him like ciliates in pond water, and he collapsed.

11: BROAD & DESPAIR

Ian took a pen to the map of Algeria at his side, scratched out the number *7* and replaced it with *6*. A short glass of pinot noir from the bottle he uncorked the day before was already losing its character, so he gulped it down, annoyed.

He used an old desktop computer in Mario's basement to create a new, encrypted email account and sent a secure message to the *Ambassade de France à Alger* about Erik. It was past midnight in Algeria, and he did not expect Deena's contact at the French Embassy to reply with any speed. Unlike in the movies, international affairs involved long periods of waiting.

The professor followed him upstairs. He stretched on his bed and opened the envelope that had arrived for him that evening. Inside was a 1970 Topps Steve Blass baseball card. No message accompanied it. The smudged postmark was incomprehensible, and the return address corner was blank. He had collected old Pirates cards when he was younger, but had not for years and never ordered one to his grandfather's house. It was neither rare nor noteworthy. He read the stats on the back and stuffed it in his wallet.

He turned on his television and folded dozens of pieces of clothing purchased at a thrift store earlier that day. After thumbing through the channels, he shouted downstairs. "There are only 25 channels, grandpop."

"The signal is from the antenna on the roof," Mario replied from the kitchen.

"We need Wi-Fi, so I can stream. I'm staring at a channel that only shows classics. Fritz Lang is great and all, but I want to watch the Buccos this spring."

"I have an 802.11az tri-band router with 2-gigabyte peak data throughput," said Mario. "What makes you think I have no Wi-Fi?"

"You have plastic on your furniture," said Ian.

"That doesn't make me a Luddite," said Mario. "Television will rot your brain. You can stream on your phone when you have to watch something."

"My phone blew up!"

"Read something."

Ian finished his laundry and flipped through his copy of *The Economist.* Military operations in the South China Sea turned Western sentiment against Beijing. President Espinoza rattled the saber.

The Professor scratched at the base of the bed. Unable to jump, he meowed until Ian lifted him to the mattress.

Metropolis played in the background. False Maria danced. Ian flipped pages and grumbled. Somebody had destroyed the Nambutanese embassy in Madagascar. Authorities suspected the British government. In Bitanga, Equatorial Kundu, opposition forces had shot the president dead in a parking lot.

Ian swatted The Professor's tail to the side as Mario

peered into the room.

"What do you know about Steve Blass?" asked Ian.

"Didn't he have a disease that made him forget how to throw a baseball?" asked Mario. He held a letter and a library book.

Ian closed the magazine. "What do you have for me?" he asked.

"I got word from our moving company," said Mario. "Everything is on time. Your stuff arrives at the shipyard Saturday morning, and they'll deliver here around noon. Good news, yes?"

"*Boh*," Ian shrugged.

Mario handed him the book. "Make yourself useful. Run this to the library box beside Southeastern at Broad and Snyder."

"We were just there," Ian grumbled. "Can I drop it off tomorrow when I go to school? At this time of night, that corner is more like Broad and despair."

"You need the air. You're grumbling."

Ian looked at the book. *Stop Procrastinating* was the title. It was six weeks overdue, and a bookmark remained in the middle of the first chapter. He unfolded a canvas field coat he had found at the thrift store. L.L. Bean. It had fleece lining, leather trim, and epaulettes. He yanked a dry cleaning tag from the sleeve.

At the corner of Broad Street and Snyder Avenue, Ian opened his backpack and placed his grandfather's book in a scuffed, rusted library drop box. A man sleeping against it did not stir as it hit the bottom.

People wandered around him without purpose. They

smoked, fought, and asked passersby for money among the pawn shops, sneaker stores, funeral homes, and pharmacies that lined the street. The hairs on Ian's neck rose.

"Don't lock your focus. Always scan," Erik had once instructed. "Whether you're at the Queen's coronation or a public beheading, every situation has a baseline. Orient yourself, then ask: what sounds wrong? What smells off?"

People sat on the concrete. They hummed and talked and waited. There was no rustling in treetops. There were no movements on rooflines. A woman who smelled of urine bumped his shoulder. Her gray hair stuck out as though she had mis-wired a car battery. In the raspy voice of somebody who had smoked a half-pack of Luckies end-to-end, she said, "excuse me, sweetheart, do you have a match?" A fresh cigarette bobbled up and down in her mouth.

Ian produced his Zippo. "I use a lighter."

"Better still," she said, leaning forward.

He struck the flint, and nothing happened. "Until they go wrong." He shrugged, and they continued in opposite directions.

He disassembled his Zippo as he walked and stopped in a drugstore for a new flint and a tin of Ronsonol. A few minutes later, the lighter worked to his satisfaction, and he resumed course. He gave cursory glances to the legions of the damned who surrounded him. Security tossed a screaming man from a fast-food restaurant. Beside a dollar store, an unwashed woman in a heroin brume hung like a weeping willow with her fingers at her toes.

Further on, a motionless, indistinct body propped open a side door at his new school.

A dirty woman pissed on the concrete beside him. Her

young daughter played nearby, along a fence. The woman hiked up her pants and yelled for the girl to take her hand. They moved on. Nothing good could come of walking in that direction, and he turned around.

The woman of stench and hair had taken leave of her senses. The unlit cigarette fell from her mouth as she screamed profanities at passing busses.

He cursed, changed course, and again walked toward the school.

12: IAN & WILL

A year ago, as he made his way to the train station in New Delhi in the black morning hours, Ian stepped over rows of frail people sleeping on sidewalks. They were inert, covered over in thin blankets. Next to one of them was a rat, its head crushed flat, covered in insects. After a while, Ian could not distinguish between the living and the dead, and at last failed to recognize their humanity at all. His only concern became getting to the station so he would not have to turn around and step over them again.

The Philadelphians on the street that night had become obstacles, too. Those that walked, he dodged. Those that slept, he vaulted.

There was no difference between the sleeping bodies in Delhi and the one beside the urine puddle in the doorway of Southeastern high. In India, they were barefoot. Here, they wore denim Converse low-tops with old soles and new laces.

Ian stopped.

Homeless people and addicts did not waste their money on new shoelaces for old shoes.

He drew near, struck his Zippo to life, and squinted into

the shadows. The half-conscious Chinese boy from the soccer match earlier that day did not stir.

Shallow breathing. A busted nose. A trail of blood.

Ian's hand went to his pocket for his phone. Nothing. "*Minchia*," he muttered. He searched the area for a competent adult on whom he could foist the problem. Finding none, he dropped his backpack.

Will's eyes opened and closed. His teeth chattered. "Sambas," he murmured. "Made in Europe. Stitching's different." When he opened his eyes again, Ian was in his face, crouching and staring. Will continued, "You got the cheesesteak out of your shirt?"

"Huh?" asked Ian. He looked down at his chest. "Oh, right. I changed shirts."

Ian looked up the staircase, removed his coat, and threw it over Will. Blood soaked into the canvas. "My name's Ian Racalmuto. How are you not dead?"

"God isn't so merciful," mumbled Will.

"Do you have a phone?" asked Ian. "I'll get an ambulance."

Will snapped awake. "Don't call," he said. His lips were numb. "I'll move."

Ian extended a hand. "Don't—"

"I'm fine," said Will. He shifted left. Pain shot through his abdomen. He shifted right. His back popped. He leaned forward. Fire tore through his ribs and forced him against the wall.

Will's stepmother said lamentations were an affront to God and emotions were not for public display, so for years he consigned grief to the depths of his stomach. He held his breath to prevent an intractable outburst. For an instant, it worked. Then his soul revolted. Tears rolled down his cheeks and mixed with blood. Horrified, ashamed, and no longer in control, he covered his face and sobbed.

Ian jumped back. "Okay. No ambulance." He inched forward again. The boy carried the smell of old cigarettes on his clothes. "Give me your hand like we're arm wrestling."

Will turned away and grizzled, embarrassed. Ian took Will's fist, clenched it, and ticked through a checklist in his head. Airway, breathing, circulation. No shock, no protruding bone. His pupils were even by the light of his Zippo.

"I don't normally cry," said Will, trying to breathe. "I'll pull it together."

"I'm a little envious," said Ian. "I haven't been able to shed a tear for a month, no matter how I try. At my old school, we had to watch *West Side Story* - the old one, with that actress that fell off the boat and drowned. Anyway, When Tony died, I fell out and had to leave the room. My reputation never recovered." He pressed a sleeve to the back of Will's head. "No medical insurance?"

"No, and my family will get deported if I go to the hospital and ICE finds out," replied Will. He lost composure again. "I'm such a screwup. I tried to help, but I only made things worse. It's what always happens."

"You need a glass of wine," said Ian. Their hands remained locked. "Who did this?"

Will sniffed and wiped his nose on the back of his hand. "Two guys on my soccer team. Craig threw me down the steps. Daequon kicked me in the ribs."

"Craig's the *pezzonovante* who was giving you hell at the game?"

Will nodded. "He's a skillful player."

Ian closed his lighter. "I need both my hands to see what's up with your nose." He let go of Will's hand, placed his fingers in a triangle, and traced the fracture. "Breathe in and then exhale as hard as you can through your mouth." Will inhaled. When he blew out, Ian yanked downward, re-setting Will's nose with a loud snap.

Will screamed in agony.

"*Va bene*," said Ian, letting go. "It needs ice. What's your name?"

Will felt his nose. It was straight again, and he took a breath. "Will. Will Xiang. Why do you carry a lighter if you don't smoke?"

Ian raised an eyebrow. "What makes you think I don't?"

"Your fingers aren't yellow and your teeth are too white. The sole of your shoe hasn't melted where you'd step on a butt. There's old gum stuck in it, but no ash."

Ian smiled. "You're good with details."

"A lot of good they do me."

"I like details, too. My brother Erik calls them the currency of the trade. Do you have any sibs?"

Will sniffed. "It's only me, my dad, and my stepmom."

"Girlfriend? Boyfriend? Houseplant?"

"No, but Rebekkah Batiste—this popular girl who goes to school here—was giving me advice about homecoming. I was thinking of going this year."

"With her?"

"She'd never go with me. She dates Craig. I don't know who I'd go with. I didn't get that far."

Ian snickered. "You're still a step ahead of me," he said at last. "I can't even think about homecoming. My brother's missing and I have six days to find him before the world blows up." Wind blew, and he shuddered. "Can you move if I help? I live a block from here."

"My ankle's useless."

"I think you have a cracked rib or two as well. We'll be cautious."

Will extended his hand again.

Ian grabbed it. He pulled Will to his feet and placed the injured boy's arm around his shoulder. They began a slow hobble.

"You're short like me," said Will.

"I like being short," said Ian. "Short men cause all the trouble in the world, my grandpa says."

Will spat and cleared blood from his mouth. "Where do you go to school?"

Ian nudged his head to the building. "Here, starting tomorrow, but hopefully I'll be back abroad soon."

"Southeastern is a sewer," said Will. "You're better off anywhere else. You have an international accent I can't place."

"You have a Philly accent I didn't expect."

"How do you know how to fix a nose?"

"I fixed my brother's nose after a bomb exploded in Chatuchak market in Bangkok. It took three tries, and he didn't get ice until hours later, in Vientiane. Yours was easy."

"You're from Vientiane?" asked Will.

"I'm not from anywhere. Mom was a diplomat with the State Department, so I've lived everywhere. Algiers, of late. She was a consular officer, so I get how tricky citizenship is. Sorry your status is uncertain. That has to be stressful."

"Everybody thinks my family can fill out some papers and apply to become legal. Craig calls me anchor baby, certain I'm on welfare at the expense of his dad. It doesn't work like that. We get nothing." Will shifted. He felt his ribs. "Wasn't there a coup in Algeria? It was on the news."

"I was there. I got out of hospital a few weeks ago. I lost my mom and moved in with my grandpop while my dad gets things sorted out."

"That's awful," said Will. "I'm sorry."

"Don't worry about me. Today, you. Tomorrow, me," said Ian. "I still have stitches from bomb rubble. Use my story and say a bomb exploded if you need to explain what happened."

"I'll say a bear attacked me."

"Wear a bearskin when you do, so people know who won."

Will laughed.

Ian had never heard a laugh like Will's, and it made him laugh, too.

"Owww," Will whimpered, grabbing his ribs.

13: ARE THERE ANY BRIGHT SPOTS IN YOUR LIFE?

Ian pressed eight numbers on a digital keypad and unlocked his front door. "Don't tell anyone my passcode," he said.

"I wasn't watching," said Will.

Ian raised an eyebrow.

"Fine," said Will. "I won't tell."

Ian placed Will on a plastic-covered sofa in the living room and walked to the kitchen to find ice.

Will exhaled. The floor plan was like his house, only the rooms were warm and well-assembled. The first floor was an open rectangle—a living room, dining room, and kitchen defined only by furniture and area rugs. Calm, incandescent lamps and the flame from a burning vanilla candle cast shadows of trinkets on bookshelves. A library table stood atop a Persian carpet in the middle—big and square and heavy, as if ready for board games. The only television was an antique with a severed cord and a note taped to the glass that read *talk to the person next to you.* On top rested a miniature suit of armor, a wooden giraffe, and souvenirs from around the world.

Ian returned and handed Will ice and ibuprofen from a heavy bottle. His grandfather stored his medical supplies in a tiffin from Mumbai. Ian looked for antiseptic.

"This is strange," he said, holding a tiny pewter shoe in his hand. "It's the shoe from a Monopoly game. Take it. Maybe it will bring luck."

Will brought it toward him. "Nobody wants to be the shoe. It's lowlier than the iron."

"I always cheer for the underdog," said Ian.

Will put it in his pocket with his broken silver chain. Ian dabbed at him with gauze.

"It's getting late," said Will, once his wounds were clean. "I should find a way home."

"Stay here," said Ian. "Take my bed. Stay elevated. Grandpop has a sofa in the basement. I can sleep down there."

"Aren't you worried about bugs?"

"The carbon monoxide from the furnace kills them."

Will concealed his phone and talked to his parents. When he finished, he jammed it in his pocket. "They don't trust white people, so I told them I was staying with my cousin Benson," he said. "Whatever. They're distracted. Dad has cancer."

"Jesus," said Ian. "Are there any bright spots in your life?"

"It gets worse. My stepmom gave me $250—everything she had—to buy a curative licorice tincture from China. I knew it wouldn't work, so I called my landlord. Our rent is overdue, so I thought we could at least keep a roof over our heads for a couple of weeks. Craig and Daequon stole it."

"Is there anyone who can help you?" asked Ian.

"At school?" scoffed Will.

Ian poured two glasses of wine and handed one to Will.

Will looked at it and gave a skeptical glance. "I don't get drunk for fun," he said.

"We aren't having fun," said Ian. "We're being honest. *Salute.*" He clinked glasses. The plastic crunched as he settled on a chair across the room. "What *do* you do for fun, Will?"

Will sipped the wine and puckered. "I play soccer. My stepmom hates it because it distracts from my studies, but my dad takes pride in me being on the team. He has a million stories about old soccer players and games he remembers from China."

Ian nodded, remaining silent.

"What?" asked Will.

"You told me about your parents," said Ian. "I asked about *you.*"

Will swirled his wine. "Honesty," he said. "I suck at soccer no matter how hard I try. Practice would be fun if I were getting better, but the team hangs me out to dry and hates my guts—Craig, in particular. I dread going."

Ian laughed. "And that's what you do for fun? I'd hate to hear you describe something you don't like."

Will ran a hand through his hair. "I'm boring. I go to soccer, school, and church. That's about it."

"Friends?"

"My stepmom liked a kid in my algebra class named Arjun. He was studious and woke up at five every morning to do math and spelling. She wished I was like him. For a while, she made me get up at five to do math. Arjun moved back to Hyderabad."

"You're talking about your stepmom, again."

Will threw back his glass and smirked. He was already

flushing. "I just got the shit kicked out of me. Can you go easy?"

"No way," Ian grinned, emptying his glass and moving to the sofa beside Will. "Let's approach from a fresh angle. You're smart. I can tell. Smart people don't have to study to do well at schools like Southeastern. Where does your time go? That's what I want to know, because that's what you do for fun."

Will leaned forward like he would speak, then stopped.

"What?" asked Ian.

"You won't get it."

"Try me."

"I listen to NPR and want to host a radio show. I want to meet Sylvia Poggioli in Rome and Ofebia Quist-Arcton—"

"In Dakaaaar," Ian interrupted, imitating Quist-Arcton's deep alto.

Will sat to attention. "Nobody under 30 listens to NPR. Were you trapped in your parents' car or something?"

"I love NPR. I asked for a sustaining membership last Christmas," said Ian.

"Steve Inskeep or Audie Cornish?"

"Audie Cornish," said Ian. "Hansi Lo Wang or Lulu Garcia-Navarro?"

"Nell Greenfieldboyce," Will snickered. "There's another thing: I'm good at magic tricks, but I lost my cards."

"Make your phone disappear instead," replied Ian.

Will reached into his pocket. His phone was missing.

Ian revealed it. "I'm good at picking pockets," he said, grinning.

Will snatched it back, embarrassed by the rhinestones covering it. "It was my mom's," said Will. "I hate pink."

"It's the color of confidence," replied Ian.

"Yeah? What color's your phone?"

"Charcoal."

Mario came downstairs. The arthritic cat followed.

Ian said, "Will, meet my grandpop, Mario, and our cat, The Professor. Definite article required."

"What happened to you?" asked Mario. "You're bleeding all over my plastic."

"I got rolled," said Will.

"Well," Mario sighed, "Lucky for us. We have a house to ourselves, and Ian has no friends and no life. Stay as long as you want." He retreated to the kitchen and added, "Towels are in the closet if you need a shower. Don't worry about getting them bloodied. The airline gave Ian an extra toothbrush, too. It's in a bag in the medicine cabinet."

"Your clothes are shot," said Ian. "I made a run to the thrift earlier today, and got about ten pairs of jeans. We're the same size. I can give you a shirt from my collection."

"I can't ask that of another person."

"It's thrift. They already come from other people."

Will hobbled to the shower where he rinsed the dried blood away, then stumbled into Ian's bed from the foot and smiled about how it filled the room from wall to wall. The pillow smelled like deodorant, but he didn't care. Ian entered the room, carrying his Sambas, and set the clock radio to NPR.

"Hey Ian?" said Will, drifting out of consciousness. "I won't tell anybody."

"What?"

"That you cry watching *West Side Story*. That's lame."

Ian lifted his arms. "Are you kidding? At the end? When Maria sings *Somewhere* to Tony and—"

"Hey Ian?" Will interrupted.

Ian paused. "What?"

Without opening his eyes, Will threw something hard at Ian's forehead. Ian tossed his shoes to the floor and caught his Zippo lighter.

"I'm good at picking pockets, too," said Will.

Ian gripped the lighter. His heart raced at the prospect of losing it, and he backed into the hallway.

"Natalie Wood," Will shouted from the bedroom.

That was the woman who drowned. Natalie Wood.

Will laughed his laugh that made Ian laugh again.

Ian crawled under a blanket on the sofa in the basement. Mario had covered it, too, in a plastic slipcover. The odor of the cat's litter box drifted from nearby. The furnace rumbled to life near a dusty, old bookshelf. He bit a knuckle, and the Professor curled on his stomach.

Mario descended the stairs and sat beside him. "How's your friend?"

"I don't have friends," said Ian.

"But you're scheming on his behalf," said Mario.

"How do you know?" Ian examined the tooth indentations on his knuckle. "He has to choose between licorice tincture and two weeks of rent. That's on a good day, when someone hasn't robbed him."

"You'll collect his money tomorrow?" asked Mario.

"Plus interest. I'll be back to finding Erik before noon."

Mario grinned. "Sounds like fun. Find Nic Delvecchio. Nic is a student of my acquaintance who attends

Southeastern's auto technology and body repair program. Mechanics are the best people to know."

"I told you, I'm not making friends," said Ian. "Friendships complicate things."

"In that case, make allies." Mario removed $50 from his wallet and handed it to Ian.

"What's this for? *Si chiama Pietro*?" asked Ian, using an old Italian idiom to ask whether he needed to pay it back.

"It's a gift. For importunate exigencies and entanglements unforeseen," said Mario. He kissed Ian's forehead and adjourned upstairs.

Ian stared at The Professor. "I'm serious. I'm not getting involved with that school or anybody there." He turned out the light. "After I get Will's money back."

The cat, still curled on Ian's stomach, yawned.

14: TZVI

In the Mojave Desert, the remains of California Highway 66 stretched from the horizon to the west and progressed in a straight line toward the summit at Cadiz. There, covered in dust and brush, was a dark road house where motorcyclists fueled idle nights with shit-talk and liquor. A dilapidated eight-room motel stood empty behind it. Termites destroyed a pile of furniture outside.

A Pontiac Grand Am pulled from the highway into a gravel lot and parked next to a green Humvee flying an enormous American flag. Rocks crunched beneath the tires. Victoria Fant, a squat diplomatic security agent from the Algerian embassy, turned the rearview mirror to examine her teeth and adjust a thick pair of glasses. She gathered a briefcase from the back seat, brushed her navy pantsuit, and waited for the cloud of dust hanging in the air to settle.

Fant and Deena Racalmuto hated one another. Fourteen months earlier, Deena ignored Fant's protests and thwarted protocol to bring Ian and her husband to Algiers—a high-security post that forbade trailing family members. As Fant reeled with indignation, Erik arrived to work at the same embassy.

In a closed-door meeting with the Racalmutos, Fant phoned her superiors and insisted they rectify the breakdown of convention. She cradled the receiver to her ear, then exploded with rage as Washington met her concerns with indifference. Deena performed cruel impersonations of Fant in that moment, mimicking her pouty bottom lip to the delight of her coworkers and family. She referred to her, even in professional settings, as *Victoria Fart.*

Fant opened her mouth to allow more oxygen to pass and stepped inside.

The road house smelled of stale cigarette smoke, cooking grease, and aftershave. It was dark and unoccupied, but for a bartender and a hulking man with a trucker cap at the far end of the bar.

Yellowed newspaper clippings on the wall carried halftone images of the bartender—Crystal Pounder, the caption read—dancing on a pole. She now had a c-section mark beneath a midriff dimpled with cellulite and a bullet scar through her shoulder. Numerous implants had become incongruous over time with leathered skin.

"I stopped dancing ten years back," Pounder offered as Fant scanned the clippings. "Muh pole snapped, and I wheeled into the crowd. The heels I had on hurt a woman in the eye, and the pole came down on a man's head." She wiped the bar. "He still got a dent where it hit. Can't spell his name or add two and two anymore. I look away when I see him."

Pounder kept a sharp knife in the liquor well. A saw-barrel scattergun dangled from a four-link chain under her bar, and a panel of mismatched plywood tacked along the front suggested she had used it before.

Fant sat on a tall stool. "Has anyone else been in today?"

"Only mister aftershave." Pounder pointed her pinky at the man with the trucker cap. Line art tattoos covered his arms, and an enormous gem-studded silver ring choked his middle finger. He swirled a packet of powdered aspirin into a shot of Wild Turkey and downed the gritty mixture with a single tilt.

Pounder shouted toward him. "How about a beer to chase that?"

"Pull whatever tap," the man answered in a thick accent. A soft belch followed.

Pounder lifted a heavy, frosted mug from a freezer.

"Where are you from?" Pounder asked him.

"Anacostia," he replied. "Near D.C."

"I mean your accent."

"Israel." A jukebox kicked to life and played Merle Haggard.

"That's quite a stone you have on your finger," said Pounder, pointing at his ring. "Did you win the Super Bowl?"

The man licked his teeth and ignored her. "Is the motel behind your bar in operation?"

"They're tearing it down," replied Pounder. "Served its use when the highway was busy, but ain't no tourists no more, and it don't pass fire code." She leaned toward Fant and became dramatic. "There's sidewinders inside, usin' it for their whorehouse. You can hear 'em hissin' and rattlin' when you come close."

The man blew foam from his beer.

The front door opened, and dry air tore through the bar like a furious wraith. A thru-the-wall air conditioner rattled to life. A thin man wearing a Panama Borsalino hat, a white

Pendel and Braithwaite suit, and a crimson tie stood in-frame. His cracked, bloody hands trapped sand and dust, and his shirt was translucent with sweat. His shoes clicked as he walked. He climbed atop a barstool, ordered a gin and tonic, and gulped water.

Pounder could not find a lime and retreated to the kitchen in the back.

"I know the sound of those shoes," said Fant.

Richard Fenzel grinned, revealing three missing teeth. "Agent Fant," he replied, replacing his empty glass. "Just arrived?"

"Yesterday, from Landstuhl. How did you make your way here?"

"Yes," replied Fenzel.

Fant leaned toward him and raised her voice. "I asked how."

"Forgive me," said Fenzel. "I've suffered the most terrific ringing in my head since that horrific child detonated a bomb in my ear. I walked."

"*You walked*?" Fant gasped.

"From Calexico I traversed Joshua Tree and continued north through Sheephole Valley. I found my way here with a compass."

"*A compass*?" she gasped again.

He took a compass from his grimy pocket and displayed it. "I need a change of clothing. My suit became filthy when I picked up the *tren de la muerte* at Tapachula. I've been wearing it since I left my tailor in Panama."

"*Panama*?" Her voice raised an octave.

"Christ, Fant! Has an echo replaced the ringing in my ears?"

Fant dabbed at her lips with a napkin. "Where are your teeth?"

"The explosion that took my hearing fairly well blew them from my skull. I'll need to see my dentist, Dr. Rosen, when I get back to Washington. Have they written me off back at State?"

"But for the paperwork."

"Good," said Fenzel. "Where do we stand?"

Fant gathered the briefcase at her feet, opened it, and placed a file folder and a small paisley box on the bar beside her. As Fenzel reached for the folder, Fant withdrew it. "My money survived your wilderness crossing?" she asked.

Fenzel smiled and pointed. "Do you see the man on the other side of the room, with the cap? His name is Tzvi."

"Tzvi?"

"Tzvi."

"Does he have a last name?"

"He's a contract killer."

Fant slumped. "I see."

Fenzel tapped a finger to his Borsalino.

Tzvi removed his cap. Above his brow was a grotesque fusion of metal, scar tissue, and flesh where a contoured gold plate replaced a third of his skull. The gold plate gave him relentless headaches. The powdered aspirin he took for relief wore away the lining of his stomach, afflicting him with ulcers.

"Tzvi is my factotum," Fenzel continued. "He received his gold skull working for Kidon, undercover in Beirut. With his bare hands, he killed three men trying to take the remaining two-thirds of his head. Today, he instructs Krav Maga near Washington. Like you, he works for diplomatic security.

Rather, he works *with* diplomatic security. He works *for* me."

Tzvi dropped a blue pouch containing $100,000 in front of Fant.

Fant pushed the folder and the paisley box toward Fenzel. "Everything you asked for is in order." She stood from her stool, but he stopped her with an outstretched hand.

"Ian Racalmuto?"

Fant nodded. "I will head to Philadelphia tonight."

Fenzel became stiff. "You were to have killed him already as part of our deal. Our superior wants him dead, because he knows too much. I want him dead, because I hate him."

"I planted a bomb in his suitcase in Germany. The airline misplaced his luggage, and it exploded on the tarmac."

Fenzel slapped his Borsalino beside him on the bar and aligned it to his satisfaction. "Sit down, Agent Fant."

She sat again, her knees together. Her swollen ankles made her feet porcine.

"Are you still playing the horses, Agent Fant?"

"I stopped gambling."

"When you arrived in America, did you go to the races?"

She said nothing.

"If I were to interrogate the Haitian janitor at Foggy Bottom who gives race book tips for a cut of winnings, he would deny having contacted you?"

Fant's bottom lip pointed to the money on the table. "Track conditions are favorable for Baby Beth Biscuit, a thoroughbred running in a maiden race this afternoon at Dover. We can double what's in front of us."

Fenzel sighed. "Our organization runs as a clock, Agent Fant." He removed a pocket watch, wound it twice, and opened it. "There is no margin for error resulting from moral weakness."

Tzvi drew close. Fenzel loosened his necktie.

"Understood," said Fant. "I will make the boy's demise my priority."

"I fear not. Our relationship has outlived its usefulness."

Tzvi's thumb moved to his ornate ring. He tapped the center stone twice. It flipped backward by a thin spring, revealing a needle. With a fast punch, he jabbed it into Fant's neck.

Fant slapped at the wound and turned to Fenzel, who looked at the watch. Her eyes rolled into her head. She fell from her chair. Foam covered her lips as she jerked on the floor. At last, she was still.

"Twenty-three seconds," said Fenzel, re-tightening his tie. "We must find a faster venom."

Tzvi examined his ring. "I have an alternative in mind, outside in the car. What do we do with Fant?"

"Take the money. Put her out back in the motel. Then, meet at your car."

As they pulled away, Crystal Pounder returned with a lime. The room was empty. Fenzel had left no tip.

Tzvi sat in silence next to Fenzel as he drove his Humvee west toward Ludlow. The beer had upset his ulcer, and he belched. The oversized American flag flapped behind them, Inaudible to Fenzel over the buzzing in his head.

Desert temperatures and the stench of Tzvi's aftershave overpowered the air conditioner. Fenzel adjusted a vent.

"You disagree with me," said Fenzel.

Tzvi said nothing and continued to drive.

"Dispensing with Fant was a matter of integrity, Tzvi. We

must do what we say we will do. You have my *bona fides*?"

He pointed to an enormous glove box.

From under the blue pouch with the money, Fenzel withdrew a cellular phone, credit cards, a new driver's license, and a social security card. He opened a passport aged with stains and stamps.

"We changed your identity," said Tzvi. "You're no longer Rick Fenzel. You're now Rick Finzel."

There was a lengthy pause. "You're joking," said Finzel.

"I spent hours forging the passport," said Tzvi. "It's a clean profile. I made you a year younger. What's in the folder agent Fant gave you?"

Finzel combed through spreadsheets revealing sorghum yields. Beneath them, a schematic of the central computer mainframe at Main State—the Truman Building in Washington that served as State Department Headquarters—showed the location of a red switch that would disable the security firewall. He read a note from their boss, typewritten on yellow paper.

Victoria: I require Deena Racalmuto's phone. P.S. Kill the Racalmuto brothers.

Paper-clipped was a transcript of a conversation between Ian Racalmuto and security agents. The phone was in a cremation urn. Completing the packet was a container ship cargo manifest and port schedule. He tucked everything back into the folder. "How much time do you have off from Main State?"

"Until next week," said Tzvi.

"Wonderful. We will recapture Deena Racalmuto's phone in Philadelphia."

"I have a cabin reserved in the mountains, Richard!"

"It won't take long. We'll kill Ian Racalmuto while we are in town. You can go to the mountains thereafter. Point the car to LAX."

Tzvi instead turned East. "We'll drive," he replied. "I have difficulty with cabin pressure, and I cannot bring the scorpion."

"Scorpion?"

In the back seat, in a terrarium, an Indian scorpion the size of a softball paced in angry circles.

That night, Tzvi would handle the creature with thick gloves and use rubber tweezers to milk poison from its tail. The scorpion survived on crickets, which he kept in an inflated plastic bag. As the sun set, the crickets would become stentorian and overcome Finzel's tinnitus, preventing sleep.

"It produces a more reliable venom," said Tzvi.

Finzel cleared his throat, displeased.

15: SOUTHEASTERN HIGH

THURSDAY.

Ian was no stranger to unfamiliar schools. Every two years, as his mother traveled with the State Department, he started afresh. He had always attended international schools, where children of expats from the world over worked to grasp cultural and religious nuances. The curriculum challenged him, but like an expensive hotel, friends checked in and out and never stayed for long.

Southeastern High was different. Students there could not find Canada on a map—a fact parents found less important than hot lunch, a modicum of safety, and a place for their kids to go while they scattered between part-time jobs. The school nurse expected no payment, which was to many families far more relevant than the capital of Slovakia and math problems involving *f-of-x*.

Outside the dismal, brutalist concrete box that devoured an entire city block at Broad and Snyder, clusters of students screamed and fought and chased one another through an asphalt schoolyard. The boy with the neck tattoo from the night before again threw a football with friends. He debated the merits of dropping out and getting a GED while his pregnant girlfriend shouted and chewed cheap lacquer from her fingernails.

At the opposite side of the yard, under a flagpole, a group of obese girls with neon hair made plans to get new piercings. Two boys locked pinkies and stared at one another. Ian could not imagine holding another boy's hand like that. It appeared delicate and limp and lacked determination. He shook his head and pushed the thought aside.

Earlier that morning, Ian took his blood-stained coat to Mario's dry cleaner, Mrs. Hwang. She eyeballed it but asked no questions as long as he rendered payment in advance. Now he shivered.

In a dim atrium that stank of bleach, a rough security guard named Mandrake Timmons pulled Ian's backpack from his shoulders. He emptied it, handed Ian the contents, and admonished him for carrying a bag not made of transparent plastic. "Pick it up at the end of the day," he said, directing Ian through a set of metal detectors.

Security cameras watched from every angle. Craig Brooks's smile beamed from a magazine cover in a glass display case. Craig was younger in the photo and not wearing a Southeastern uniform.

The classrooms existed in various states of collapse. Ian's Geography teacher, a patchouli-scented woman named Calliope Moon, had taken leave for a hysterectomy and had a stroke under anesthesia. Stunned colleagues visited her at her convalescent unit to find her vocabulary reduced to a single word.

"How are you feeling, Calliope?"

"Vagina," she replied, smiling.

"Can I get you some ice chips?"

"Vagina," she nodded.

Ms. Baxter, the principal at Southeastern, squeezed her hand. "Your students need you, and we can't wait to have you back, Calliope."

"Vagina."

Baxter phoned her superior from her car. "Moon's a potted plant," she said. "Demagnetize her entry credential and reassign her parking space."

A 76-year-old man named Aloysius Grant replaced Ms. Moon until a student hit him in the face with a stapler. The secondary substitute, Mr. Brady, now managed the mixed class of sophomores and juniors by screaming at them while they did as they pleased.

"This is not as bad as the embassy raid," Ian muttered to himself. In the hallway, a fire extinguisher flew past, spewing white foam.

Will was still asleep when Ian left home, so Ian could not retrieve his Sambas. Instead, he wore a pair of his father's Nikes, taken from a suitcase in the back bedroom. His toe blistered. He had been up since 3 AM reading *Wine Girl* and brought it to finish over lunch. For now, he stuffed it in a basket under the desk where he sat. He closed his eyes and yawned, pulled his Pirates cap over his brow, crossed his legs, and became smaller than he already was.

Hip-hop music jarred the room to attention. Craig Brooks entered, while Daequon followed and played DJ with his phone. They sang along and struck at the air with their fingers. Rebekkah walked behind him.

Daequon surveyed the room. "Where's anchor baby?" he

asked. Even after leaving Will for dead, he anticipated seeing him bruised and bandaged at school. Will never skipped, if only for free lunch.

"Who cares?" asked Craig. He gave Daequon a cautious glimpse. He had not told Rebekkah about the assault.

"He gets straight *As* in his sleep." Rebekkah replied. "Missing a day won't kill him. He only comes here to shuffle his cards and shower. Maybe he's picking dandelions with his mom."

"Dandelions?" asked Craig.

"She picks bags of them in Marconi Plaza. I think they eat them."

"Marconi Plaza?" asked Craig. "The park where my dog takes a dump?"

"I'd die if my mom went to Marconi Plaza and picked bags of dandelions to eat."

Daequon was distant. "He better not be dead," he said.

"Why would he be dead?" Rebekkah asked.

Craig elbowed Daequon and whispered, "You're being a pussy, again." He produced Will's shabby deck, showed Rebekkah, and replaced them in his pocket.

"Where'd you find those?" she laughed.

They stopped in front of Ian, only then taking notice of him and growing quiet.

"You're in my seat," said Daequon.

Ian stood. "I didn't realize there are assigned desks."

"There aren't," said Daequon, overtaking Ian's chair. Rebekkah and Craig crowded him out. Daequon draped a leather Armani coat over the backrest. It was three sizes too large, but pristine. $2,000, at least.

Craig dropped his books two seats away. He and Daequon

sat together for years until other students called them queer. Now Rebekkah sat between them. Craig drew his hand along her thigh.

Ian wandered to the back of the room and spun an outdated globe atop a low bookshelf. Where was Erik? Czechoslovakia? Zaire? The USSR?

The music stopped.

Craig turned Daequon's phone in his hand. "What's your passcode?" he asked.

"Fifteen-fifteen-fifteen," said Daequon. "My jersey number three times."

"You stole that idea from me," said Craig.

"Your combo is fifteen fifteen fifteen?"

"No, idiot. *My* jersey number. I use it for my locker."

Idiots, thought Ian. Foreign governments spent vast sums of money on drugs and liquor and sex to get people to give out passwords and codes and combinations—all the things Craig and Daequon spit into the open air. He gave the globe another spin.

Craig flipped Daequon's phone around again. "How much did this cost?"

Daequon took it back and started another song. "A grand."

"It should suck your dick for that price."

Rebekkah sniffed the air. "What smells like lemon?"

Ian sagged. He had showered with Mario's *Il Frutetto* soap that morning. "Citron and bergamot," he confessed. "Sorry if it's strong. I only had old man soap to use in the shower. *È così e basta*, as they say."

"*È così e basta*," Daequon imitated Ian's accent before breaking into exaggerated laughter. "Where the hell are you from?"

Ian pointed east.

"Europe, or some shit?" asked Daequon.

"I hear European guys like to fuck a lot. Is it true?" asked Craig. Ian didn't answer, so Craig continued, "Can you even reach to see over a pussy?"

Rebekkah laughed.

"What does that mean?" asked Daequon

"Dude is short," Rebekkah explained.

Ian spun the globe faster.

"Maybe he doesn't like pussy," said Rebekkah. "Europeans are androgynous and femme and act sort of ace, so who knows for sure?" She locked eyes with Ian. "You're kind of cute. If I weren't with Craig, we could get pizza and find out if you like pussy."

Ian exhaled. "It would have to be amazing pizza to get me hard with you in the room." He slapped the globe to a sudden halt. "I doubt even breadsticks would make it worthwhile. Would you pay for the food, at least?"

There was gasping and mumbling. Rebekkah shrank. A boy sitting off to the side laughed out loud.

Craig turned his attention to Ian and snarled. "Shut up. Running your mouth like that will get the shit kicked out of you."

"Do you have experience shit-kicking?" He shifted his gaze to Daequon, who snapped upright.

Craig leaned forward. "Do you have any idea who I am?"

"I watched you win yesterday's soccer game with a weak toe kick while your friend here stood in scoring position, scratching his balls and stinking," said Ian.

Craig jumped from his seat, his jaw clenched. Daequon

followed.

"Don't get friendly," said Ian, waving them back. "I won't be here long, and I only have time for business. Last night you took something that doesn't belong to you. I'm here to get it back." Ian sat.

"What's he talking about?" Rebekkah asked.

Craig swallowed hard. "I don't know," he said, refusing to look at Daequon.

Mr. Brady arrived and passed out worksheets. Word searches. Crossword puzzles. There was no lecture. Students from other classes entered the classroom at-will and joked with friends. Daequon fidgeted and drowned out Brady's screaming with earbuds the entire class could hear. Rebekkah powdered her face with a compact shaped like Minnie Mouse.

Ian clicked his Zippo open and closed. He replayed the moment he found it on his mom's desk in Algeria. "You didn't see a cigarette lighter here, did you?" Fenzel had asked. "A Zippo? Mother of pearl? Letter R?" Why had the man asked for it?

When class ended, Ian searched for his book. He had left it under Daequon's desk, and it was no longer there.

He tapped Daequon on his way out the door. "Did you find a book under your desk?" he asked.

Before Daequon could answer, Craig swung the spine into Ian's scalp. His stitches opened. Blood flowed, and his lighter fell to the floor. Ian scrambled toward it, but Daequon recovered it and handed it to Craig.

Craig drew near and stuffed the lighter between the pages of the book. "*Wine Girl*?" he asked. He cleared his sinuses and spit a warm, slimy wad of mucus that crawled down Ian's nose and cheek.

Daequon erupted into laughter.

"Don't laugh," said Ian. "Nobody likes being kicked when they're down."

Daequon's eyes grew wide, and he slapped Ian in the mouth. His breathing had become rapid. "Shut your mouth or I'll do it for you," he said.

"Picking pockets is like playing poker," Erik once instructed. "Don't count your money at the table." In a dank boys' room, Ian used frigid water and coarse brown paper towels to clean his face. His lip turned blue. He put pressure on his scalp to stop the bleeding and looked to see what he had lifted from Craig's pocket as the boy spat.

Playing cards. He was certain he had stolen Craig's wallet, perhaps stuffed with Will's money. Right shape, wrong pocket.

He left and observed Craig, who stood across the hall.

Craig jammed Ian's book beneath a dirty tee shirt on the top shelf of his locker. The Zippo, wedged between the pages, created a bulge and a crease in the front cover. He twisted his padlock and left.

The lock had six dials. A six-digit combination. Craig's jersey number. Ian could only remember him with his shirt off. He stopped a blond girl walking with her friend.

"What's Craig Brooks's uniform number?"

"Ten?" she said.

He moved the dial to read 101010. The lock did not open. He scrambled it, kicked the door, cursed, and left for the main office.

16: NIC DELVECCHIO

Officer Mandrake Timmons sat in a dark, state-of-the-art security center near the main office at Southeastern High. A control board flashed and beeped and gave access to hundreds of cameras around the school. On three enormous television monitors, students tore through the halls and held middle fingers to the electronic eyes in the ceiling. Timmons focused instead on his phone and assessed the Eagles' prospects a month into their regular season.

Outside, Ian examined a paint-streaked ladder propped against the wall next to Timmons's office door. He knocked. When the man did not answer, he entered. Timmons pointed his nose at the boy while continuing to watch his phone.

"Craig Brooks has a book that belongs to me. He stole it and locked it in his locker," said Ian.

Timmons stood from his seat and adjusted his belt.

"He also spit on me. Daequon Griggs—"

The guard gave Ian a delicate push out the door and closed it in his face.

Ian knocked and opened the door again.

"Open my door again," said Timmons, "and you'll have

bigger problems than spit."

"You have a security board," said Ian. "There was a fight last night in the southeast stairwell. Did your cameras pick it up?"

"Someone ripped the camera off the wall in the stairwell."

"Before or after the fight?"

"That's not your business," said Timmons. "Go to class."

Ian held out his schedule. "Where's the automotive tech center?"

"Off-campus," said Timmons. "Two blocks south." He went back to his phone, not bothering to check Ian's schedule. If he had, he would have noticed the boy was skipping biology class.

On his way out the door, Ian stared up at the security camera in the southeast stairwell. It hung from a hole, unscrewed from its mounts with care. There were no signs of damage. Nobody could reach it to destroy it—not without a ladder.

Students scattered throughout the automotive center—a space Southeastern shared with a for-profit trade school. In four of six auto bays, hydraulic jacks lifted cars into the sky. In a fifth, the legs of a mechanic stuck from under a 1978 Chrysler New Yorker Brougham. Sudden bursts from an air impact drill made Ian cringe.

"Help you with something?" asked an old black woman wearing coveralls and grease-flecked reading glasses. Her name was Flora Carter. She had fourteen grandchildren, made potato salad for picnics at Mount Tabor A.M.E. church, and for 49 years had trained some of the best mechanics in Philadelphia.

Ian introduced himself and extended his hand. Hers were rough.

"I'm looking for Nic Delvecchio," said Ian. "Know where I can find him?"

She grinned and pointed at the legs under the car. "Nic?" she yelled. There was no reply. "You can go over."

"Are you certain he heard you?"

"Nic hears everything."

"He didn't answer."

"You'd know if you weren't welcome."

Ian walked over and squatted beside the legs. They ended in a pair of Timberland boots. "Nic, my name is Ian Racalmuto. I'm sorry to be a bother. You're friends with my grandfather, Mario."

Nic continued working under the car and said nothing.

"I need a 1/16-inch slotted screwdriver with a 1-inch shank and a ball peen hammer. It's urgent," said Ian. He brushed off the floor and sat with his back to the front tire. A gloved hand reached out and pointed at a spanner wrench. He handed it over.

"I'm having a lousy first day of school," he continued. "Last night, Craig Brooks and Daequon Griggs threw a student down a flight of stairs and robbed him. I wasn't going to involve myself—I have five days to find my missing brother in North Africa—but the kid can't walk and he's about to get tossed from his house. So, I'm going to get his money back. I thought it would be easy, but I was careless and the operation rolled up. Craig spit on me and stole my cigarette lighter, which wouldn't be important, but I think it's a clue. Anyway, it's stuck between the pages of a book in Craig's locker and the only thing I have to show for my efforts is a deck of playing cards."

Nic Delvecchio slid out on a creeper. A familiar plastic bag covered her hair. "You really are fascinating, Stephen," she said. She pulled herself up and bumped Ian's elbow as a greeting. "Nicole. Call me Nic. Everyone else does."

Ian turned red.

She continued, "You don't want a ball peen hammer. A cross peen hammer is a better bet if you want to bust a lock."

"Who said I was trying to bust a lock?"

Nic yelled across the room, "Miss Flora, can Ian borrow a cross peen hammer?"

"Whose lock is he trying to bust?" shouted Flora. "And where's my spanner?"

"Three more minutes!"

Ian stared at the bag on Nic's head. It said Shop Rite in bold letters. Nic looked up and touched it.

"The car drips oil."

Ian followed Nic. She walked and talked. "Craig is more likely to forget about or lose your lighter than he is to do something malicious with it. The money's what's urgent. Daequon will spend it all on Skittles and liquor."

"I'm guessing the money's already spent, so I made a contingency plan."

"Who's your friend that got robbed?"

"I don't have friends. I'm doing it for Will Xiang."

"Will," she smiled. "He was in my 4th grade class. Kids back then called him *Dirty Billy* because his parents never washed him and he smelled. They still roast him on social media about that. Friend or not, it's nice someone's going to bat for him."

"It's only because he's all banged up and can't do it

himself. I thought there might be security cam footage, but Officer Timmons said someone busted the camera. I think he did it himself, after the fact."

"Find Chelsea Granados. She has a talent for electronics and may have recorded footage—" she stopped cold. "Let me start over. Matt Granados."

"Her brother?"

"No. Trans. Came out this summer. It's still taking me a minute to get used to the change. He's kind of cute as a dude. I have a thing for Latino guys. The eyes, you know. Where's your phone? I'll give you my number."

"My phone was in my valise when it blew up."

She shook her head. "Fascinating." She wrote her number down on a slip of paper. "Use your grandpop's house phone if you need me. I have his number stored, and I'll pick up if you call. Your hammer and screwdriver will be ready in the morning. Meanwhile, find Matt. Every day at lunch, he sits alone on the hood of a car in the corner of the school parking lot. Run and you might catch him."

17: MATT GRANADOS

Matt Granados sat alone on the hood of a car in the corner of the school parking lot at Southeastern High. He video chatted with his 12-year-old sister Amy. At the same time every day, she excused herself from English class, went to the toilet, and talked to Matt.

Matt refused to go to the cafeteria for lunch. Rebekkah Batiste would walk past and say hello, but always said, "*Hello, Chelsea,*" before giggling and walking away. He never shrank from her, but when Craig Brooks began repeating, "somebody should fuck Matt until she's Chelsea again," lunch in the cafeteria became a whistle past the graveyard.

Matt fashioned a shiv out of dense plastic and now carried it in his sock.

A thousand avatars on social media told Matt he had a right to be who he was. Actual life was more complicated. When he cut his hair, changed his name, and tried to join the boys' soccer team last summer, it created an uproar. The situation horrified his parents and adults at school lectured about how there were consequences to choices. There were dozens of conversations on internet message boards about locker rooms and bathrooms.

Matt's mother Lisvette, famous for dropping the F-word as most people might pepper a sentence with "um" or "uh," expounded on the situation on the car ride to school.

"Stop using the boy's room, Chelsea," she decreed. "Principal Baxter keeps fucking calling."

Amy unfastened her safety belt, leaned toward Matt's ear, and whispered, "mom's a professionally licensed esthetician."

"I'm a professionally licensed esthetician, sweetheart," Lisvette continued. "Every day, trannies come into the studio for waxing or laser treatments or whatever the fuck. They're fine people, but..." she paused. "You're fifteen. You used the girl's room all last year. You have two years until you fucking graduate."

"This is your doing, mom," replied Matt. "You doubted Jesus while I was in the womb."

Amy stifled a laugh as their mother frowned and touched a rosary hanging from the rear-view mirror.

"It isn't fucking funny. You could get raped in the boy's room! Whose fault would that be? And abuelita! Do you know what you're putting her through? She says she hasn't felt this way since they shot Kennedy!"

"Bobby or Jack?" asked Amy.

Hours later, Matt ate a sandwich, and Amy, entombed in a bathroom stall, called to make certain he was okay. "Are you going to kill yourself?" she asked. Toilets flushed in the background. "People with gender dysphoria kill themselves because people like mom say it's their fault if they're raped."

"It's nothing," Matt replied. "Don't worry about it."

"I *am* worried. Being a boy suits you. You were a total bitch when you were a girl. I'll support you if you cut off your tits and needle the juice, just don't kill yourself."

Matt blinked. "Okay."

"I *will* keep calling you a bitch if you don't help with my Halloween costume. I want to go as Sylvia Plath, and I need to make a gas oven out of a cardboard box."

Ian Racalmuto approached from a distance.

Amy spied him over Matt's shoulder. "There's a boy behind you."

Matt touched his sock.

"I'm sorry to interrupt," Ian said, keeping several car lengths between them. "You're Matt Granados?"

"Who wants to know?" asked Matt.

"My name is Ian Racalmuto. I need help."

"Help isn't free!" Amy shouted from the phone. "One hand washes the other!"

Matt waved him over.

Ian continued, "last night, in the southeast stairwell, Craig Brooks beat up Will Xiang and stole $250 from him. I asked Officer Timmons if he had security video, but—"

"The camera's busted," Matt interrupted. "Timmons erased the footage. That happens anytime Craig does something questionable. He's worth a lot of money to this school."

"It's nice to see we're on the same page," said Ian. "I need that video."

"Why?"

"I want to show it to the headmaster."

"The *headmaster*?" laughed Matt. "Where do you think we are? Green Gables? *Principal* Baxter is why Timmons erases videos. She's a bigger problem than he is. Nobody will touch Craig. The video won't bring justice to anybody. Don't waste your time."

Ian kicked a pebble at his feet and scoffed. "Craig stole a Zippo lighter from me. I want it back. I didn't think much of the lighter at first, but someone in Algeria—someone I don't like—is looking for it."

"What's that have to do with anything?"

"He's looking for it. That makes it important, even if I don't know why. It's the same way with Timmons. If he knew Craig would face no consequences, he wouldn't have erased the footage and sabotaged the camera. He's afraid of that video going public. That makes it valuable." Ian looked into Matt's eyes. "I don't want the video for justice. I want it for leverage."

"Ask Ian if he's dating anyone," said Amy. "Right now."

"I'm not gay," Matt mumbled into the phone.

"Not for you. For me," said Amy. "I'll be 13 in six months. Tell him."

Matt disconnected.

"Nic Delvecchio tells me you can help," said Ian.

"Nic Delvecchio has a big mouth," replied Matt.

"Nic Delvecchio thinks you're cute and you should ask her out."

Matt turned red.

"Why *are* you the person I need to talk to?" asked Ian.

Matt bit into his sandwich again. "I wanted to join boys' soccer last month. It touched off a storm, and I felt my personal safety was at risk. I hacked into the school's security network. A monster hard drive at my house now records days of surveillance cam footage, so if there's a problem Timmons can't erase history and deny something happened."

Matt's phone chimed, and a compass with a needle

appeared. He called Amy back.

"Why aren't you in school?" he asked when she answered.

"I'm going across the street to the papi store for ice cream. Stop tracking me."

"You want me to track you."

"There's a guy in a black van kidnapping girls. He cuts off their ears and saves lockets of their hair, and takes Polaroids of them as they scream."

"It's urban legend, Amy."

"You're to track me in case he abducts me. Not when I sneak to the papi store for ice cream."

Matt covered the mic with his thumb. "I made a piece of radioactive lint in Physics class, and I use it to geolocate my sister."

"Radioactive lint?" Ian mouthed.

Matt went back to his call. "Want to help me look through some security footage tonight?"

"Does the Pope shit in the woods?" replied Amy.

Matt turned to Ian. "Find me tomorrow morning."

18: I BORROWED YOUR SHOES

After school, Ian checked his email on Mario's computer in the basement. The French *attaché* in Algeria had replied with an encrypted message.

I was saddened to hear about Deena. She was a true friend and confidant. I wish you luck finding Erik. Your mother was friends with a hotelier near the Medina in Tunis. His inn was to serve as your family's fallback in event of crisis. In recent weeks, Erik had made contacts in Mezerana, outside Tablat in Algeria. I'll attach what information I have.

Ian wasted no time digesting the information. He sent further messages and pinned both Mezerana and Tunis on his map.

Upstairs, Mario made repairs under the kitchen sink. The professor supervised from behind a garbage disposal.

"Any news?" Mario's disembodied voice sounded as Ian entered the room.

"Nothing yet," said Ian.

"How was school?"

"You've gotta send me somewhere else, Grandpop. Virgil's ghost didn't even show up to guide me," said Ian.

"You met Nic Delvecchio?" asked Mario.

"I did. You knew it was her the other night, when I was caught in the rain with my suitcase?"

Mario laughed. "I know everything. I won't bother the woman next door for her doorbell camera."

A thud came from under the sink, followed by the sound of draining water and cursing. The professor jumped to the opposite side of the room.

Mario said, "hand me a dollar bill, a piece of bread, the towels beside the oven, and the acetylene torch from atop the fridge."

"Bread?"

"*Sbrigati!*"

Ian gathered the items. Amid clanging, banging, and the smell of burning metal, Mario continued, "Will left a note on the table. He had me drop him off at the corner of his street earlier today. He needed a cane, so he grabbed your baseball bat."

"That's dad's Willie Stargell bat!" Ian replied. He picked up the note from Will. Beneath his phone number it read, *I borrowed your shoes.*

Ian raced upstairs, where a pair of well-used canvas low-top Chuck Taylors replaced his Adidas Sambas.

"The balls on that kid!" He ran back down to Mario's house phone. It had a rotary dial, and it took forever to call Will's number. It rang and went to voicemail.

"Ian, it's Will. Shit. No. The other way around." He searched for a button to press to re-record the message. "Where's the..."

He hung up and dialed again. Again, it went to voicemail.

"Will, it's Ian. You have my shoes," he barked. Then he relaxed. Could he not get them back in a day or two? Was the baseball bat even a big deal? Will was in rough shape. "If I get blisters..." He let out his breath. He already had blisters. "Anyway, I'm just calling to say I'm thinking about you—wait. That sounds—that's not what I mean. This is a mess." He spun the rotary dial, attempting to delete the message.

He disconnected and called again. It rang. Voicemail.

"Yo! Will. Ian. Ah, you know, kinda bored. I'm hoping those past few messages didn't record. If they did, pretend they didn't happen. I met Craig today." He sighed. "I'm pissed about what happened to you. I can't fix it—I mean, you never asked me to—but I have a plan. Call me back. I really enjoyed sleeping with you last night—having you sleep over—Goddammit! No! No, no, no!!! Nothing's coming out right! Why won't my words work?" He dialed the rotary again. "Why doesn't this old man have a phone with buttons in the 21st century!"

"I'd replace it," Mario said, "but I don't talk on the phone anymore. My friends and I all do the WhatsApp."

"I'm in hell," Ian continued. "Call me back."

Will Xiang sat on a mattress on his bedroom floor, his back propped against a paneled wall. His ribs ached worse than the night before. Li kept only herbal medicine and hoarded it, insisting prayer was the best remedy. His chest hurt from her cigarette smoke. An electric space heater in the corner did little to warm the room, and ice for his nose had melted in a Ziploc bag.

A year ago, he trash-picked a compact stereo someone set

to the curb with three enormous boxes of Jazz cassettes. All Things Considered concluded on the radio, and he started Art Blakey's *Buhaina.*

Frigid wind blew outside, and a piece of duct tape covering a hole in his window broke free. It flapped until he pressed it back into place.

His heart dropped at the thought of losing his parents' money. It was the first thing Li had asked about when he hobbled through his front door that morning. He bowed his head and said he wired it minutes before a car hit him.

"So stupid," she had replied. "Do you not look both ways before stepping into the street?"

The prospect of his parents discovering the truth—and they soon would—made his knee twitch. He did not want to be home when they learned he had lost the money, but school was no better alternative.

How would he face Craig and Daequon ever again? He had cowered and begged and let them throw him down a flight of steps. Then, as they had ordered, he quit the soccer team. He had no other choice.

That morning, he called Coach Osbourne. "I got injured last night," he said. "I'll be out for the rest of the season—"

"Hang on a second, Will," Osbourne interrupted. In a muffled voice, he talked to somebody in the office, then returned to the phone. "I have to go. Return your cleats next week." Before Osbourne could hang up, Will's phone disconnected. The battery struggled to hold a charge.

He plugged his phone into the wall and texted Rebekkah. *Have Craig and Daequon already spent my money? Can you ask them to give it back? Even half?* Even if she knew what had happened, she wouldn't care.

The space heater hummed. The lights in the room dimmed. He inspected the Monopoly shoe Ian had given him. The memory of the boy holding a soaked cheesesteak and blowing his hair out of his face made him laugh. The duct tape on the window popped open again, and icy air blew over him. It was useless to hope they would remain friends. Li would hear nothing of him wasting time with Ian outside of school. Ian would soon find better friends with less baggage and successful parents—smart, worldly people who visited family abroad every summer, like Molly Yang.

He tried to read, but only stared at the words. He jerked off, but something was wrong. Fantasies that had occupied him for months were now as thrilling as *Better Homes and Gardens.* Classmates he eroticized days ago had become lackluster and insufficient. By the time he finished, his mind had progressed to troubling perversions. Did his fall down the steps scramble his brains? Was this why things had become so terrible? He begged God's forgiveness and cleaned up.

His phone chimed. Rebekkah.

I don't know what you're talking about. What money? Ask Craig yourself. He's a reasonable human being. I'm not his answering service.

Can I have his number? typed Will.

Ask him at school, she replied.

Li opened his door and poked her head in. "I just talked to Mrs. Yang. What did you break in the computer lab?"

"I dropped a mouse. It didn't break."

"Molly said you slammed it on the desk."

Will shrugged.

"I can't afford to replace things!" She held Ian's Sambas. "Where did these come from?"

Will smirked. "Someone let me borrow them."

She stared him in the eye. "Your phone has been ring-a-ding. Who are you calling?"

"I'm texting a girl from class."

"Do I know this girl? Where does she go to church? Where is her family from?"

"It's nothing," replied Will. "What do you need?"

Eddie appeared beside her, hacking and coughing. Li cleared her throat. "Tomorrow, take daddy to his doctor's appointment."

"I have to go back to school," protested Will.

Eddie grinned. "You want to see this girl you are texting?"

"No—"

Li's lips remained flat. "Daddy's doctor is more important than school. I don't trust the Chinese doctor at the clinic. His family is from Gansu province." She rubbed the tips of her fingers and thumb together. "People from Gansu are greedy. I asked for an appointment with a white doctor." She pointed to his phone. "Give me that. You will find many girls once you have a good job and prove to be a stable provider."

"I'm waiting for a message," Will protested.

"You're wasting time." Li took his phone downstairs.

"Plug it in," he called after her. "It won't hold a charge."

The cassette flipped to the B-side and Art Blakey resumed drumming.

Will adjusted himself on his mattress. His heart dropped. If he had to wait until Monday to go back to school, there would be no chance of getting his money back, and Ian—having forgotten him—would find easier friends.

Downstairs, his phone rang. It went to voicemail. It happened twice more. Li silenced it and lit a cigarette.

19: SECOND PLACE IS FIRST LOSER

FRIDAY.

Fire trucks, SWAT vehicles, and an ambulance screamed past Ian as he walked to Southeastern High. He dodged a large puddle on the sidewalk and tugged on the strings of a bright pink hoodie that once belonged to his mother. The hoodie zipped on the wrong side, and an iron-on patch on the breast read *fancy* in exaggerated script. His Pirates hat covered his brow.

He had been up since three. Deena's contact in Tunis had seen no sign of Erik, but promised to keep watch. No other replies arrived before he headed out the door to school.

Heavy chains locked the door to the southeast stairwell. Will's blood remained visible on the concrete at the foot. At the front of the building, red and blue lights flashed atop SUVs parked in a semicircle near the main door. A bomb squad ran inside, and Officer Timmons rushed out, waving his arms. Ian stopped in his tracks, and a boy behind him collided and tripped.

"Watch it!" said the boy.

"Sorry. I've had trouble with explosives recently," said Ian.

"It's nothing." The kid untangled a pair of cheap earbuds. "This happens every two weeks." He carried forward into the school. "I wish it *would* blow up," he muttered.

Inside school, Nic Delvecchio stood beside Matt's locker. Ian didn't recognize her at first without a bag on her head. She had styled her natural hair in perfect twists.

"You look pink today," she said.

"Pink is the color of confidence," he replied. "Mrs. Hwang, my grandpop's dry-cleaner, needed another day to get Will's blood out of my coat."

"New shoes?" asked Matt, pointing down.

"Will's. He stole mine. I tried calling him several times. His phone was off. What's all the commotion out front?"

Matt gave a thin smile. "Some guy and his 12-year-old sister crack Timmons's security board every couple of weeks and send disaster signals to emergency services. It keeps him busy."

Ian laughed. "And the footage of Craig attacking Will?"

"You can thank Amy for finding it. She's sending it now."

Ian looked at Nic. "The tools?"

Nic said, "Timmons missed my screwdriver when I went through the metal detector, but he got my flat peen hammer."

"Ms. Flora will be unhappy about that," Ian said.

"At least it wasn't her spanner," said Nic.

Ian leaned against the locker next to Matt's and examined the screwdriver. "This won't break a lock on its own."

"I double-checked Craig's combination," Nic continued. "Ten-ten-ten doesn't work. Ten *is* his jersey number."

The crowd in the hallway walked past. Matt's phone

chimed. He watched the video Amy sent and turned gray. "This is disgusting."

He turned his screen to face Ian and Nic. Craig and Daequon swung Will over the stairs. When Craig let go, Nic gasped. Ian recoiled as Daequon's rib kick connected.

Matt sent the video to Ian's email address. "There's still no good way to stop Craig or Daequon."

Ian dug his heel into the ground and ground his teeth. His ears reddened. "If we can't find a good way to stop him, we'll find an effective one. As my mother used to say, when they go low, we go—"

"High?" Matt interrupted.

"Hard," Ian corrected.

Rebekkah Batiste rounded a distant corner. She examined her hair with her Minnie Mouse compact. Craig walked beside her and slapped peoples' locker doors shut.

Ian's eyes narrowed. "I need details—the kinds that keep social workers awake at night. Does Craig's mom abuse OxyContin or leave home in manic episodes? Did she sob all night for months with postpartum depression? Did Daequon cry into his pillow when he was little because he couldn't stop his dad's drinking or his parents' fighting? Is Rebekkah writing an affirmative blog because she's self-conscious about the dimples on her thighs? Do any of them live with violence and uncertainty or lose a family member to the streets? Teeth too big, tits too little, skin too dark—tell me everything."

Matt and Nic stared at one another.

"Fuck them," Ian's voice shook. "They decorated the concrete with my friend's blood, left him for dead, and are about to turn his family onto the street. I'm getting his money back."

"I thought you didn't have friends," said Matt.

Ian smirked. "Welcome to the wilderness of mirrors."

Nic lifted an eyebrow. "Craig's dad works on the line at an aerosol can factory. He got passed up for promotion and blames the Chinese."

"The old bastard raised hell to keep me off the soccer team," added Matt.

"Does Craig like him?" asked Ian.

"He respects his dad for getting him to his level of success. Pros are scouting Craig at tomorrow's game," said Matt. "What's your plan?"

"I'll make Rebekkah cry," said Ian.

"She never cries," said Matt. "Plus, there's no dirt on her. She's even part of the homecoming court this year. She was runner-up for queen."

"Second place is first loser," said Ian.

Nic examined Ian's face. "She'll cry," she said.

Rebekkah and Craig drew near.

20: WITHOUT A CONSCIENCE

"Hello, Chelsea." Craig Brooks slammed Matt's locker door shut. "I didn't realize the lemon-scented midget and the grease monkey are your friends," he said.

"Watch it," said Nic.

"What?" asked Craig. "Grease monkey? It's a common term for a mechanic. I'm not being racist."

"I didn't say you were," said Nic. "Funny you should go there."

Rebekkah popped her lips into her mirror and turned to Ian. "Conversation would have been different yesterday if I knew you were a trannie chaser. Why didn't you say something? I would have introduced you and Chelsea properly." She reached up toward Nic's head. "Look at your hair," she said. "So twisty!"

Nic batted her away. "Touch it, and I'll end your life."

Craig turned away from Nic and brushed against her. She could feel the beginnings of an erection and stumbled back in disgust.

"Sorry," he smiled. He bent down with his hands on his knees and stared at Ian. "Have you been thinking about what

I said yesterday?"

"I haven't been thinking about you at all," Ian replied. "Has your girl figured out you and Daequon robbed Will and left him for dead?"

Craig swung a hand to slap Ian's face, but Ian caught his wrist.

Rebekkah closed her compact. "Will texted me some weird message about money last night. What happened?"

"Nothing that's his business," said Craig.

"Your boyfriend and Daequon stole $250 from Will Xiang, threw him down the southeast stairwell, and left him for dead," Ian said to her. "He also has something in his locker that belongs to me."

"Is it true?" Rebekkah asked Craig.

"No. I swear."

"You'll be screwed if it is and anyone finds out."

"Nobody's going to find out. Nobody died." Craig knocked Ian's hat from his head. "Not another word out of you."

Ian tilted toward Rebekkah. "Can I talk to you for a minute, Becky?"

Craig forced the two apart. "You've got nothing to say to her."

Rebekkah pushed Craig aside. "I can speak for myself. And it's Rebekkah, not Becky."

Ian led her to the heavy double doors by the stairwell and stood so Craig could see her face. His head tilted down to the floor and back up. He spoke, and her face flushed. The corners of her mouth turned down. She looked left and right and fluttered her hands as though she needed air. At last, she shrieked and ran for the stairs, toward the first floor. Ian shrugged.

"Why's she crying?" screamed Craig. "What did you say?"

"Nothing she doesn't already know." Ian walked backward toward the stairwell. "Anyway, good luck with your scouting session tomorrow, Craig. Someday, it will be a nice memory when you're making cans next to your dad at the factory."

Craig's face became purple. "Are you shitting on my dad?"

Ian turned to the door. "I'm shitting on your mom, for fucking him." He shot both middle fingers over his head.

Craig rushed like a beast let from a cage. People in the hallway moved to the walls.

Ian continued to meander. Soccer players run at 30 kilometers per hour. 20 with hallway traffic. 7 meters distance. Eight seconds. Seven... Six.

He dropped his hand to his side. He had picked Rebekkah's Minnie Mouse compact and opened it with a thumb. The powder puff fell to the floor.

Five... Four...

He entered the southeast stairwell through the double doors and stood on the landing. 35 steps down. A 20-foot drop. Rebekkah was at the bottom, wiping tears. Ian raised the mirror. Craig was six feet behind him, running full-bore with hands outstretched, ready to push him to the bottom.

Two... One...

Ian stepped sideways and ducked.

Craig screamed. Off-balance, he barreled toward the drop. A sharp tug. A hard stop. Ian held tight to the back of his shirt. He hung out over the steps, leaning forward into space. His feet slipped on the lip of the landing, and his arms thrashed.

"Did you ever read A Separate Peace?" asked Ian.

"What?" shouted Craig. He could not regain his balance or turn to face Ian without plunging to the bottom.

"A Separate Peace. John Knowles. It's a book about a boy with a conscience."

"I hate reading," said Craig.

"I don't have a conscience," said Ian.

"Pull me up," Craig shrieked. "If you let me fall, this school will have nothing. No money. No soccer team—I lettered freshman year. They never give letter jackets to freshmen."

"Who cares?" Ian bellowed. Craig's shirt was slipping from his grasp. "All I want is my book and Will's money. Leave us alone, and you can do what you want."

"Timmons will have your ass!" said Craig.

"Someone disabled his camera," said Ian.

Craig bellowed for help. Rebekkah's head snapped to the top of the staircase.

"What are you scared of?" asked Ian. "The staircase? Nobody died the last time someone tumbled down."

Craig slipped another inch. People below stared back at him. Rebekkah ran toward him in slow motion.

"I'll give you your book," said Craig, his voice high-pitched. "Daequon has the money. I'll get it for you. Pull me up."

Ian hauled Craig back onto the landing.

Craig brushed his shorts and tugged at his shirt to straighten it. Then he swung a powerful hook at Ian's head.

Ian dodged and spit in his face.

Craig's momentum carried him over the edge. He tumbled down the stairwell, hitting every third step and colliding with

Rebekkah on the way. His head struck the handrail, and blood covered it in long dashes. When he stopped at the bottom, his leg formed an unnatural angle at the knee. He could not feel his foot.

Sharp bone stuck from Rebekkah's forearm. Her gums bled where Craig's scalp smashed into her teeth. Students shrieked and dialed an ambulance. A few moments later, the PA system called for Timmons.

Matthew and Nic appeared at Ian's side and turned from the carnage. Matt handed Ian his hat.

"Put that on the cover of a magazine," said Ian.

"I can't look," said Matt. "I have a thing about blood. It makes me dizzy."

Nic stole a glimpse and gritted her teeth. "Yeah. It's a puddle."

"Stop!" said Matt, swooning. "I'm serious."

"He won't play soccer anytime soon," said Ian.

Matt caught his breath. "They'll accommodate him any way they can. They'll probably change the school colors from green and white to black and blue."

"He's in the wrong uniform on the magazine in the display case, anyway," replied Ian.

Nic's eyes grew wide. "The display case!" she shouted. "The screwdriver! Hurry!"

Ian fumbled in his pocket and handed it to her. She took off back through the double doors.

"Where is she going?" asked Matt.

"Beats me," said Ian.

"Want me to follow?"

"We have another job," said Ian. "Come with me to Mr. Brady's class."

21: I NEVER POP OFF HALF-COCKED

Daequon Griggs scanned social media for news about Will Xiang on his walk to school Friday. No high school student died unnoticed, however unpopular they were in life.

A classmate at Southeastern died inhaling spray paint last year. Nobody liked her. She would take deep breaths into a paper bag at her locker, then fall out of her chair in class. Her funeral was a circus. Girls who didn't even know her wailed in performative grief for their social media accounts. Afterword, there was an investigation.

If Will died, would there be an investigation? What would it uncover? And what of the new kid with the funny accent? Did he really know as much as he led on, or was he shooting in the dark and landing shots? Would he talk?

He ached to talk it through with Craig.

Daequon hung his coat in his locker—Southeastern had started its torrid boiler system overnight—and blasted Kendrick Lamar from his phone. He turned the corner into Mr. Brady's room. Will wasn't at his desk. Neither were Craig and Rebekkah. Once seated, he silenced the music and put his phone in his pocket. He picked at his jeans and stared at the door.

Matt settled in.

Ian tilted his ball cap over his brow and pulled his mom's hoodie around him. Sweat rolled down his back. "Daequon is twisting in the wind," he said. He bit his knuckle. "What's his home life like?"

"His mom's a licensed practicing nurse. Works long hours. His dad used to work with Craig's dad at the can factory. He moved to Orlando."

"Why?"

"Craig says management replaced him."

"You don't have to go to Orlando to find another assembly line job," said Ian. "There has to be more to the story." He stood. "I'll talk to him."

"What do you want me to do?" asked Matt.

Ian pulled at a sleeve. "When things turn south, make it worse."

Daequon stared into the hallway. Ian slid into an empty desk beside him.

"Hello," said Ian. "I didn't introduce myself yesterday. My name is Ian Racalmuto."

Daequon did not face him. "Clear off, shorty," he said. "I don't want to hear anything from you."

Ian felt his lip and stood to leave. "Fine. If you're waiting for Rebekkah and Craig, though, they're in the emergency ward."

Daequon snapped around. "Huh?" he uttered.

Ian sat down again, this time locking eyes. "There was blood everywhere."

"Where?"

"The southeast staircase," said Ian. With a twist of the

head, he added, "You know where that is."

A chill overtook Daequon.

Ian continued, "You have two hundred fifty dollars that belong to Will Xiang. I want it."

Daequon whipped his head between the door and Ian. He checked his phone for messages and pocketed it again.

"Craig needs a transfusion," Ian continued. "Becky's bone was sticking out. They won't text." He tapped his finger on the surface of the desk. "The money."

Daequon let off a singular huff. "I'm not giving you shit." His stomach churned. He had hidden the money in his dresser and wouldn't surrender it without Craig's consent, but the boy in pink cast an unwavering gaze. He twitched. His lips parted and his tongue dried. "What makes you think I have anything?"

Ian leaned forward. "Craig has a big mouth."

"What did he say?"

Ian recounted the details of the video Matt showed him, finishing with the rib-kick.

Daequon drummed his fist on his desk. Why had Craig snitched? Who else had he told? His heart raced. He had to buy time. "Craig has the money, not me."

Ian stood. "You're a thief and a liar."

Matt stood and gasped and shouted from the back of the room, "He called you a liar!"

"Shut up," answered Daequon.

"He said it in front of guys from your neighborhood!" Matt continued.

The room came alive with chattering and pointing.

Are we in this together, or do you want to handle things on your own if something happens? Craig had asked. Where was Craig now?

The room spun. Daequon sprung from his chair, towered over Ian, ground his teeth, and drew close. "Fuck you, calling me a liar," his voice boomed. Under his breath, he added, "Will needs to learn to stand up for himself. He's lucky what happened wasn't worse." He nudged Ian backward and screamed, "Make friends who win fights!"

Ian straightened himself out. "Like who? You? You don't know what to do without Craig beside you." He waited until the room was silent again. "Your dad might have taught you how to think for yourself if he hadn't left your mom. Then again, if my son was a liar and a thief, I'd move to Florida, too."

Daequon would have crushed Ian against a portable whiteboard had it not collapsed as they wrestled to the floor. His fists flew into Ian's sides, but without room to swing, he could not land a damaging blow. Tears left trails on his cheeks. He grabbed Ian's hood and pulled him into the clear so he could break every bone in his face, but Mr. Brady arrived and tore them apart.

"I'll kill you!" screamed Daequon.

"Office!" shouted Brady.

"What about him?" Daequon pointed at Ian.

"Now!" Brady thundered.

Daequon's glasses had fallen off. An arm had snapped. He gathered the pieces from the floor. "This isn't over," he said. He kicked his desk over and stormed out.

Ian returned to his seat. He massaged his ribs and gave Matt a thumbs-up.

Matt stared, shaken. "I've watched people get into fights at school every day for the past two years. I'm cool with broken bones and scraps over money and drugs and girls, but that was low. His dad's behavior isn't his fault. You may not have lived in America long, but you have to watch what you say to whom."

"I have goals to advance," Ian replied. "It's only words."

"Words have weight," said Matt, "and they get heavier depending on who uses them. There's punching up, and there's punching down—"

"I'd take the weight of words over the spine of a book slamming into the back of my skull," said Ian. "Do you think the CIA has conversations about whether their words punch up or down? I'm not noble, Matt, or good, or here to play fair."

"But what did you accomplish? He'll never give you the money, now. And isn't *how* you do something as important as *what* you do?"

Ian exhaled. "You sound like my grandfather."

Matt drew his brow and shook his head. "I was wrong about you. You aren't clever."

Ian's cheeks turned red. "Yes, I am."

"No, you aren't. You're no different from Craig with *his* fists and reckless mouth."

Ian's eyes widened. "The hell you say!" he shouted. Brady looked up from his desk, and Ian drew close to Matt. "Cut class for the rest of the day."

"Why should I?" Matt asked.

"Because I never pop off half-cocked. I'm fucking clever."

Like every student sent to the office, Daequon Griggs instead roamed the hallway. He dripped sweat. His muscles tensed. His busted glasses fell from his face, and he put them in his pocket. Everything was a fog. He ducked into a nook by a water fountain and focused on Mr. Brady's classroom door. Soon, the bell would ring.

What did Ian know? Ian hadn't been with him in the stairwell Wednesday night.

He wanted to call an ambulance. Craig had gone too far. But what if the police had come? Who would they have arrested? Who would have appeared before a judge? Been kicked off the soccer team? Lost their scholarships? Not Craig. He threw a kick into Will to leave the scene, and would again if he had to. At least he wouldn't have to watch his mom cry while he got locked up.

Things could have been different. Ian could have kept the conversation about Will and Craig and the robbery. Instead, he blasted Daequon's family in front of the class.

Ian would leave school on a stretcher. To hell with the consequences.

The bell rang. People tumbled out of the room. Ian's pink hoodie stood out, and his Pirates cap bobbed up and down.

Daequon stepped from hiding and closed the distance between them. He prepared to throw a punch, but the boy in pink spun and faced him.

Matthew.

"I swore I'd never wear pink again," said Matt.

Daequon pushed Matt to the ground and squinted, searching the hall. He could not find Ian. He needed to talk to Craig. He reached into his pocket to send a text. His stomach hollowed.

His phone was missing.

22: DAEQUON GRIGGS

Daequon Griggs had a goldfish in his bedroom. Its name was Happy, and it was six years old. It peered out from its fishbowl and bubbled.

When Daequon was four, his dad, who had always lived in Florida, moved to Philadelphia to live with his mother, Angela. Leon was an attentive father. Weekends would include ice cream and trips to the playground. He got a job managing the can factory and won Happy at a street fair. Every other weekend, the enormous man's thick fingers scrubbed Happy's tiny aquarium at a faucet in the backyard.

Leon would nod at laundry hanging on the patio next door and say to Angela, "A good woman lives there."

Angela would roll her eyes and respond, "He's a lucky man," and they'd laugh. The call-and-response was a source of comfort.

Leon's ex remained in Orlando. She worked in publishing and was prone to wild swings between anxiety and torpor. When Daequon was 14, the timorous woman stopped taking her meds because they made her fat. Within a week, she was no longer eating or communicating with her office. She wrote a 70,000-word manifesto about young adult books on social media, 280 characters at a time. She changed her online profile to describe herself as a "student of the pedagogy of the oppressed" and picked her eyebrows bald. Paramedics from the fire department took her to the hospital. Nobody was available to care for her two young children. Leon returned to Florida while Daequon continued to live with Angela.

"Take care of your mom while I'm away," Leon had instructed. "I swore I wouldn't leave her again, but your brother and sister are in danger. You're grown, now. They aren't. Your mom needs you, and the kids need me. I promise I'll be back."

Daequon understood the situation better in his teenage years than he had for the first four years of his life, but he hated the crazy woman in Florida. Why couldn't she throw herself into traffic or swallow all her pills like she threatened? Whenever Leon visited Philadelphia, she would relapse into sickness and call him back to Orlando early. Angela and Leon had terrible fights about her. Leon promised to return for good as soon as he could. Daequon stopped believing him after a year.

Leon left Happy on Daequon's nightstand. He also left his enormous leather Armani coat on a peg in the kitchen. Angela announced nobody was to touch it, but Daequon found it too appealing to leave in place. He removed it every day after Angela left for work and returned it before she got home.

Daequon lunged into Mr. Brady's room, searching the floor for his missing phone, his heart racing. His dad was to Facetime him that night; Molly that afternoon. He turned in circles, holding his busted glasses to his nose. He scanned baseboards and under furniture. Nobody had delivered it to the main office.

At dismissal, he sprinted to his locker. A stream of water leaked into the hallway from the boys' room across the hall. He hurdled a yellow *piso mojado* sign in his way.

Rebekkah and Craig appeared. Surgeons had encased Rebekkah's arm in plaster and tied ice bags to her face. A metal frame immobilized Craig's knee.

Rebekkah slurred and slobbered. Daequon leaned forward to better understand her.

"She's asking why you haven't been answering her texts," Craig shouted. "Do you have any idea what we've been through?"

"My phone's gone!" Daequon snapped back.

"When did you last see it?" asked Craig.

"Brady's class, before the new kid, Ian, started running his mouth at me."

Craig punched a wall. "*That* asshole."

"Why'd you snitch to him?"

"About what?"

"Everything! Will! The staircase! Me kicking him!"

Rebekkah mewed unintelligibly and threw her hands at Craig.

"Shut up!" Craig shouted at her. He returned his attention to Daequon. "I'm no snitch! When could I have told him? They took me to the ER so fast, I didn't even have time to get my stuff from my locker. We nearly froze to death in the ER." He clutched Daequon's locker door. "You didn't give up the money, did you?"

"Hell no! You think I'd let that faggot get past me?"

Daequon grasped his combination lock. It fell open, already set it to 151515. He yanked at his locker door, and his jaw went numb. A pink hoodie hung in place of Leon's Armani coat. Pinned to it was a ticket from Lenny's Pawn Shop. Someone had drawn $250 against his iPhone.

He pulled the ticket free.

The school's janitor—an old man named Troy—appeared from inside the boy's room. He spoke into a walkie talkie. "Toilet drain's causing the flood. Someone gummed it up with a coat."

A tornado ripped through Daequon's brain. Tears formed in his eyes. He called on Jesus. He promised to leave Will alone—to leave everybody alone, forever. Troy swung a plunger over a garbage can. The coat draped across the bell wasn't leather. It was Craig Brooks's varsity jacket. Pasty shit fell from the sleeves and spattered in mounds on the floor. Students screamed. Rebekkah gagged. Craig ran toward it, then stumbled back, overcome by the smell. He choked as though his tongue were blocking his throat.

Lenny Alexopoulos, the pawnbroker at Broad and Snyder, was a loud, hirsute man with dirty fingernails and a polyester shirt from another decade. Daequon had $250 he had taken from Will, but Lenny would accept no less than $300 for the phone's return. "I have a business to run," Lenny repeated as Daequon begged.

Angela Griggs, who burned through her earnings paying for the week's groceries, had no cash saved. Daequon would ask her for the money, anyway, and confess he lost Leon's coat. Then, he would spend the evening ashamed while she borrowed from friends and struck unnecessary items from a shopping list on the refrigerator.

Will's money, which Craig and Daequon dreamed of wasting on video games, was five times the amount his mother would have to cobble together ten dollars at a time. It grew heavy in his pocket, and he was certain it was pulling him into hell. Missing phones, missing coats, broken bones, pawn tickets—what might come next?

Daequon returned home and paced the kitchen floor. When his mother arrived home a half-hour later, she stumbled on a box in front of the door. "Baby?" she asked, "Can you move this?"

"What?" asked Daequon.

"This package. Your name's on it."

"Don't touch it!" he screamed. "It's the devil collecting my soul!"

"Don't you say the *d-word* out loud in this house!" She swatted at him as he ran past. He gathered the package, whimpered, and ran back into the kitchen.

While Angela opened bills in the next room, he cut through thick packing tape with scissors.

In the box was Leon's coat, in perfect condition. Clipped to it was a $50 bill and a note. It read, *you're lucky what happened wasn't worse. Make friends who win fights.* It was signed with the letter *R*.

Daequon slammed his fists down, then returned the coat to the peg before his mother appeared. An enormous grin covered her face. "You did it!" she shouted, holding up the mail. "From Lincoln! A provisional scholarship!"

His legs tingled. He propped himself on the kitchen table. "They decided already? What about the game on Saturday? Doesn't it matter?"

Angela raced over and hugged him.

"What about Craig?" he continued. "Does the game matter to him?"

"Brooks?" she asked. "I don't know. It only says *you* need to finish *your* season and play senior year, and they'll pay for four years of college." She stomped her feet and screamed in excitement.

He burst into tears.

She cried with him and sniffed. "Don't cry! You earned this!"

"I hate Ian Racalmuto!" said Daequon. "I hate him bad!"

"Who?"

He collapsed into a chair and sobbed. She brewed a cup of tea, but he ran to his bedroom before it was ready. He taped his glasses back together, then wrapped himself in Ian's pink hoodie—four sizes too small—and tapped the aquarium glass where Happy bubbled and observed life outside. His phone waited for him at Lenny's.

23: I THINK MY HOUSE BLEW UP.

After school, Nic retrieved her hammer from Timmons, then led Ian and Matt to the top of a tall, enclosed fire shaft. She broke a padlock on a heavy iron door and forced it open with her shoulder. Autumn air rushed over them.

A spool of chain-link fence rested at the base of a four-foot-tall brick parapet high above the school parking lot. The three jumped atop the parapet, and the afternoon sun lit their faces.

Wind had blown a faded blueprint beneath the fence, and Ian unrolled it. "They're building a garden up here?"

"It's been in the works for years," said Matt. "It isn't accessible to people with disabilities, so the school stopped construction."

"With all the money Craig brings in, you'd think they'd build an elevator," said Ian.

"They're adding a wheelchair ramp to the athletic grounds, instead," said Matt.

"He'll need it," Ian muttered.

A cargo plane left the airport in the distance and turned over South Philadelphia before pointing east toward the

Atlantic Ocean.

"DC-10," said Matt.

"MD-11," said Nic. They won't be in service much longer.

"You're a planespotter?" asked Matt.

"My brother Franco's a flight instructor and small plane mechanic. I was eleven when he started ground school. I learned alongside him. I'll start flying this summer."

"How do you afford it?"

"An energy company trains pilots to fly small planes over gas pipelines. They prepay Franco for six slots a year. Drones are making the job less necessary, so only two or three people show up. He packs his classes with family and friends."

Matt said, "I built tons of airplane models when I was a kid. I've read everything there is to read about aerodynamics, control surfaces, avionics, communication, airport operations, weight, balance, and navigation. My brain absorbs it. He has to teach me!"

"What would your parents say?"

"They don't have to know. What do your parents say?"

"They met at flight school. Mom's a commercial pilot. Dad heads the flight school at Cheyney."

Matt stepped sideways. "So, you're learning to fly planes and auto mechanics is a hobby?"

"Piloting is a hobby. Astrophysics is what I really like. I'll be the David Duncan Professor of Astronomy at Cornell University in fifteen years." She looked at her watch. "Twenty, if I'm handicapping for this school."

She faced the city.

"What *don't* you do?" asked Matt.

"When I sing, it sounds like domestic battery," she said.

Ian and Nic jumped down from the wall while Matt

remained standing.

Matt opened his backpack and returned Ian's Pirates hat. Nic reached into her coat and handed Ian his book. He took the Zippo lighter from its pages and stuffed it deep into his pocket.

"How did you break into Craig's locker?" asked Matt.

"I used my screwdriver to bust the small lock on the display case in the lobby." Nic gave Matt the magazine with Craig's head on the front. Inside was a picture of him kicking a ball. "You mentioned the team colors when we were in the stairwell. I remembered the magazine—he's in a different uniform, playing for another team."

Ian smirked. "With a different number?"

Matt tapped at Craig's jersey. "Nineteen-nineteen-nineteen."

Ian counted the $250 he got for Daequon's phone at the pawn shop.

Nic smiled at him.

"I told you before, it's only because Will can't do it himself right now," said Ian. "He's perfectly capable. I'm not nice. I'm not good, or here to play fair," he turned to Matt and pointed, "but I am clever."

"Maybe," said Matt.

Ian flicked his eyebrows and continued counting.

Nic grinned and cracked her knuckles. "Will has a friend."

"Yeah, well," Ian trailed off and shoved the money in his pocket. "Will has a reputation for being indecisive. He isn't. He has strict parents and doesn't always get to decide what he wants or who his friends are outside school."

"His parents should lay off," said Matt. "It's a free country."

"I get it," said Ian. "It isn't easy living in a different culture. When I lived in Algeria, my parents never told me who I could be friends with, but it was easiest for all of us when I was running around with English-speaking classmates who shared a western point of view. Otherwise, there were religious insults, language barriers, misunderstandings—it was work."

"It sounds like you have experience with this," said Matt. "Did you fall in love with a local girl or something?"

Ian looked away.

"He knocked out a local kid's tooth," said Nic.

Ian threw his hands into the sky. "Does my grandpop ever shut his yap? My point is, my parents only knew how to raise me and Erik with American values. That's how they kept us safe. That's what Will's parents are doing."

"I get it," said Matt. "I always tell my mom this isn't Mexico, but it's her default mindset—especially when there's a problem and she has to act instead of think."

Ian said, "It might be different if I were Chinese and understood his parents. I'd like to be friends with Will, but he's going to want to do what makes his family happy. I don't blame him. It's a lot less complicated that way."

"Weird," said Nic.

"What?"

"You said Will doesn't get to decide what he wants, then you decided what he wants. What do *you* want, Ian?" Nic checked her phone. "I need to go. Matt, let's continue our conversation about airplanes." She gave her number. "The last four digits are 2998. If you text me, I answer—are you ready for this?"

"At the speed of light," Ian moaned.

"I don't get it," said Matt.

"It's a joke for smart people," said Ian.

"Give me your phone," Matt said to Nic. "I'll give you my number." He misjudged his footing as she handed it to him and stumbled on the wall. When he regained his balance, he dropped her phone over the side of the building.

"What the hell?" she screamed.

"Better change those last four digits to 9806," said Ian.

"Shut up, Ian!" said Nic.

"I don't get it," said Matt.

"It's a joke for smart people!" said Nic.

Ian clicked the lid on his Zippo and traced the engraving with his thumb. "We'll continue this fight at my house. 10 AM tomorrow," he said. He pointed east. "I live over there. 1154 Tree St."

A mushroom cloud rose from his block. Seconds later, the report of an explosion reverberated from the walls of the school.

"What was that?" asked Matt.

Ian's eyes widened. "I think my house blew up."

24: SHELLSHOCK

Ian barreled down the fire escape, leaping two and three steps at a time, and raced to Tree Street. Police cordoned it off with yellow tape. A tall officer, her blond hair pulled tight in a bun, stopped him until he caught his breath. He explained he lived in the neighborhood. *S. Hosay*, her name tag read.

His front awning warped, and the upper windows of his home had cracked, but nothing else was amiss. On the other side of the street, flames shot from a collapsed house. A fire truck arrived, sirens wailing. Three news helicopters circled overhead. The wind carried smoke and heat toward him in a tremendous cloud, and he turned away. His eyes burned and watered. When he opened them again, he was lying on the sofa in Mario's basement. Matt looked down at him. Mario dabbed his forehead with a towel.

He bolted upright. "*Che cazzo è?*" he screamed. He saw stars, and his chest pounded.

Mario helped him back down. "*Aspetta*," he said. "You've been out for an hour. The house across the street blew up. You had a panic attack."

"I don't get panic attacks," said Ian. "Why the hell am I

down here? And are you okay, Grandpop?"

"Fine," said Mario. "I was taking *la passeggiata* when the bomb went off."

"Nic and I ran after you when you bolted from the rooftop," said Matt. "When we found you, you were wandering in circles in the middle of 13th Street, blocking traffic. You were looking under cars for Erik."

"That's embarrassing," said Ian. "Where's Nic?"

"She had to go home."

Ian looked around the room.

"You don't remember any of it?" asked Mario.

"It happens sometimes," said Ian. "Sudden noises set me off, but I've never passed out."

"You have PTSD," said Mario.

"I prefer to call it shellshock," said Ian.

"You need help," said Mario.

"I can get help after I find Erik," said Ian. "I have four days left and I'm making scarce progress."

"I talked to officer Hosay while you were..." Matt paused and smiled, "shellshocked. The house that blew up belonged to an old woman named Mildred Santucci."

"I thought she was dead," said Mario.

"She is now," said Ian.

"Officer Hosay says workers were performing illegal electrical and gas work on Mrs. Santucci's house," said Matt.

"1145," said Mario. "Our address is 1154."

"That means nothing," said Ian. "Lighting strikes at random."

"But I can smell it before it does," said Mario. "Your namesake once wrote, *Once is happenstance. Twice is a coincidence. Three times is enemy action.* Your suitcase, the house across the street..." Mario twitched his mustache. "The lady next door with the doorbell camera will be home tomorrow morning. I'll talk to her. In the meantime, Ian, from the beginning, tell me everything you can about Richard Fenzel."

"Over dinner," said Ian. "I want rendang. Let's go to Hardena." He stood and leaned on the wall, then drew a breath. He searched his pockets to play with his lighter and found the hundreds in cash from earlier. "Do you still have Will's address?"

After dinner with Mario—Indonesian was a mutual favorite—Ian walked east through South Philadelphia. Boarded windows, broken awnings and cracked stucco became commonplace. A man slept on the porch of an abandoned house. Along a desolate tertiary street where storm doors lacked glass and fell from hinges, he found Will's house. Somebody had painted the address on the brick beside a mailbox in a sloppy hand.

Ian continued to a narrow concrete alley behind the house, where he used his Zippo as a torch. Rodents scattered among bags of garbage, old buckets, and spent syringes. A rusted-out washing machine and an unusable motor scooter blocked his way. Yellow light glowed from Will's bedroom, where duct tape covered a hole in a broken window.

He returned to the street.

Earlier in the day, while *Morning Edition* played on the radio, Li pulled to the front of Will's house in a blue Daihatsu Charade. Her window was down, and she blew puffs of cigarette smoke into the air.

"Whose car is this?" asked Will, gathering his belongings and climbing in the back.

"This is Elaine's," Li replied.

"Next door Elaine?"

"No, Marshall Street Elaine."

"How old is it? The seat belts in the back lack shoulder straps. Did you have to turn a crank in the front to start it?"

"Don't be smug," Li replied. "We are lucky Elaine lets us use her car."

"You don't have a license," said Will.

"Daddy cannot walk to the clinic. He didn't sleep a wink last night." Eddie closed the front door and left the house, his skin pallid in the daylight.

"You'll screw up the upholstery with your smoking," said Will.

Li screamed, "The upholstery is pleather, and the smoke blows out the window when we move. Elaine won't notice."

The next day, Li and Elaine would get into a tremendous Cantonese quarrel in the middle of Marshall Street. Elaine would declare the interior ruined by smoke. Li would give her a half-bottle of Febreze, and the matter would conclude in uneasy silence.

They stood in line and waited for the clinic to open. Will balanced himself on his baseball bat. Fifteen people had arrived ahead of them. When the doors opened, they sat among rows of metal chairs in a bland cinderblock waiting room.

When the hands on a round analog clock swung to 9:15, Will hobbled to a busy registration counter. His ribs ached, his nose burned, and his shoulder throbbed where he had landed on it.

"Do you have any ibuprofen?"

A receptionist gave him a smudged, photocopied map on

a half-sheet of paper with directions to the nearest pharmacy. The bottom edge of the sheet, cut by hand with scissors, was rough and uneven. Before he could say more, a Physician Assistant approached the receptionist.

"Is the orthopedist here today?"

"Not on Fridays. Why?"

"He's needed at the hospital. Two kids fell down a flight of steps at the high school."

On returning home, Will again sat on his bed and ached, this time while listening to John Coltrane. Mario Racalmuto had given him the number to his house phone, but Will remained without his cellular. He had no clue what he'd say to Ian, anyway, should he dial. He imagined Ian saying, "Who? Oh, right." Maybe there'd be a perfunctory "glad you're feeling better" before an excuse to disconnect.

What had become of his lucky deck of cards? He removed a snow globe from his bedside table. Cousin Ruthie gave it to him when he was young. Tiny glitter coins floated around the Stardust Hotel in Las Vegas. The heavy base read STARDUST $1 BILLION GIVEAWAY! He imagined standing inside, catching the billion dollars and having all he would ever need.

A visitor pounded on the door downstairs. Li jumped from her chair and chattered to Eddie. Will listened from his room, but did not understand their conversation.

Friends at church talked to Li about deportation raids that had become frequent on blocks like hers. Officers came in the evening hours, when people were secure at home, and took them to detention centers where they awaited trial.

She left her fate to God and walked to the door, her nerves

unsteady. From the window, she did not see a black van that would carry her family away. Instead, a short white boy with a Pittsburgh Pirates hat stood on the concrete steps.

"I do not know who this person is," she told Eddie.

She cracked the door.

Ian recognized the smoke that Will carried on his clothing. "My name is Ian Racalmuto. I'm here to see Will. Can you give this to him?" He held up a small brown bag.

She threw the door shut, locked it, and returned to her husband.

"One of Will's teammates?" asked his father.

"It does not matter," said Li, igniting a cigarette. "We do not need strange visitors in the middle of the night." She exhaled a cloud. "Without soccer, Will's going to need something to occupy his time. I cannot imagine leaving him to roam the streets like the boy outside. I'll call Mrs. Yang. Molly is president of the math club. Will can go there."

Li dialed Mrs. Yang and imagined the acerbic cut-and-thrust that always came with talking to her. *Perhaps send him to Chinese school on Saturday instead of math club? It's only $500. He knows no Mandarin. No hanzi. No history. How is he to get along in society?*

Li's fears did not come to pass. Earlier that night, Mrs. Yang learned of Molly's homecoming plans with Daequon Griggs and quashed the idea. Molly now cried into her pillow. Mrs. Yang wasted no time adding Will's name to the math club roster, dispensed Molly's phone number, and encouraged Will to ask her to homecoming.

The conversation was pleasant. They agreed their children needed guidance and would always find unsuitable people to date if left on their own.

Will had rallied at the sound of Ian's voice at the door, but his stepmother's behavior humiliated him. Ian had journeyed to his shitty neighborhood and found his nasty house, only to have Li slam the door in his face. Had pain not shot through his swollen ankle, he would have chased Ian down the street and apologized.

His phone rang downstairs. Li silenced it.

He planted a fist hard into his pillow, and his sternum burned. Would she deny him friends forever? His landlord would want money tomorrow. How would he ever reclaim it? He couldn't even walk. He closed his eyes. Nothing was right, and never had been, and never would be, for the rest of his life.

A sharp crack at his window raised the hair on his neck. Another followed. He backed into the corner of his bed. The duct tape covering the hole tore open.

A heavy bottle of ibuprofen sailed through the opening, bounced off his wall, and crashed to the floor beside him. Inside were 400 tablets and a note. It read, *My house. 10 AM tomorrow. -Ian.* Wrapped under the note was $250.

25: LASAGNA

SATURDAY.

Will's pain subsided overnight, but when he awoke Saturday morning, his ankle remained swollen and weak. He sat on his mattress and turned his radio to NPR. It was lousy on weekends.

His father, who cluttered the downstairs table with new medications and a blood pressure cuff capable of inflating a bicycle tire, was well enough to spend the day playing *xiangqi* at cousin Ruthie's house. Before leaving, he knocked on Will's door, then opened it without waiting.

"You quit the soccer team?"

"I had to," said Will.

Eddie's eyes turned down. He pursed his lips, cleared phlegm from the depths of his throat, and swung his finger in a circle at the floor. "Clean your room."

Will shut the door with his baseball bat.

Li visited ten minutes later and did not bother to knock before opening the door. She would work a half-day shampooing at the hair studio, then travel to her church in Chinatown where cheap coffee brewed in a large silver percolator in fellowship hall.

"Nice to see dad feeling better," said Will.

"He will be better when the licorice tincture arrives, and he can stop taking chemicals," she said. "You aren't making his recovery easier. He worries about you."

She lit a cigarette. "Last night, the Jesus came to me in my sleep. He said a person serving Lucifer prayed for a car to strike a person of weak faith. Pray more. Prayers to heavenly father must surpass prayers to hell. You were careless, and Satan took advantage. Pray while I am gone." The cigarette paper crinkled as it burned. "Go to school today. Molly Yang has added you to the math club. Text her." She gave him Molly's number, smiled, and departed.

Will again closed his door with his bat. He tried to pray, but his mind detoured. Why would Jesus come to Li with explanations of events that never happened? His pastors always instructed him not to doubt his elders. He did not want to anger God, but where did spirituality end and psychosis begin? Had she been telling his father that insufficient faith caused his cancer?

He walked with his bat to his landlord's house and surrendered the money. The man opened a calendar. He used his rubber hand as a paperweight for the bills and circled a new date two weeks in the future.

At ten o'clock, Will neared the school. A piece of paper on the door pointed math club attendees to the cafeteria. The humid room would stink of bleach. He imagined working problems next to Molly Yang under buzzing fluorescent lights. He gripped the handle, but did not enter.

Ten minutes later, he knocked on Ian's door with the end of his bat. Nic Delvecchio answered.

"Will!" she said. "You look like hell!"

"I got beat up," replied Will. "What's your excuse?" She blew a raspberry. He placed his baseball bat in an umbrella vase next to her skateboard and sat. "What happened to the house across the street?"

"Faulty wiring," said Nic.

"The old woman who lived there had blue eyes," said Ian. "One blew left and one blew right."

Will laughed. On hearing his laugh, Nic burst out laughing, too.

"I've never heard you laugh," she said. "It's adorable!"

The Professor sat on a cookbook in the kitchen and swished his tail. Ian made lasagna. The room was a mess of ingredients.

Will limped over. "I only came by to say hello," he said. "I'm on my way to math club, so I can't stay."

Ian handed him a ball of dough. "Run this through grandpa's pasta machine. Double it over and run it through again while I mix some ricotta. Did you see Matt Granados outside?"

"No." Will cranked the dough through heavy metal rollers on an antique press. "Where's your grandpop?"

"Next door. He's been dying to watch yesterday's explosion on my neighbor's doorbell camera. When I came up from the basement this morning, he was already out of the house."

"You're sleeping in the basement?"

"I can't fall asleep in my room. Where's the math club?"

"The school cafeteria. Li enrolled me. Four hours every

Saturday. I might drop by here again when it's over, but there's a lot of homework."

Ian showed Will how to layer the cheese and handed him the bowl, then noticed his shirt—light brown with a red wine glass and text that read *barbaresco*. "That's my shirt."

"You told me to take one from your collection," said Will.

"It's my *favorite* shirt." said Ian.

"I understand why. It's soft," replied Will.

"And you're wearing my shoes," said Ian.

"How lucky is it we're the same size?" grinned Will. "Now you get to wear my Chucks. They're more your style."

"No, they're not!" laughed Ian, flailing his hands.

"You're talking with your hands," Will said.

Ian hid them behind his back.

Nic and Ian brought Will up-to-date. The moving company hired to bring the Racalmuto's goods was loading at the nearby shipyard and would arrive at any moment. A mover with a prominent underbite had gathered a key to their storage crate early that morning. Nic recounted Friday's events to Will's amazement.

"How have you spent the past few days?" asked Nic.

"Eh," Will shrugged. He had never complained to outsiders about family matters, but with Ian and Nic focused on him, he took a breath and in a cathartic rush explained his father's prognosis, Li's obstinance and unhinged religion, and his clandestine negotiations with his landlord. When he finished, he slumped in the chair.

"$250 for licorice tincture?" asked Nic. "What will your parents do when they don't get it?"

"Ground me for all eternity," said Will. "Nothing matters if we have nowhere to live. What am I supposed to do? Feed my dad squirts of licorice juice in a tent at the heroin camp in Kensington?"

"Grandpop uses anise tincture when he makes pizzelles," said Ian. "I only like the vanilla ones." He rummaged through the cabinet and found licorice extract in a dropper bottle. He removed the label under scorching water and handed it to Will. "Guaranteed to cure cancer better than the stuff from China."

"Wait a week and put it in your mailbox," said Nic. "Matt can forge a Chinese mailing label. Where is he?"

"Can you call him?" asked Will. "My phone stopped working."

"He dropped my phone from the roof of the school," said Nic.

"I only have grandpop's with the rotary dial," said Ian. "Where are the movers?" he asked. He opened the door to glance down the street. Matt Granados looked up, his fist poised to knock. His hair was out of place, and he wore clothes from the day before. Dark circles surrounded his eyes.

"You look as bad as Will," said Nic, giving Will a side-eye.

"Sorry I'm late," said Matt. "I've been up all night."

"I have to go to math club," said Will.

"Hang on," said Matt. "I have something for you guys." He removed a heavy bookbag from his shoulder.

Matt moved a heavy stack of *Foreign Affairs* magazines from the library table. He opened his backpack, set aside a piece of dust sealed in a Lucite box, and placed three thin, nondescript smartphones in a row.

"Ian's phone blew up in his luggage," he said. "I dropped Nic's by accident. Will hides his because it's pink and bedazzled in rhinestones."

Will bristled.

"Sorry, kid," said Matt. "Word gets around."

"It doesn't hold a charge anymore, anyway," said Will.

Matt continued, "I got five busted phones off eBay for $15, repaired them with two bucks worth of parts, and hacked them into network. They're a little slow, but functional. They're also encrypted end-to-end and undiscoverable—totally off the grid." Matt continued on about proxies and virtual private networks.

"Android or iOS?" asked Nic.

"I wrote the operating system, called Boothroyd. It's easy. You'll get the hang of it."

He gave them each a Bluetooth earpiece. "The phones include a wireless local loop."

"A WiLL," said Ian, pointing at Will.

"What is it?" asked Will.

"It's a voice over internet app. A party line, where we can all talk at once like we're in a room together." He toggled a button and his voice came from their earpieces. "If you don't want to include me, toggle me off."

"One last thing," said Matt. "These phones have near-field comm chips. You can use them to unlock computers, open compatible doors, or pay for things at Target with a valid credit card."

Ian programmed the combination to his front door lock into his phone and waved it a few inches away. The deadbolt turned and unlocked.

"You're giving these to us?" asked Will, admiring the phone.

"Thank you!" Nic grinned. "There's an EFB on mine!"

"A what?" asked Ian.

"An electronic flight bag," said Matt, growing quiet. "I figured Nic's a pilot, so—you know—she needed digital charts and weather and stuff."

"Amazing," she said. "You're so thoughtful!"

Will kicked him under the table and he blushed.

The lasagna bubbled inside the oven. The Professor pawed at the window.

Ian turned to Matt. "When you opened your backpack, there was dust in a box. Is that your radioactive lint? Can I see?"

"Radioactive lint?" asked Will. "Didn't Madam Curie die from carrying around radioactive lint?"

"It's not like that," said Matt. He tapped his phone. An on-screen needle pointed at the lint, and the app chirped like a Geiger counter. "It's an old-school tracking device used by MI6 in the '60s. I hope to weave it into a dollar bill someday. My phone will point to the dollar as it travels across the United States. I track my sister, so she doesn't get abducted by a man in a black conversion van."

"The one who cuts off girls' ears and takes Polaroids of them screaming?" asked Nic. "I remember that legend. When I was a kid, he cut off their hands, too." She removed the lint from the box and squeezed it.

"One last important thing," said Matt. "The State Department."

Ian sat upright.

"Engineers at Foggy Bottom mounted a webcam on the lip of the Truman Building to observe a Peregrine Falcon nesting there. I've been recording it, and if you ever want to watch, you can click on the app marked P. Falcon."

"Does it fly?" asked Nic.

"No."

"Does it sing?" asked Will.

"No!"

"What does it do?" asked Ian.

"It sits on its eggs." said Matt.

"And people watch?" asked Ian.

"They can't get enough," said Matt. He turned his phone to reveal a Peregrine Falcon fluttering as it sat.

Will lifted his shoe. "I have a question for you, Ian, unrelated to the falcon. On the bottom of your shoe is a crease that looks like a bullet grazed it. What is it?"

Ian took a gulp of orange juice. "It's a crease where a bullet grazed it."

Will ran his finger across. "I need more than that. I just told you everything about my family. Quid pro quo."

"Okay," said Ian. He offered a plate of bagels and bit into one, getting crumbs on his lap. "I doubt you'll believe me."

26: A MATTER OF TRUST

Phones at the Racalmuto house in Algiers rang through the late summer evening. The 92-year-old President of Algeria had died with no clear successor. His two sons hated each other, and each claimed leadership. Two military generals sent troops in armored carriers, hoping to gain control, themselves. Reports of unrest in *Bab El Oued* lit up social media.

Erik Racalmuto put his phone down, buttoned his collar, and adjusted his watch. Air raid sirens blared. "The French *attaché* called. I have to go to the embassy. Natalie is already there."

"Take the Glock from on top of the fridge," said Deena from the other room. "Ian, can you please load it for your brother? Don't chamber a round. I almost lost a foot because of you last time."

"I hate guns," said Erik. "Leave it in case dad needs it." He tossed a 3x5 index card filled with random numbers in Ian's direction. "Practice while I'm gone."

The card was an encoded message for Ian to decipher with a one-time pad - a series of numbers shared between them.

The encryption technique, invented in the 1800s, remained unbreakable to the best computers.

Deena rounded the corner. "You can play cryptography and spycraft in the car, Ian. Come with me."

"Where are we going?" asked Ian.

"Boumediene Airport. Rick Fenzel called. With hell rising downtown, the Secretary of State is flying in. Somebody needs to get her."

"The embassy has a motor pool."

"Fenzel can't reach any of the drivers. He was asking if I have heard from any of them, and I haven't. So, I put my martini on the nightstand and said 'fuck it, I'll pick her sorry ass up myself and drive her to the embassy.' You can keep me company. You've never met the Secretary of State. She's quite a pistol. You can distract her with gentle humor and fart noises so I don't have to talk to her."

"Why would SecState fly into a hot zone? Isn't it irregular to ask you to drive?" asked Ian.

"I'm going as a matter of trust," said Deena. "That is, I don't trust Rick Fenzel. He's lying, and I want to know why. We also need to talk about what happened at school. Your headmaster called."

"You shouldn't do this, Mom," said Ian. "It's a terrible idea, and you're not entirely sober."

"I'm not entirely drunk."

Cardiff entered the room. "Everybody's up. What's going on?"

"Nothing, dear," said Deena. "There's a coup. Go back to bed. Erik's off to the embassy, and Ian's coming with me to the airport."

"Do I need to worry?"

"No more than usual, darling. No good about goodbye," she said, kissing him.

Erik gave Ian a sharp flick of the ear as they headed out the door, but Ian didn't react.

Deena drove her SUV along National Highway number five. It was late and the road to the airport was empty.

"Are you okay to drive, mom?" asked Ian.

"I'm fine. There's no traffic this hour, and it's a straight shot to the airport."

"Straight shot," repeated Ian, saying nothing more. He removed the encoded card that Erik had given him.

"Do you have your phone if we need it?" asked Deena. "Mine is at the embassy."

"Yeah," said Ian. He combined arithmetic with a conversion table called a checkerboard to work out the cipher on the card. When he had finished decoding, he rolled his eyes. It read DICK FACE. He smiled with the certainty he had succeeded.

"Why did you let your brother flick your ear as you were leaving?"

"It's a game." Ian pulled a 50 Dinar coin out of his pocket. "When Erik flicked my ear, I picked his pocket and stole his coin. He wants me to think and act while under attack. There are endless alternatives. A Racalmuto loves alternatives."

"You sound like your grandfather."

"Grandpa thinks the spy stuff is neat. Did he used to be a secret agent?"

Deena rolled her eyes. "Your grandpop is an instigator, and will be the death of me. I've spent my life trying to mitigate his influence. Do you remember what he gave you for your eighth birthday?"

"A stiletto that you and dad wouldn't let me touch?"

"A stiletto that your dad and I wouldn't let you touch. A stiletto! And not a pair of heels! It was an ejector knife, Ian, that you could have used to kill somebody! What might that man have taught Erik in their unsupervised moments? How to kill someone with a rolled newspaper? How to build a grenade from a soup can?" She uttered a nervous laugh and considered the martini she had left behind. "Your father wanted to name you Mario, after your grandpop. Gentle Jesus. Gentle, loving Jesus! Could you imagine?"

"You tried to take the plastic off his furniture when you were new to the family. You got off on the wrong foot."

She scrunched her face. "About school. You knocked out Kintu's tooth in a fight over a girl yesterday. He's your best friend."

Ian sighed. "He was trying to punch me. I raised my arm to defend and caught his jaw. He wasn't my best friend."

"You've known Kintu for three months and you've been inseparable."

"No, we've been hanging out for three months. I've only known him since yesterday."

Several miles away, Ian could see the runway end identifier lights at the airport. Along the road, a woman wrapped in a white haik stood motionless beside a baby carriage.

"Mom!" Ian shouted, "Brakes! IUD!"

Deena locked the brakes and spun the car 90 degrees, so the driver's side door was nearest the woman. She dropped, and the baby carriage exploded. The blast caused the SUV to roll upside-down, then upright again. Ian's window shattered. The SUV's alarm filled the otherwise quiet night.

"Ian, it's an IED, not an IUD." said Deena.

Ian brushed himself off. "What's the difference?"

"An IED is a bomb that hinders diplomacy. An IUD is not a bomb and hinders grandkids. Hand me my gun from the glove box."

Ian loaded a magazine into Deena's P226 and spun it upright on his index finger with the grip facing her. She stepped out of the car and surveyed the damage. Ian's phone rang. It was Erik.

"Why isn't mom picking up? I've been trying to reach her!"

"Tell Erik to get the phone from my desk," said Deena. "Promise me you won't allow it into Richard Fenzel's hands."

"But—"

"Promise me!" she shouted

"All right, all right," said Ian. He screamed her instructions to Erik, but the line filled with static.

"I can't hear a damn thing," said Erik. "The embassy is under attack. Natalie McLauren is with me. I don't know how much longer the building will be secure. Stay away."

"No way," replied Ian. "I'll be there in fifteen minutes." There was a loud ping off of the side of the car. "Better make that twenty, Erik. Somebody's shooting at us."

"Don't forget to air down the tires."

"I know!" said Ian. "I'm not a child."

Will reflected on the bullet scar in Ian's shoe, and Nic bit down on a bagel. Matt had fallen asleep and snored, his cheek smashed against the table.

"What happened next?" asked Nic.

Ian continued, "My mom died later that night. I showed

up at the embassy and found Erik, but lost both him and my mom's phone when I triggered a bomb. After that, I woke up in a hospital in Germany."

Will's eyes, skeptical and inquisitive, locked on Ian's. When they did, Ian was no longer in a field in Algeria, but at the snack bar at the soccer game, beef dripping on his shirt. He shook his head and diverted his attention to the kitchen clock. "Where the hell are the movers?"

The front door rattled and opened. Mario rushed through, his neighbor's laptop in hand. "Ian," he said, "you need to see this."

27: LET'S STOP A WAR

Mario situated his neighbor's laptop on the table between Ian and his friends and poured a mug of dark coffee from the pot on the countertop. "Good to see all of you." He motioned toward Matt. "Who's sleeping beauty?"

"That's Matt. He was up all night," said Ian. He nodded at Mario's coffee. "Pour me a cup?"

"You're too young," replied Mario, moving an empty wine bottle into a recycling bin. "There's decaf in the cabinet."

"There's no adventure in decaf," replied Ian. "What do you have for us?"

Mario turned the computer to face the room and started the neighbor's security video. An enormous man, half his head enveloped in a gold plate, stood in the middle of Tree Street with a black cherry bomb. He attempted to light it with matches that snuffed in the wind. He talked on his phone, disappeared, and returned five minutes later with a *crème brûlée* torch.

"Borrowed from the bakery down the street," said Mario. "The man with the gold head never returned it. The bakery is unhappy. They're using a salamander broiler to caramelize sugar, but it isn't as effective."

Tzvi knocked on Mildred Santucci's door. It took the decrepit woman a few seconds to open an abundance of locks. The fuse burned down, and Tzvi twitched. No sooner was Santucci in view, tennis balls at the feet of her aluminum walking frame, than Tzvi forced her backward, threw his bomb inside the house, and ran. The house exploded.

"Can you identify that man?" asked Mario.

"I've never seen him," said Ian. "Why did he come to town to kill Mildred Santucci?"

Will groaned. "He wants to kill you, asshole!"

"Oh," said Ian.

"Do you think it's coincidence he's in town the same day your stuff is arriving at the shipyard?" asked Nic.

"There's nothing they would want," said Ian. "It's only pots and pans and clothes and furniture."

"Do you have a cargo manifest?" asked Nic.

Matt raised his head from the table, squinted at the computer, drew it toward him, and hacked into the shipyard intranet. "Freighter Ningbo arrived last night." He matched the container identification number to a receipt Ian gave him and read a list of items. "Kitchenwares. Toaster, Cuisinart, blender, racist cookie jar."

Mario laughed. "I gave that cookie jar to Deena several years ago. You should have seen her face."

"Was it an Aunt Jemima?" asked Nic.

"It was!" Mario laughed as tears formed in his eyes. "She comes apart at the waist, and you fill the cavity with gingersnaps."

"You're terrible!" said Nic.

"Further decorative items," Matt continued. "Antique

clock, giclee of Nero bathing. Office supplies and accoutrements. Bowling trophy, Dictaphone, soda siphon, cocktail set..."

Ian turned white. "Cremation urn?"

"How did you know?" asked Matt.

"I hid mom's phone in a cremation urn in her office. I told security about it. Surely they have the urn in-hand by now."

"But suppose they don't," said Nic

"But they do!" argued Ian.

"But if not?"

"If someone gets it, they can use it to start a war from Main State in D.C."

"And that someone could be our mad bomber. Will you take that chance?" asked Will. "You made a promise to your mom to keep it out of Fenzel's hands."

Ian tore open a thin plastic dry cleaning bag that covered his barn coat. "I'll get an Uber to the container yard."

"You can't walk into the Philadelphia Container Yard by yourself," said Will. "It's dangerous. Did you ever see *On the Waterfront*? Karl Malden's nose is terrifying." He pulled his bat from the umbrella vase. "I'll go with you."

"Don't you have math club?" asked Ian.

Nic said, "I know Hodges, a guard who works in the security booth. Count me in."

Matt had fallen asleep again.

"Leave him," said Ian. He took Matt's backpack from nearby and threw it over his shoulder. Nic gave him a questioning glance.

"Timmons still has my bag, and I need one," said Ian. "I'll give it back. Promise."

The Uber pulled up to the front of the house.

"Be back in time to take your lasagna out of the oven," said Mario. "I'm not cleaning up the mess you made in the kitchen."

Ian nodded. "Let's stop a war."

28: WE LEAVE AT THE FIRST SIGN OF TROUBLE

"What do you think happened to your brother?" Will asked Ian. Stained blankets covered the back seats of a rattling car that stank of marijuana.

The driver looked at Ian in the rearview mirror. Ian withdrew his phone and texted Nic and Will.

He's hiding. Fenzel commands agents at Nightwater, a security service. I know they're searching for Erik. The Bab el Bhar *in Tunis was always our fallback, but nobody's seen him. Tablat was also a possibility, but they have yet to reply—they use a complex series of signals from a nearby town called Mezerana, and the timing has to be right.*

He produced the Topps baseball card he got in the mail. "Check this out," he said. "It's a 1970 Stephen Blass. He pitched for the Pittsburgh Pirates until one day he lost all his skill, out of the blue. Nobody knows why. He's now an announcer."

"What does it have to do with anything?" asked Nic.

"It's an innocent postcard," said Ian. He returned to his

phone. *It's a signal that an agent is still alive and operating. Erik knows I collected baseball cards when I was a kid, and he knows I like the Pirates. He sent it. It had to be him.*

Was it mailed from Tablat? asked Nic.

"Third party," he said.

Why doesn't he shoot you an email? asked Will. *There have to be a million internet cafes in North Africa.*

He's abandoned his accounts if he's gone dark, and it's possible he's off the grid. Ian put his phone to the side. "Even in the best circumstances, trails go cold. I have three days remaining, and I've made scarce progress."

The freighter *Ningbo*, moored at the Philadelphia Container Yard, came into view, and the Uber slowed. Two quay cranes stood abeam of the ship, fore and aft. "The main checkpoint is just ahead," said Nic. "I'll talk to Hodges and find out who's been through. He has thick glasses and bad peripheral vision. You can get under the barrier as long as he's looking at me."

"If anything is wrong, we leave," said Ian.

Ian, Will, and Nic exited the car and walked toward the guard booth. Nobody appeared. The security gate pointed skyward. In the distance, a group of young trespassers raced loud dirt bikes through the industrial park.

"That's Dirt Bike Tre and his gang," said Will, removing his phone to take a picture. "They're street celebrities. Police have chased them for three years. On hot days, they'll ride their bikes and quads on city streets, snarling traffic and stopping for nobody. Security must have the day off if they're racing here."

"I wonder if he's seen anything suspicious?" asked Ian. A

biker with a red leather jacket stopped a yellow Yamaha to situate himself. Ian approached, and the biker greeted him at knifepoint.

"Is that a Yamaha?" asked Ian. "I once had to ride one through a busy market in Bangkok, and— "

Will grabbed Ian's arm and yanked him away. "You don't talk to Dirt Bike Tre," he said.

"That's him?"

"That's his cousin, Sawbuck. You don't talk to him, either."

"Nice to meet you!" Ian shouted. The man glared and sped off. He turned to Will again. "Where's Tre?"

Will pointed to another man on a neon green bike who wore a ninja mask and carried a hefty Katana sword on his back.

Back at the guard station, Nic banged on the door. Nobody answered. The knob rattled, but a hefty weight prohibited her entry. She threw her body forward, and the door yielded. On the other side, Hodges's cadaver tilted sideways on the floor. His neck was black and blue.

Ian ran over, and Will hobbled close by.

An unfinished cigar burned in a glass ashtray. Blood crept toward a drain. Beside Hodges lay two associates, their throats sliced open.

"My God," said Nic, turning away.

"What?" asked Will, struggling to get a glimpse inside.

Nic described the scene.

"I want to see!" said Will, pushing forward.

"Think Sawbuck did this?" asked Nic.

"His blade was clean, and it does nothing to explain the strangulation," said Will. "This was the work of more than one person. You don't knife two people then strangle the third, or strangle a guy while his friends stare and watch."

"The killer used a serrated blade," added Ian. "Sawbuck's is smooth. Chances are, the bikers have no clue this happened. They saw the open gate and came in."

"The bruise circles his neck," said Nic. "Someone strangled him with a rope."

"Or a necktie," Ian muttered.

Two more riders appeared on red Kawasakis and screamed past to join their friends.

"Remember how we agreed to leave at the first sign of trouble?" asked Ian.

Will stood fascinated beside the mess and did not answer, and Nic stared at the cranes over the Ningbo.

"Me, either," he concluded.

29: THE CONTAINER YARD

Ian pulled the straps on Matt's backpack to fit his frame. Will, baseball bat at his side, peered deep into the guard booth. "Someone ripped the security system out of the wall and smashed the computers. The monitors are blank."

Nic made for the *Ningbo*. Ian followed. The crane at the bow loaded intermodal containers onto the boat while an offloading crane remained still at the rear. Onshore, 20-foot ISO crates stood in rows. Between the stacks and the ship, a dented flatbed moving truck idled in a transfer lane.

Dirt Bike Tre's motorcycle gang raced in the distance.

"Be careful!" Will called to his friends. When Nic and Ian carried forward, he hobbled after them, using his bat. "This didn't happen long ago. Whoever did this is still here. Your movers could be in danger."

"They're already dead," Ian shouted back to him.

"How do you know?" asked Will.

"Experience," said Ian. He drew close to the moving truck. Diesel exhaust hung in the air. Face down beside the truck was the mover with the underbite, the key to the shipping container still in his hand. Further on was his crew, stabbed to death.

"We need to call the police," said Nic.

"We needed to call the police three cadavers ago," Will said, still trailing behind.

Ian rushed over and felt for a pulse. There was none. "The only blood is at his mouth where his face struck the ground."

Will at last caught up, squatted, and inspected the corpse. "Foam on his lips," he said. He noted a pinprick of blood dotting the back of the man's neck.

"Good catch," said Ian. "Poison. Hit from behind. A needle or a dart."

Will removed the key from the man's hand and surrendered it to Ian. "Odd they left this."

Ian observed the perimeter. "They're watching us. They want us to lead them to mom's phone. It's here. It's the only thing worth the cost of butchery like this." He pointed up. "Why isn't the aft crane moving? Is it manual or automatic?"

"The forward crane is automatic," said Nic. "The aft one's manual, driven by a woman in the glass cabin suspended overhead." The crane operator appeared outside. Nic waved. The operator did not wave back. Instead, she pitched out into space.

Nic gasped, and the three scattered. The woman's body hit the concrete and burst, spattering blood and skull fragments over them.

"What the *hell?*" cried Nic, shaking off the sludge.

"Can we please not have any more carnage?" asked Will. "I've never even seen a dead body in the wild before today."

"No promises," said Ian. "Rub some dirt on it and make sure you aren't next." He surveyed the mess buried in the broken asphalt, then made for the forward crane. "Put your earpieces in and set your phones to party line. Nic, with me. Will, monitor things here. You have a baseball bat if you need it. Hide." He checked the time. "Let's be quick. My lasagna comes out of the oven in 45 minutes."

Ian and Nic ran to the *Ningbo*'s bow. In under a minute, the spreader on a quay crane picked up an ISO container the size and shape of a tractor trailer, swung it high over their heads, and dropped it in the ship's hold.

"Think we can get a lift?" asked Ian.

Nic led him to the container next to be loaded and showed him where to sit. "I've never done this before, but if I'm right, the spreader will pick up the container around us, lift us into the air, and carry us aboard," she said.

"What if you're wrong?" asked Ian.

"You'll get squished by the spreader," Will said through the earpiece. "And if you don't climb off the crate as soon as it's aboard, you'll get squished by the next one that's loaded. It'll be a closed casket funeral, either way."

Ian grumbled. "Aren't you late for math club?"

Will laughed. "I'm hiding under a loading bridge. I can see you."

The giant crane descended around Ian and Nic's crate and lifted them off the ground. It swung over the Ningbo's cargo hold. Nic cautioned Ian to hang tight, and the container dropped. Ian gripped a nearby cable, fearful of floating away. Two feet from the ground, the falling stopped, and the container came to a rest in the hold.

The spreader detached. Ian and Nic climbed off and into a narrow passageway. Bodies—sliced, strangled, stabbed and poisoned—led aft. The container information Matt discovered earlier led them to the steel crate containing his family's belongings. He inserted his key into a round lock.

The unloading crane above them rattled to life, absent cargo.

"How is the *unloading* crane moving?" asked Nic. "I'm still wearing bits and pieces of the operator on my shirt."

Ian's eyes followed it as it moved to shore. "Hurry," he replied. He pulled the heavy container doors open, lit his Zippo, and climbed in.

All his family belongings were there. He recognized furniture and familiar objects and his dad's handwriting on stickers.

A thin paper box rested in the drawer of an old nightstand, and Ian stuffed it in his backpack. He ripped open larger boxes, looking for anything from Deena's office.

"Ian? Nic?" said Will from ashore. "Look up."

They peered from the crate. High above, riding the crane toward them, was the gigantic man with the gold plate in his head who had bombed the house across from Ian's. He gripped a cable with both hands and carried a knife in his teeth.

Ian jumped back into the container and tore through boxes in the rear. Nic did likewise at the front.

Why did Erik have so many shoes? Did Cardiff really need a Roberto Clemente poster? Ian found the seltzer bottle from Deena's office and triggered it with his thumb by accident. Water sprayed into his face, and he shook it off.

Nic rummaged through office supplies. Rolls of tape. Pictures of Ian's family.

Ian discovered a sitz bath with information tailored to his mother. He threw it to his feet, gagged, and wiped his hands on his jeans. A melted Dictaphone topped a carton. He was getting close. A bowling trophy, a business card holder—finally, the familiar heavy metal lid of Aunt Judy's cremation urn. He opened it. *Lo Batt* flashed on the screen of his mother's phone. "Got it!" he cried.

"Guys!" said Will. "The dude with the knife is about thirty feet above—"

A thud sounded on the roof.

"Never mind. He jumped."

"Thirty feet?" asked Ian. "That's impossible!" He turned to Nic. The man with the gold head held her from behind, his knife at her throat.

"He's fast," muttered Nic from the side of her mouth.

Ian's hands fell to his side, and he slumped. "Let her go," he said. "I'll give you what you want."

The man cocked his head. "Why not simply kill you and take it?" Light from outside reflected off his skull and onto the ceiling.

Ian mumbled.

"What?" asked the man.

"He said it's a shame you don't have an earpiece," said Nic. "Our friend back home remote-hacked the crane controls. Hold tight."

A spreader connected. The crate shook, then rose from the deck and spun like a top.

At Ian's house, Matthew cackled and directed the enormous crane with his tablet. He forced the container into others, toppling them.

Inside, the man with the gold head released his grip on Nic to keep from tumbling out the door. She fell out instead. Her wrist hyperextended and snapped against the ship's deck. Heavy furniture smashed to timbers around her.

Ian stuffed the cremation urn into his backpack, bolted forward, and felt the gargantuan man's knife crease his ear. "Take us up, Matt!" he screamed.

The crane hauled the container into the air and swung it over the Delaware River. Ian grabbed a brace on the side panel outside and lifted himself to the roof.

"Holy cow!" shouted Will, watching from below.

"What?" asked Matt.

"Ian's outside, climbing to the roof of the crate!"

"Is he safe?"

"He's a hundred fifty feet above the river! What do you think?"

The man with the gold head followed Ian, again with his knife in his teeth. Atop the crate, he released the blade into his hand and backed Ian toward the ledge.

"Bring them down," said Will.

"No!" screamed Nic, watching from the deck. "Ian has nothing to grip. He'll fall too fast and go over the side."

The man with the gold head shouted to Ian. "Give me the urn and I'll spare your friends."

"What if I jump?" asked Ian.

"I'll collect the urn beside your body and kill them both."

Ian looked down at Will, hidden and Nic, walking ashore, then back at the man. He ran a hand through his hair and reached into his backpack. The man extended his blade. Ian withdrew Deena's seltzer bottle.

The man guffawed. "You plan to squirt me with a soda siphon? Like the Three Stooges?"

Ian laughed. "That would be great. But, no." He swung the glass carafe. It shattered against the man's gold plate. He clutched his head, stumbled and fell over the edge and into the river.

Matt lowered the crate near the ship's bow. Further on, Will and Nic cheered.

"Can we get ice cream?" Will asked. "We need to celebrate. I love rum raisin."

Nic clutched her wrist. "I need a hospital."

"Get Ian a glass of wine," said Matt.

Ian did not reply. Richard Finzel met him at gunpoint where the container landed, ripped the earpiece from the boy's ear and snatched the urn from his backpack.

30: CAPTURE!

Ian sat on a wooden chair in an empty shipping container. The residual odor of urinal cakes filled the air. Richard Finzel sat in front of him at a small folding table, his red necktie tucked into his vest. The man with the metal head, tangled in strands of kelp, held Finzel's gun. His sodden clothes created puddles on the floor. He rubbed his gold plate with his free hand every time a dirt bike buzzed past outside.

A naked incandescent lightbulb, suspended from a thumbtack, hung between the three.

Finzel spoke to Tzvi. "You told me he was dead. Why is he in front of me?"

Ian answered, "he bombed the wrong house." His eyes burned in the lightbulb's glare.

"Shut up," said Tzvi, rubbing his head where Ian had hit him. "I'll have to look back on my notes to see where matters went wrong."

"Your notes?" asked Ian. "Even if you had the right address, I was still at school. In the best of circumstances, you would only have blown up my cat. My grandfather was taking a *passeggiata*."

"I said shut up!" yelled Tzvi.

"Nincompoop," Finzel muttered. He turned his attention to Ian. "For a boy who knows nothing about his mother's affairs, you have a curious way of showing up in places that suggest otherwise."

Ian sighed. "How are things with the sorghum?"

"Yes," Finzel grinned, revealing his missing teeth, "he has my gun."

Ian raised an eyebrow. "The *sorghum*," he repeated, loud and slow.

"Ah," Finzel squinted. "Forgive me. My head rings night and day, as though a Mongoloid were kicking a cathedral bell between my ears. Have you seen news of war with China?"

"No."

"That's correct. There is no news of war with China. Ergo, things remain unchanged in the sorghum trade. You delayed my plans when you triggered the bomb in Algeria. It shan't happen again. You will help me find your brother. After that, I will remove my tie and strangle you until you are dead. Tzvi will sink your body in the river."

"Tzvi?"

"Tzvi." Finzel nudged his head to the man with the gold plate.

"Does he have a last name?" asked Ian.

"He's a contract killer."

"I see," said Ian. "Well, Tzvi screwed the pooch yesterday. I'm surprised your organization tolerates failure."

"Silence!" screamed Tzvi. A dirt bike whizzed past outside, and he grabbed his head once more.

"Where is Erik?" asked Finzel.

"Dead," said Ian. "That's what they tell me. You're going

to strangle me, so why would I say if I knew otherwise?"

"Strangling you isn't my only option. There are good deaths, and there are bad deaths." Finzel presented an ice pick and a rubber mallet. "I, too, thought your brother dead. Then, a colleague intercepted something on its way to you."

Tzvi handed Ian the paisley box Fant had given him. Inside was Erik's Breitling watch, the bezel still set to mark the time.

"Erik's Watch?" Ian shrugged. "What's that prove? A watch ticks when its owner dies."

A helicopter flew low over the container yard. Ian next remembered Finzel picking him up from the floor, slamming him back into his chair, and slapping his face. "I require your focus and cooperation," said Finzel.

"Shellshock," muttered Ian.

"Isn't it called PTSD, now?" asked Finzel. Behind him, Tzvi bent at his waist and gripped his head with both hands. "What's the matter, Tzvi?" he asked.

Tzvi squeezed his eyes. "The boy hit me with a soda siphon, Richard. It triggered a megrim. The helicopter... the motorcycles... There are zigs and zags in my vision, and—"

"Shut up, Tzvi." Finzel turned back to Ian and handed him a note. "Inside the box with the watch was this message:"

Ian:
Greetings from Estonia. Come to this place!
01961 93439 83630 43949 08449 30569 53304 01580.
/Steve

Steve! Steve Blass! The innocent postcard! Erik was alive! Ian held the note but shared no excitement. "I don't know who Steve is, and if this is a cipher, I have no key," he said. "I suppose he wants me to meet him in Estonia?"

"Steve is his codename? Estonia is his fallback? Tallinn? Tartu?"

"I don't know."

"Do the numbers mean anything? The first four numbers are 1961. What is 1961?"

"The Bay of Pigs?" said Ian.

Finzel nodded at Tzvi, who hit Ian on the side of the head with his gun. Ian fell from his chair. Finzel returned him upright, slapped him back to consciousness, gathered the urn with Deena's phone, and handed it to Tzvi.

"Take the urn to the hotel." said Finzel. "Wait for me there."

Tzvi exchanged it for his gun and left. Outside, his Humvee ground to a start. The weather had grown warm, and he unzipped the plastic windows before pulling away.

Dirt Bike Tre's gang dismounted and climbed a rise in the terrain to admire the vehicle rolling over their makeshift obstacle course. Their unattended bikes idled and backfired. Tzvi clutched his head. A blue vein pounded at his temple.

Inside the intermodal container, Finzel continued holding Ian at gunpoint. He lifted his ice pick. "I always start by driving this through the thigh, back to front," he said.

"Mine or yours?" asked Ian.

Finzel gritted his teeth and blinked twice. "Why would I drive an icepick through my thigh?"

"People get off in strange ways," said Ian. "I had a headmaster in Algeria who was paying the school secretary to pee—"

"Stop!" He buffed the sharpened point of the pick with

fine sandpaper. "In the past, when people did not tell me what I needed to know, I tapped this pick under the upper eyelid, into the emotional centers of the brain. I stopped because it deprives me of witnessing expressions of horror. Now, I save that part for last." His shoes clicked.

"What's that clicking?" asked Ian. "Do you have taps in your shoes?"

"These shoes are Pendel and Braithwaite," said Finzel. He reached for a rope to tie Ian to the chair. "Taps preserve the life of the leather sole."

"Erik used to place taps on his shoes. It's a shame you didn't buy rubber ones."

"Erik wore rubber taps?" Finzel asked. He ran the rope through his fingers and admired the weave. "Bourgeois, wouldn't you say?"

"Maybe," said Ian. "But rubber soles, like wood chairs, don't conduct electricity."

Finzel looked up from his rope.

Ian's hand surrounded the cord suspending the light bulb. He tugged, freeing the tack that held it to the ceiling.

Finzel's eyes grew wide. The bulb shattered. Electrical current traveled along the wet metal floor into Finzel's shoes. With a cracking spark and a puff of smoke, the man flew backward. His gun discharged into the ceiling. A breaker tripped, and Ian bolted from the shipping container, stuffing Erik's watch and note in his pocket on his way out. At the door, he collided with Will.

"What the hell are you doing here?" asked Ian.

"Trying to find you! I heard shots! Your grandfather dropped by. He's taking Nic to the hospital. She broke her wrist. He says you're grounded."

"Get out of here! People want to kill me!"

"It took me a long time to limp here. Where am I supposed to go?"

Dirt Bike Tre's bike sputtered next to Sawbuck's nearby. Ian grabbed Will's baseball bat, turned him around, and crammed it down the back of his shirt. "Can you ride a bike?"

"I learned on my dad's delivery scooter. But Dirt Bike Tre won't let us borrow his ride."

"You don't talk to Dirt Bike Tre," Ian replied.

Tzvi's Humvee approached the front gates of the container yard. Dirt Bike Tre and Sawbuck were watching it pull away when their bikes screamed past them, filling the air with dust and debris. They stood dumbfounded before scrambling to their friends' Kawasakis to pursue the thieves.

31: DIRT BIKE TRE

Until Ian Racalmuto appeared in his rearview mirror, Tzvi ascribed the dirt bike engines growling in his ears to the headache that now made him too nauseous to take aspirin. He strained to focus on the scene behind him. An Asian boy accompanied Ian on his left wing. Behind them, two more sinister bikers gave chase. One carried a heavy chain. The other drew a Katana sword.

Columbus Boulevard curved past a rail yard and a strip club and straightened to become Pattison Avenue. Tzvi pressed the gas. His GPS routed him between Philadelphia's baseball and football stadiums, then across a major intersection at Broad Street a mile and a half on. A college football game at the sport complex made traffic thick. Police closed Broad Street for a Columbus Day parade.

Will pulled alongside Ian. "What's the plan?" he yelled.

Ian produced the Lucite box from Matt's backpack. The radioactive lint. "Get it through the back window of the Humvee!"

Sawbuck nudged Will's back tire, and he lurched forward. Dirt Bike Tre readied his sword.

"I think they want their bikes," said Will.

Ian waved and smiled, then shifted into high gear and raced toward Tzvi.

Dense stadium traffic forced Tzvi to slow. Seeing no path forward, he bulldozed his way onto the wide sidewalk and crushed the accelerator. Pedestrians scattered. Side mirrors ripped from cars and he ran over sapling trees. Ian followed, evading people, split branches, and automotive plastic. He pulled alongside the Humvee's left rear quarter-panel and drew near the window.

Will blocked Tre and Sawbuck from reaching Ian.

Sawbuck unwound his chain. He swung it at Will, but the boy ducked. The chain passed overhead, hit the ground, and sparked against the concrete. Sawbuck reeled it back over his forearm. He threw it again, this time striking Will's injured ankle.

Will screamed. Tre raised his blade.

Ian gripped his brakes, and the others shot past him. He throttled forward and closed the gap with Will.

Sawbuck spun his chain overhead. It gathered momentum, and Ian and Will ducked twice. When it came around a third time, Ian drew the baseball bat from the back of Will's shirt, struck the chain, and twisted it. With a sharp tug, he pulled Sawbuck from his bike.

The chain unwound. The man spun in the air and hit the concrete. His bike came to a rest twenty-five yards on.

Will drew close to the Humvee. Tzvi nudged him out of the way and returned to Pattison Avenue. He searched for an object to throw. The cremation urn. If he could remove the phone, he could lob the heavy base. He worked to free the lid.

Police at the Broad Street intersection used a bullhorn to call for a stop to the pursuit. Ian felt the swish of Dirt Bike Tre's Katana near his head. Tre held his bike steady with his thighs, gripped the hilt of his sword with both hands, and reset it with a series of kata learned from martial arts films. He slashed again and missed.

They drifted to the middle of the road. To Ian's left, oncoming traffic flew past. To his right, Dirt Bike Tre readied his blade.

Tzvi loosed the lid on the urn. The wind caught Great Aunt Judy Ricciotti's ashes, and a tremendous cloud filled the Humvee. Tzvi buckled and coughed.

The ash whipped from the window into Dirt Bike Tre's eyes. He blinked and teared and wiped at his face. Ian dodged a parking cone in their path. Tre did not. His front tire hit a deep hole. His bike flipped and fell atop him, and he slid down the road, crushed between the asphalt and the bike's searing muffler.

Tzvi slowed his Humvee for neither the stopped police cruisers nor the gathering parade. Will was too far away to reach the rear window, and Ian continued to grip Matt's radioactive lint.

Ian zipped to Will's left wing. "Catch!" he shouted, throwing Will the baseball bat. Will caught it one-handed. "Hit!" Ian shouted again, throwing Matt's Lucite box, accounting for the rushing wind.

Will swung, sending the plastic square into Tzvi's back seat. The gigantic man, still gagging from the ash, did not notice. He collided with the police cars and powered forward, speeding through Broad Street and missing a drum major.

Ian and Will made a sharp right, jumped onto the

sidewalk, and raced into a parking lot. When they came to a stop at the far end, away from the commotion, they leaped from their bikes, screamed, and high-fived.

"Did you see that?" said Will, pointing to the intersection. "Did we *actually* de-throne Dirt Bike Tre and bat a radioactive tracker into a Humvee?"

The police slapped handcuffs on Dirt Bike Tre and took his sword as evidence. They fit the scabbard on the blade as far as it would go, but the metal bent in a 90-degree L.

They screamed again. Will threw his full weight on Ian and bear-hugged him, laughing. "Shit!" he shouted.

"What?" asked Ian, holding him up.

"My ankle! I can't get my balance."

Ian grinned and propped him up on his motorcycle.

"I'd love to keep my bike, but I don't want one of Tre's people to find me on it," said Ian. "Can you give me a lift home if I leave it here?"

"Sure. I'll leave my bike on the corner of the street with the keys in it. Someone will steal it before church tomorrow," said Will. "What about your stuff from the dock? Salvageable?"

"Useless," said Ian. He pulled the box he had found from Matt's backpack. Somebody had affixed a handwritten sticker that read Racalmuto, D. "I found my mom's ashes. My family thought we lost them."

"Where were they?"

"Next to an issue of *Gun and Garden* in a nightstand drawer. Appropriate, if you knew my mom."

"Where will you put them?"

"Aunt Judy's cremation urn is vacant if we can get it back," laughed Ian.

Will said nothing.

"What?" Ian asked. "That was funny! Why are you quiet?" He studied the remains. "I can't change what happened. It is what it is, you know?"

"Sure," said Will.

He gave Ian a lift home. When they arrived, Mario opened the door. He held a burned lasagna in an oven mitt. Smoke alarms sounded through the house.

"I'd better keep moving," said Will. "My ankle better heal fast, so I'm not such a useless sidekick in the future."

"You can't stay?" asked Ian. "Mom's phone is in enemy hands, and we've been busy all day and haven't had a minute to chill."

"I need to get home before Li figures out I wasn't at math club," said Will.

Ian's eyes turned down.

"Let's hang out tomorrow night," Will said. "I like your place. It's quiet."

They fist-bumped and parted ways.

Ian's coat had become filthy. He walked to the dry cleaner and again left it with Mrs. Hwang. She did not smile, stuffed it in a bag, and collected his money. On his way home, his phone rang. It was Will.

"What'd you forget?" asked Ian.

"I forgot to say thanks."

"For what? *I* should thank *you*. I was considering what you said earlier. You weren't a useless sidekick. Not at all."

"I don't mean about today. Thanks for being nice last week. For getting my money back. For being good about my stepmom when she slammed the door in your face. All of it."

"Don't be like that," said Ian. "That was nothing."

There was a pause. Ian's phone beeped in his ear. Will had sent him a picture. It was a Chinese woman behind an industrial sewing machine, smiling and holding an infant. A surgical mask rested at her chin, and Tufts of black hair stuck from under a net. The infant, too, wore a tiny mask.

"Who knew they made dust masks that tiny?" said Ian. "Who's this?"

Will said, "I never knew my mom. She died in a factory accident when I was little. It's the only picture I have of her. That's me, visiting her at the factory." he trailed off. "Anyway."

The woman in the photograph worked 12-hour shifts six days a week, and would have worked twice that if it bettered the life of the kid in her arms. She gave a mischievous glare into the cameras, as Deena would have—ready to make luck if hers ran out.

Ian could not tear his eyes from her and could not speak. He cleared his throat at last. "See you tomorrow."

32: AMBASSADOR REID

Every hospitality chain had at one time owned the round brick hotel tower near the diner in Southwest Philadelphia. Its receptionist, Mrs. Stuyvesant, had seen so many brand names chipped away from the wall behind her desk she now answered the phone by saying only "hotel."

The hotel served as a bulwark between poverty and homelessness for most of its inhabitants. It had few rooms available for nightly rent. The stained carpets and broken furniture were on no schedule for replacement. A vending machine in the lobby dispensed condoms.

Richard Finzel shuffled three miles from the container yard to the weed-infested hotel parking lot. He pulled at the door of Tzvi's Humvee.

Locked.

Finzel's hair frayed at the tips. His shoes and cuffs were black with ash. He smiled at bird song and distant conversation. The ringing in his ears had disappeared following the electric shock, replaced by a profound love in his heart for Jesus Christ.

He whispered into the ether about the Gideon's Bible

certain to be in his room. When there wasn't one in his nightstand, he dialed Tzvi. When Tzvi didn't answer, he called the Gideons and cursed at them.

Tzvi had arrived at the hotel hours earlier. He withdrew money from the blue pouch in his glove box and tapped a front-desk bell, summoning Mrs. Stuyvesant. She cast a suspicious gaze at his gold head and the scorpion in his terrarium. He massaged his temples as though the bell had made his forehead explode. He secured adjoining rooms, burped acid into his throat, and swallowed it back down.

On the way to his room, he passed the housekeeper—a man in his late 90s who had been with the hotel since construction and attributed his good health to a vegan diet and a daily regimen of edible flowers.

Tzvi placed Deena's phone in a shoebox-sized safe in his closet. He created a four-digit combination on a digital keypad. After the safe locked, he drew the curtains and darkened the room. A small, inextinguishable triangle of light shone through a hole. Tzvi could not bear to look at it without treacherous pain. His crickets chirped, so he moved them to Finzel's room with his scorpion. He emitted a thunderous fart, and somebody knocked from the room above. The knocking rattled his brain against his skull.

The old housekeeper delivered ice. Tzvi emptied powdered aspirin into water and vomited. Visual haloes mimicked the flashing and drifting of the Northern Lights. His affliction needed to run its course, but his vacation was slipping past, and he wanted to go to the mountains. His phone rang with calls from Finzel. He silenced it, unable to bear the man caterwauling in his ear.

He approached sleep when Finzel appeared through their

adjoining door. He offered to buy food from a diner across the street. Tzvi belched and gagged and asked the man to leave. A minute later, Finzel reappeared. He complained about the scorpion and the crickets, then asked Tzvi if he would like to talk about Jesus Christ. When Tzvi refused, Finzel shoved his way toward the man's nightstand in search of a Bible. Tzvi drew his knife.

"I am suffering the torments of the damned. Bother me again tonight, and so help me I will slit your throat from one ear to the next."

Tzvi stood from his bed, pushed Finzel back into the adjacent room, and locked the door.

Richard Finzel kneeled at his bedside in prayer. His phone rang twice from a blocked ID, stopped, and rang again. It was a call he had expected since his arrival in the States.

He shifted to sit on the floor and answered.

"Ricky," said the gravelly baritone voice of Ambassador Caleb Reid, "You're stateside?"

"Hello, Mr. Ambassador. Yes. Things are fine."

"You're at the round motel in Philadelphia?"

"Per our plan."

"I'm in the phone booth at the diner across the street."

"It works?" Finzel asked.

"There's no phone inside. I'm talking on my cell-phone."

Finzel hated the way the man said *cell-phone*, as though they were two words, hyphenated. From his window, he could see both the phone booth and the glowing tip of Reid's cigarette. "Why stand in the booth?" he asked.

Reid's lips popped off the butt of the cigarette. "Meet me here, Ricky, *sur-le-champ*."

Finzel left his room, crossed the street, and spied Reid in a blue vinyl booth in the back corner of a large dining room. Once settled, a waitress with hair like Texas and teeth covered in tartar approached. "What are we having?"

Finzel flipped the menu over and back again. "The garden salad. No. Wait. Peaches. Cottage cheese, dry toast, marmalade to the side. No! Wait. No toast. Peaches and cottage cheese."

"Soft food," Reid chortled. "Best not to challenge your remaining teeth."

Finzel grimaced and again turned to the waitress. "Iced tea."

"Sweetened or unsweetened?"

"Unsweetened. Do you have any Sweet 'N Low?"

"We're out. An old man comes in and steals it every weekend. Thinks we don't notice." The waitress turned to Ambassador Reid. His menu remained where she had placed it before Finzel had arrived.

"I'd like eggs and scrapple, burned. Home fries. Coffee, very black, and an ashtray."

Finzel grabbed the waitress's wrist. "Have you heard the good news of the risen Lord?"

She jerked away, put the order on a spinner and rang a bell.

Reid situated his cigarettes in front of him. "What was that bit about the risen Lord?"

Finzel's face lightened. "I'm so glad you asked."

"Forget it," interrupted Reid. "You met Agent Fant in California. Talk to me about the Racalmuto problem. You located the older brother?"

"Did you read my cable?" asked Finzel.

"Of course not, Ricky."

"Why did you have me wire a cable, then?"

Reid withdrew a cigarette and tapped the butt on the table to pack the tobacco. "On with it, Ricky."

"We don't yet have Erik Racalmuto's location. We believe it to be Estonia."

Reid grumbled. "Our men from Nightwater can investigate. And the younger boy?"

"Here. Escaped today, but my factotum is swift with a blade. He'll handle the boy.

"Your factotum?" asked Reid.

"One of our men embedded as a security agent at Main State, called Tzvi."

"Tzvi?"

"Tzvi."

"Does he have a last name?"

"He's a contract killer."

"I see," said Reid.

"Tzvi obtained Deena Racalmuto's phone," said Finzel.

Reid grinned and slapped the table. The silverware jumped. "What news, Ricky! Perhaps I was mistaken about you after your unmitigated failure in Algiers."

Finzel puckered.

"You brought the phone with you?" Reid continued.

"It's locked in Tzvi's room."

"Knock at his door."

"Impossible," said Finzel. "Tzvi fell prostrate to a megrim earlier. If I knock at his door, he'll slit my throat from one ear to the next."

Reid struck a match and lit his cigarette. "Send the phone to me first thing in the morning via courier, then remain in

Philadelphia to assure Ian Racalmuto's death. I won't need the phone until Wednesday, when I chair a meeting at Main State. I'll launch our war on China a half-hour after it concludes." He waved the match until only a wisp of smoke rose from the gray tip.

"Must I deliver the phone on a Sunday morning if you aren't launching our operation until Wednesday?" asked Finzel.

Reid sucked on his cigarette and exhaled through his teeth. "You will do as I say. It's embarrassing that you cannot collect the phone from the hands of your man tonight. Then again, not all of us graduated from West Point with efficiency as our guiding principle."

"I graduated from UNC Chapel Hill," said Finzel.

"And, for a graduate of a modest public university, your work has been satisfactory." Reid ashed his cigarette into a saucer. The two sat in silence. Finzel bit his tongue. Reid took a sip of water. "I know you're trying very hard to be professional."

Finzel raised his voice. "I am professional!"

"Calm down, Ricky," said Reid.

"You're belittling my efforts and making me perform unnecessary tasks to humiliate me!" Finzel screamed. "I could deliver the phone Monday or Tuesday to equal effect."

"You're being petulant, Ricky. It debases you," said Reid. "Make certain the phone is in my hands no later than 10:30 tomorrow morning. I'll be at my apiary. Identify the boy's corpse and meet me at Foggy Bottom." He blew another cloud of smoke. "Perhaps on Wednesday, I'll let you push the button that launches the cyberattack. If you're good."

Finzel clenched his jaw.

"At Foggy Bottom, there's a Peregrine Falcon you can watch as you wait for my business to conclude," said Reid.

"Does it fly?" asked Finzel.

"No."

"Does it sing?" asked Finzel.

"No!"

"What does it do?" asked Finzel.

"It sits on its eggs." said Reid.

"And people watch it?" asked Finzel.

The manager approached.

"We don't allow smoking," she said to Reid.

"There's nobody sitting to the right of me. I'll blow it that way." Reid exhaled a puff toward the empty booth to his side and returned his attention to Finzel. "Don't fail me, Ricky."

Back in his room, Finzel pounded his dresser in frustration. He asked Jesus to calm the tempest in his soul. He would remain steadfast, carry on, and kill Ian Racalmuto. His courier would arrive at Reid's house early tomorrow. He'd show the man what efficiency was, indeed.

He climbed into his bed, drew the sheets over him, turned out the lights, and closed his eyes. The crickets came alive and kept him awake until dusk.

33: REBEKKAH BATISTE

Will's motorcycle gathered speed. The familiar landmarks of his childhood flew past. He gambled with the amount of gas sloshing in the tank beneath him and took a long route home. Would he hate giving up the bike? No. It wasn't the bike he loved. It was that he was free to go where he pointed it. His church, the clinic, the Vietnamese supermarket—the places he knew were smaller and closer, and the world beyond was more curious.

Ian had been to places a motorcycle couldn't carry him. What must it be like to spend a life adapting to far-off places? To call anywhere home? Was he ever afraid?

He drove past the high school, and a girl staring at her phone stepped into the street in front of him. He clutched the brakes. The back tire locked and skidded. He missed her by inches.

"Jesus Christ!" yelled Rebekkah Batiste. She flapped the cast on her arm. "Can't you see I'm already jacked up?"

"Get off your damn phone and watch where you're walking!" Will shouted back.

They locked eyes.

"Will?" she stammered, stepping back.

"Rebekkah?" His mouth hung open.

"Since when did you have a bike?"

"It's Dirt Bike Tre's."

"You know Dirt Bike Tre?" she asked.

"Nobody knows Dirt Bike Tre," said Will.

She looked left and right. "Give me a lift home. It's late."

Will sped through traffic on Broad Street. Rebekkah gripped his waist with her good arm.

"This isn't how I picture you," she said. "You spent your weekend street biking?"

"I spent it with Ian. I was supposed to be at math club, but we ended up at the container yard where he electrocuted some dude trying to murder him. That's where we ran into Dirt Bike Tre."

"Ian's a monster," she said. "Do you know what he said to me in the hallway?"

"I don't care," said Will.

"He broke my arm," she continued. "Craig's leg is in a frame. Nobody knows if he'll ever go pro. He needs months of rehab." She tightened her grip around him. It irritated his ribs, and he shifted.

You want me to feel sorry for Craig? he wanted to ask. He held his tongue. West of Broad, on Oregon Avenue, they passed tag and title offices, pizzerias, gas stations and phone stores. "Can I ask you a question?" asked Will. "Why has Craig always hated me?"

"Because you suck and nobody yells at you for it."

He said nothing.

"It's mean, but it's true," Rebekkah continued. "He works hard to be excellent and everybody yells at him like he's doing everything wrong. No offense, but you shouldn't even be in this country." She wiped drool from her swollen lip. "Can I ask you a question? Why do you want Craig to like you so bad? Are you in love with him?"

"No!" Will protested.

"He isn't gay." said Rebekkah.

"Neither am I!" shouted Will.

"But why him? You could be friends with all the other Chinese kids who sit together in the cafeteria."

"It's complicated," said Will. "My life isn't like theirs. I don't go to Chinese school or cello lessons on weekends. I don't speak the language or even part of it. I can't make the tones right. My parents connected English with success and didn't want a second language to be a distraction. My stepmom's accent embarrassed her, and she wanted to be sure I didn't have one."

"A lot of Asians don't speak Asian. They speak Chinglish or whatever. That can't be the reason you don't hang out with them."

"It's one of a thousand cuts. Our parents all go to the same church. My family doesn't have much, so we're a cautionary tale." He turned onto Shunk Street. "They're afraid bad luck is contagious, or our problems reflect on Chinese people and diminish their success. Plus, I crave dense apple pie and pasta and bread I have to rip with my teeth—and those little peanut butter cups. I can't live without those. They go for delicate, fluffy cakes and froyo with fruit toppings. We don't understand each other."

"You don't know you're Asian," she laughed.

"Of course I do," said Will. "It never escapes me. Every day Craig tells me how I don't belong in America, and Molly

Yang calls me *uncle Tong* and tells me I'm idealizing and pandering to white people. I just want to live my life."

"You're smart. That's Asian."

"I'm not smart. School's a joke."

"Not for me." She shifted behind him. "Anyway, your parents must be proud of you."

"Who knows?"

She motioned him to pull over around the corner from her house and got off the bike. She didn't want anybody to see her with him.

"Can I ask you a question?" asked Will. "Why do you like Craig so much?"

"I don't. I broke up with him."

"Oh," said Will. "Sorry, I guess."

"Don't be. He's bad luck and I need some time on my own. Thanks again for the lift."

"Hope you feel better," said Will.

Rebekkah waved, and he pulled away.

Will parked his dirt bike at the end of his street and left the keys in the ignition. Inside his house, Li reclined on the sofa. Eddie rummaged through a kitchen cabinet.

"Where have you been?" asked Li.

"I was helping a friend get home. She had injuries, and it's getting dark."

Li stopped him from going upstairs. "Molly has injuries?"

"A different girl. Her name's Rebekkah."

Li bolted upright. "The girl you were texting last week? She's in math club?" Her color drained from her face. "Did Mrs. Yang see you leave together?"

"Calm down. We aren't getting married. She isn't in math

club."

"How are you acquainted? What do her parents do? Where is her family from? Fujian Province? Everybody in Philadelphia is from Fujian," she said.

He hesitated. "I didn't ask. They were born here, I think."

"Her parents are American-born?" Li withdrew a cigarette. "How can you not be certain?"

"It's not important to young people," Eddie said.

"It is important to us," said Li. She struck her lighter. "What is her birth year?"

He shrugged.

"Do you ask nothing before saying yes to a date?"

"We aren't dating! I helped her get home!"

"Well," Li exhaled. "You can spend tomorrow studying after church. I'm sure you have assignments."

"I have plans with friends tomorrow night," said Will.

"What friends are these?" asked Li, her voice becoming shrill. Her phone rang. It was cousin Ruthie. She answered, but continued speaking to Will. "You're sneaking around. Stay home tomorrow." She left to talk outside. Her muffled voice seeped through the door with the smell of cigarette smoke. "I'm guessing Fujian," she said. "If his grades suffer, it's over. I've told him already. Do you know if Molly Yang will be at Sunday school? Can you call Mrs. Yang to be certain?"

Will sank into a chair, punched the arm, and glared at the wall.

Eddie moved from the kitchen and took over Li's space on the sofa. "A girlfriend?"

Will looked up. "Only a girl I helped home."

Eddie grinned. "Mommy competes too much with Ruthie

now that cousin Benson is engaged. Best to leave women alone to their jealousies. You like this girl?"

"I would have killed for a date with her a few weeks ago," said Will.

"Mommy will never say it, but she's happy." He shifted. "We worried for a time that you might not like girls."

The house key in Will's fist creased his palm. "Why do people keep saying that?"

"You only ever talk about that boy on your soccer team."

He threw his hands up. "It doesn't mean anything. You and Li only talk about my schoolwork and soccer," said Will. "Isn't there more to the picture?"

Eddie reached into his pocket and pressed $10 into Will's hand. Will tried to return it, but the man waved it off. "I met your mother when I was your age. It was long ago. With so much uncertainty, family offers stability. A secure job, a wife and children are the keys to happiness." He cleared his throat and rubbed his lower abdomen, but continued to smile. "Ask this girl out. School comes first, though, like mommy says. I don't want to hear her complaints."

Will smirked. "What if my path's different from yours?"

"Some things are eternal. Your news gives me something happy in life. Ask her out!" Eddie exhaled and pulled a blanket over himself. "Besides," he whispered, "I don't like Molly Yang. She's full of herself."

Will smiled and put the money in his pocket. "I won't waste it." His phone beeped. A text from Matt. They typed back and forth.

He slept badly that night. At 2 AM, Dirt Bike Tre's motorcycle roared to life outside, then faded into the distance.

34: DEENA'S GHOST

Ian sat in the silence of his basement with a notepad and pen as the Professor scratched in the litterbox behind him.

He re-read Erik's note.

Greetings from Estonia. Come to this place!
01961 93439 83630 43949 08449 30569 53304 01580.

ESTONIA wasn't a place he had to go. He had known from the beginning. It was a type of straddling checkerboard—a grid of letters matched to numbers that allowed spies to convert text into digits and back again. His brother would have converted his message to the string of numbers beginning with *1961* using the Estonia checkerboard. He would then have added a second series of numbers to encrypt them. Without knowing those exact encryption numbers in the exact order, however, he could decrypt nothing.

Erik's watch ticked beside him. His time was nearly up.

He recalled seeing a bottle of Malbec in a kitchen cabinet and walked upstairs, where Mario sat reading National

Geographic. He opened the cabinet.

"Wine won't solve your problems," Mario said.

"Neither will water," said Ian, snatching the bottle.

A knock sounded at the door. Mario peered outside.

"Matt and Nic," he said, allowing them in. Soon, they gathered around the table. Ian poured the Malbec.

"How's the wrist?" Ian asked, pointing at a cast on Nic's hand.

"Annoying," said Nic. "The cast makes it difficult to hold a wrench. Have you talked to Will?"

"Not since this afternoon," replied Ian. "We're hanging out tomorrow."

"Don't count on it," she replied. "His stepmom is locking him away for the rest of the weekend."

"Why?" asked Ian. "Did she hear about the container yard?"

"Worse," said Matt. "Will ran into Rebekkah Batiste and gave her a lift home. Rebekkah broke up with Craig, and now Li thinks they're dating."

Ian reddened. "Why on earth would he give her a ride home? She's vile."

"He's always had a crush on her," said Matt.

Ian's chest tightened. "He should have done the world a service and run her down," he said.

"Craig's sure to find out," said Nic. "when that happens, he may try to beat the shit out of Will, again."

"I don't care," Ian muttered. Nic raised an eyebrow at him, so he added, "what I mean is, Craig can't move fast with his injuries." He took a gulp of wine. "Have we tracked the lint?"

"Bad news," said Matt. "We lost the signal."

"You're kidding."

"Think of how my sister feels," said Matt. "She fears abduction, now."

"Did you bring any good news?"

"They built a box with a gravel floor for the Peregrine Falcon at Main State," said Matt. "It's pretty cool."

That night, Ian tossed in bed. *Mr. Arkadin* played on the classic movie channel. Orson Welles told a parable of a scorpion who stung the frog that carried him across a river.

"What's the logic in stinging me?" asked the frog. "You've killed us both."

"I couldn't help it," said the scorpion. "It's in my nature."

Ian retreated to the basement. He brought Deena's ashes with him and situated them on the top shelf of the old bookcase that guarded the sitting area. He could not discern whether a hint of Shalimar lingered in the air or in memory.

He reviewed the day in his head and became tense.

"*Cos'è questo, Deena*?" he asked the ashes. "You always knew what was going on in my head. When I didn't want to talk, you annoyed me. Now I want to, and you can't."

Ian listened in silence. A distant locomotive whistled. Then, he imagined the sound of ice cubes hitting a rocks glass, and his mother's ghost joined him. She appeared as she always had, though her hair was bright white.

"What's the matter with you?" she would ask. "You're brooding. Racalmutos don't brood. *Veloci! Andiamo!*"

"I ran into Rick Fenzel this weekend," Ian said. "He's trying to start a war with China over sorghum."

She swished a drink. "It's the world's fifth most popular cereal grain."

"He has your phone. I don't know where he is, and I may

be too late to stop him from using it to start a war," said Ian.

"Fenzel doesn't have to beat you if uncertainty already has. Things will come together. *C'è ancora tempo.* Anyway, I'm glad you're looking for my phone. Staying busy after school keeps you out of trouble."

Ian said nothing.

"The phone and the Fenzel situation aren't what's nagging at you."

Ian exhaled. "It was a perfect day. Matt gave all of us new phones. Nic broke her wrist when she fell out of a shipping crate. Will and I chased a guy with a metal head through the city on stolen dirt bikes after I electrocuted Fenzel with a lightbulb. It ended in uncertainty."

"Because of Rebekkah Batiste?"

"How do you know?"

"Because I'm your mother. And, because I'm dead. You fear you'll screw up your friendship with Will like you did with Kintu," said Deena. "Over a girl."

Ian swallowed hard. "How would you know?"

"Do you remember that boy you became friends with when we were in Berlin last year? Ever since then, you've worried about twisting in the wind while your friends end up in love."

"If I don't make friends, it won't be a problem," he said.

She cackled and caught her chest as she hiccupped. "How's that working out?"

"Will finally has some good coming into his life. I'll wreck everything if I stay close. It's my nature, like the scorpion and the frog. Besides, people are trying to kill me, and I have to concentrate on finding Erik and your phone."

"What are you going to do about Will, then?"

"I'll disappear. He won't care now that he's hitting it off with Rebekkah. I won't lie, though—I wish she didn't exist. I wish it could be different."

"And I wish I had something other than Old Overholt in my glass, but your grandfather is parsimonious. It's all he keeps under the sink."

"He keeps it on the credenza, not under the sink."

"How did it get under the sink?" she trailed off. "Ian, you can wish things were different all you want. As your grandmother used to say, though, wish in one hand and shit in the other, and see which fills up first." She raised her glass to her lips, but put it back down. "You don't mean you wish *you* were different, do you?"

Ian shrugged.

She lifted a pinky from her tumbler. "You are Ian-*fucking*-Racalmuto. You are exceptional. Your father and I did a fine job raising you."

"Tell it to Kintu."

"Be patient."

Ian didn't want to be patient. He didn't want to be fifteen. He wished he could hit a fast-forward button to a time in which everything was sorted and certain.

Deena continued, "Life seldom forces us to better understand ourselves in convenient moments. That's what makes it fun. Heed Erik's advice, though. Keep a sharp eye when you're distracted because reality has a mean left hook."

He nodded and drew a breath. "Mom," he said, "there's something I never told you, and I probably should."

"Too late," she interrupted. She shifted in her chair. "This plastic is insufferable. My ass is sweating. Why is your grandfather so insistent on protecting this sofa? It's ancient."

She shifted, and her drink spilled.

Ian raised a brow.

"Go find Erik," said Deena. "And find whoever stuck me in that nightstand. And get me an urn. Please. A cardboard box doesn't cut it. I look like a *senzatetto*."

Ian shook his head.

"Not aunt Judy's urn, either! Don't you dare repurpose her urn. Get me something nice. The Christmas Tree Shop has nice urns."

"Bye, mother," said Ian. He placed Erik's watch beside her ashes, and propped the Steve Blass baseball card beside it.

"I'm not going anywhere," she said. "No good about goodbye."

35: APIARY

SUNDAY.

Before the sun rose Sunday morning, Richard Finzel paced in front of an old, square television at the round hotel tower. Ian Racalmuto must die. Tzvi had wasted the evening. From behind their adjoining door, the bilious man continued to promise the job would conclude in a satisfactory manner.

Tzvi spun aspirin powder into a cup of acidic in-room coffee. He hadn't had a proper bowel movement in three days and expressed copious wind. He called his doctor, who advised him to stop taking aspirin and begin a regimen of cathartic tablets and warm enemas administered from a rubber bag that hung from his shower rod. Heating the solvent proved problematic. The microwave in Tzvi's room did not work, so he used Finzel's. It made the air smell of hot vinegar.

Finzel drummed his fingers. "Fetch the Racalmuto woman's phone from your safe," he said at last. "I'll send for a courier to take it to Reid."

Tzvi disappeared into his room and returned a few

minutes later, empty-handed. "I've forgotten the combination," he said.

Finzel walked into Tzvi's room. A display on the safe glowed *ERR*.

Tzvi continued, "When my megrim abated, there were gaps in my memory."

"Imbecile," snapped Finzel. "Ambassador Reid will want bad news immediately. *You* are to call him and explain this failure."

Tzvi swallowed hard and dialed Ambassador Reid. "Hello, Mr. Ambassador? It's Tzvi."

"Who?" asked the Ambassador.

"Tzvi. I work with Richard Finzel."

"Well, put him on the line."

Tzvi handed over the phone.

Reid was to leave for Washington later in the day. He attended his apiary. In the background, the distant sound of bees filled the air.

"I was not anticipating your call," said Reid. "One of my bees has gotten under the protective net of my bee-helmet, Ricky. Be quick."

"It's about the Racalmuto phone."

"I'm expecting it within the hour, per our arrangement," Reid said.

"Tzvi locked it in the hotel safe and cannot remember the combination."

There was silence as the buzzing in the background became louder. "You're an idiot, Ricky," said the Ambassador.

Finzel opened his mouth to argue.

"How about the Racalmuto boy? Is he dead, yet? He needs

to be dead, Ricky. I've needed him to be dead for weeks."

"By the end of today, I will—"

"OUCH!" Reid cried out, interrupting. "Goddamn it!" Rapid blowing followed as though the Ambassador were puffing through out-turned lips to protect his face. His phone hit the ground amid a clatter of wood and screen, and a deep buzzing crescendoed. Reid's baritone shrieked in distress, then grew distant. The buzzing softened, and the line disconnected.

They waited for Reid to call back. Tzvi offered games of pinochle with Finzel at a penny a point. Finzel said cards were of the devil and turned to an enormous Bible he had stolen from the altar at a nearby Baptist church.

Hours later, the phone rang again. A hospital in Bethesda.

Caleb Reid's enervated voice sounded through the headset. "As you may have heard, Ricky, my bees turned on me. They breached the protective barrier of my bee-suit. I am in hospital, in traction, reduced to drinking thin broth with the aid of a straw. Doctors extracted forty-seven stingers from my face.

"I cannot travel to Main State." He sighed. "I require the Racalmuto woman's phone at my bedside so I might start our war once I have recovered."

"I'll take the phone to Main State," said Finzel. "I'll begin the war while you convalesce."

"You'll do no such thing," said Reid. "You and your Tzvi have already done irreversible damage to our campaign. I dispatched a courier of my own."

No sooner were the words out of Reid's mouth than someone knocked from the hallway. Tzvi opened the door. Victoria Fant snarled.

The poison Tzvi administered in the desert had torpefied the right half of her body. She wore a patch over an eye and dragged her leg. Her lip turned down on the right side of her face. Her left hip pocket bulged from a handkerchief. Finzel suspected she used it to catch drool. She carried a wrecking bar.

Tzvi raced to the hotel safe. Before he could make another attempt to open it, Fant ripped it free with her wrecking bar, clutched it under her arm, and departed. For two minutes, Finzel and Tzvi stood in silence, listening to her foot sliding down the hallway and into a distant elevator.

"Very well," Reid's voice said at last. "Kill Ian Racalmuto first thing tomorrow."

36: I DON'T KEEP THE COMPANY OF ORDINARY PEOPLE

While Tzvi and Finzel waited in the round hotel Sunday afternoon, Ian made his way to Philadelphia City Hall, a hulking French Second Empire building in the center of town. A 53,000-pound statue of William Penn capped the tower and looked northeast. Beneath his feet, a circular observation deck for tourists offered panoramic views.

Ian moved north to south, east to west, holding his phone high, hoping to gather a signal from Matt's radioactive lint. Nothing came of his efforts. Two miles away, he could see his school. He sat on the floor, withdrew Will's playing cards from his pocket, and shuffled through them.

Will had texted five times that morning and left a voicemail, but Ian did not reply. "Don't do it. You'll screw everything up," he muttered to himself.

The temperature fell. On his way home, Ian stopped by Mrs. Hwang's dry cleaning store. "*Annyeonghaseyo*," he smiled. She snooted and pressed a button. An infinite chain of hanging clothes passed on a conveyor from a room in the back. She placed his coat on a tree and walked away.

He returned home, scratched the number 2 on his map of Algeria, and cooked eggplant parm.

In the early evening, Eddie Xiang called from his room. He trembled with chills and broke into hives in reaction to his medication. Li phoned cousin Ruthie and hurried her through the front door, ashamed though she was of her house. They bantered in Cantonese, and with Will's help, situated Eddie on the sofa. Will ignited the kerosene heater next to him and brewed tea.

The intensity of the moment waned. Ruthie sat beside Will. "I understand you have a girlfriend, Billy?" she asked.

Will blushed. "I helped a friend get home last night. She isn't—"

"Benson had a girlfriend at your age. We told him she would be a distraction, but her family proved to be good Christians, and now they are engaged." She laughed. "God's will was greater than mine."

Li frowned. "I still know nothing of this girl. Will must stay focused on school so he can be a provider for the right girl when he is old enough to marry."

Will rolled his eyes. "I'm not dating anybody. I don't have a girlfriend, and I'm not getting married."

"We're simply happy your life is normal," said Ruthie. "We worried Benson might play on his computer forever. Young women today focus on careers and grow old and barren. They don't consider family." She squeezed his arm and lowered her voice. "For a time, your parents feared you were a gay."

Will gritted his teeth.

"I told them you would bloom late," Ruthie assured him.

"Sometimes people don't like anybody," Will argued. "Sometimes, they don't want to marry, or have other goals, or don't want babies, or want to be alone. Is that not okay?"

Li threw her hands up in resignation.

Ruthie's face rumpled, then relaxed. "Other families have different ideas." She pointed to the sky. "Ours puts faith in Him."

Will said nothing else and started upstairs. Li stopped him.

"Ruthie will stay in your room tonight," she said.

Will sighed. "Where do I sleep?"

"Stay with Benson, in his apartment," Ruthie offered. "He won't mind if you go over."

Will cleaned his room and gathered some belongings. Later, as Ruthie showed him out the door, she said, "I am delighted for you, and proud you are taking steps toward manhood. Have faith in yourself, and in God, and he will show you the way."

Will hated Benson's apartment. His sofa was sticky and smelled like beer. His misery lasted only a moment.

At 8:30, Ian recognized Will's shadow through the front window and cracked the door as far as a chain lock would allow.

"I can't talk," said Ian, poking his nose and one eye through the crack.

"Why not?" Will stretched his baseball bat across his shoulders. "Where have you been all day?" he asked. "I've called and texted. Is your phone working?"

Ian's eyes traveled down. Will continued to wear Ian's Sambas. "I want my shoes back," he said.

"I'm not finished wearing them," said Will.

"And my bat. Do you still need it to walk?"

"No. Now I need it for protection."

"From Craig, now that you're with his girlfriend?"

Will laughed. "You sound like my aunt," he said. "I had to put up with her questions all night. Why do you have the chain lock across the door?"

"Because you know the combination to my door." Ian unhooked the chain.

Will charged inside and dropped the bat in an umbrella vase. "Got any food? Your house smells like oven. You made eggplant parm. Are you brooding? You cook when you brood."

"I do. I mean, I did." Ian stammered. "Yes. I made eggplant. How do you know what I do when I brood?"

Will took a butter knife from a rack and pointed it at Ian. "You were brooding last night when I left, too."

"No, yesterday I was moping."

"What have you been brooding and moping about? You have no reason to mope."

Though he said nothing of it, Will, too, had been sulking. He hated being trapped at home and spent the afternoon staring at his phone and waiting for messages from Ian.

Ian poured glasses of chianti and told him of the radioactive lint and the lost signal. Will ate and described his night. "Can I stay over?" he asked.

"You don't have to ask."

Will toasted with his glass as he chewed. "I'll take the sofa."

"The guest always gets my bed. You're the guest."

"I hate to keep sending you to the basement. I'll be sleeping here frequently, so we need a better plan."

Ian closed his eyes and rubbed his temples, laughing. "Frequently? *Sto cazzo*. I sleep okay in the basement. I'm used to it."

"Your Xbox is in your bedroom. We can't play video games if you're downstairs. Your room is tiny, but the bed is enormous. I'm little, and so are you. I don't care if you take the other side of your bed."

"You're inviting *me* to sleep beside *you* in *my* bed?" asked Ian, raising an eyebrow.

"We'll play Halo," said Will. "We'll sit on the bed and shoot each other until we fall asleep. Then, you can say we passed out and you won't feel weird for crawling into my bed."

"It's *my* bed!"

"I wanted the sofa. You wouldn't let me have it." Will laughed his laugh that made Ian laugh.

It was getting late. When they got upstairs, they turned on the console and killed one another.

"So why weren't you answering my calls?" asked Will.

Because I won't be able to stop myself from ruining everything between you and your first-ever girlfriend, Ian wanted to say. "I was out looking for mom's phone," he said, instead. "Nic said you were in prison because your parents caught you with Rebekkah?"

"They've never even seen her. I gave her a lift home yesterday, and now my stepmom swears we're engaged," said Will. "It's ridiculous. She thinks I'm out of control."

"Don't tell her about the motorcycle," Ian laughed.

"The whole situation has me thinking I should put some effort into dating," said Will. "Nobody thinks I like girls." He shot Ian, who fell into a ravine, died, and respawned.

Ian gripped the controller hard. "You played soccer for years to make other people happy. Might as well date Rebekkah for their benefit, too."

"It's not like that!"

Ian ran up a ladder and down a ramp, looking for grenades. "It's exactly like that. You're talking about what you *should* do. What do you *want* to do?"

"I don't know what I want!" said Will. Ian shot him in the head, and Will returned his attention to the game. "You're an asshole. You distracted me."

Ian grinned as Will respawned.

Will said, "This thing with Rebekkah has become a big deal in my house. I'm letting people down if I date her. I'm letting people down if I don't. All I want is to go to college. I want to see Europe. How will I ever do either? I have no money, no papers and stupid dreams, and I have to be realistic about family and future sometime. I'm an ordinary person."

"I guess," muttered Ian.

"You're talking with your hands," said Will.

Ian checked. His hands were around his controller, which was now damp with sweat. Will shot him in the face.

"You're an asshole!" Ian laughed.

Half-asleep, Ian and Will leaned against the headboard. The game remained on, but they weren't playing.

"I don't like that you consider yourself ordinary, Will," mumbled Ian. "It's insulting to me. I don't keep the company of ordinary people. You underestimate your talents, and you want something bigger than what life gives you."

"I'd look crazy if I insisted on it."

"No, you wouldn't. People want to be told what to think. They're dying for somebody to tell them, so they don't have to think for themselves. People will believe what you tell them to believe if you say it with confidence. After a while, you'll believe what you say, yourself, and incredible things happen. The night we met, I knew you had a talent for details, like me."

"And pick-pocketing," added Will.

Ian smiled. "You stole my Zippo lighter from my pocket again tonight, when you dropped your baseball bat into the umbrella vase."

Will smirked and reached into his pocket. He found nothing.

"I stole it back," said Ian, holding it up with his eyes closed.

Will jumped to life and punched Ian in the arm. "Do you care if I shower tonight?"

"The weather's frigid. You're off the soccer team. It's a strange thing to offer, I know, but you can use the shower anytime, if it's tough at home." Ian rubbed his arm where Will hit him. "Be a proper gentleman. Don't piss in the drain, or rub one out."

Will shook his head. "Gross."

Ian fell asleep a few minutes past eleven. Will showered and found the toothbrush he used the night before. Mario had added it to the holder in the bathroom. When he went back to the bedroom, Ian was asleep. He drooled on his pillow, his phone beside him. The radioactive lint tracker was on, showing no signal.

Had a stranger seen Ian, they'd underestimate him. It would be a mistake. People underestimated Will, too. Was there a difference?

The Professor stood at the base of the bed. He looked up at Will and meowed. Will lifted him onto the bed and crawled onto the other half of the mattress. The furnace switched on in the basement. The blower started, and white noise filled the house. As small as Ian's room was, it was warm and safe, and both Will and Ian slept until morning.

37: A MEANS TO A GOAL

MONDAY.

On Monday morning, Ian opened his eyes, shivering and choking on the scent of lemons.

Will had used Mario's *Il Frutteto* soap in the shower the night before. He had stolen all the covers, and his head stuck from an enormous blanket cocoon three feet away.

Ian crawled out of bed. Downstairs, a light glowed on Mario's coffee pot. The carafe was nearly empty already. Torn Sweet 'N Low packets, empty of their contents, littered the countertop. He put a hand to the kitchen window. 29 degrees. A record low. Cold weather, no blankets, and he slept better than he had in months.

Two days ago, he was certain a friendship with Will would be a disaster. Now, he wanted every night to end in pick-pocketing and video game battles and wondered how they might continue without Will's stepmother's approbation. The future filled him with apprehension. It wasn't only Li that concerned him. Will downplayed his new friendship with Rebekkah, but a relationship between the two was easy to imagine and could still change everything. The thought of her made his blood hot.

Will appeared at the top of the stairs, his hair in a plume and one eye open.

"You stole all the covers," said Ian.

"You overheated," said Will. "You should thank me."

"I didn't overheat."

Will limped downstairs. "It's why you never sleep. I never sleep because I'm cold and I had a perfect night. In fact, I might still be asleep. Do you have any toaster waffles?"

Ian opened his mouth to argue.

Will cut him off. "With real maple syrup. Not the fake stuff with the corn syrup. Li makes congee every morning. I need something real."

Ian retrieved a box of waffles from the freezer. "You smell like an old goombah."

"*Stronzate!*" Mario's voice boomed from the basement. "*Il sapone fa bene alla pelle e all'anima!*"

"What did he say?" asked Will.

"He said Ian is always right, and you shouldn't steal his blankets or his shoes."

"Or his lighter." He threw Ian's Zippo toward him.

By the time Ian and Will arrived at Southeastern High, their teeth chattered. Nobody stood outside. A brand-new bicycle hung high above the door on a chain.

"It's a prize for the school fundraiser, which begins today," said Will. "They dangle it, and the sharks snap at it. In December, they give it to the top earner. I'll win it this year."

"How do you know?"

"I have a strategy. I almost won last year. This year, I'll refine it and come out on top."

"Where will you ride?"

"I won't. I'll sell the bike. It's worth a month's rent."

They made their way to the cafeteria, where students assembled on cold-weather days. Ian received a text—Matt needed to change a phone setting—so he broke away.

"I'll save everyone space at a table," said Will.

The cafeteria stank of too many kids, too little ventilation, and reheated, soggy French toast served from an industrial warmer. Kids with nothing to say said it too loud, creating an unpleasant cacophony.

Rebekkah Batiste appeared before Will could find a place to sit. She was less made-up and smelled of talc. She wore a new pair of Sambas.

"Hey Will?" she asked. "Do you have a second?"

Will waved her over so he could hear her. "I like your shoes."

"You're a trendsetter," she smiled. "It was time for a change. Anyway—"

A thundering voice interrupted them. "Anchor baby!" Craig. A stress fracture boot struck the floor.

Rebekkah's smile faded. She turned to face him. "Go away."

"You can break up with me, but you can't tell me where to go," said Craig. He limped closer to them, and focused on Will. "I heard you have a dirt bike."

"Someone stole it," said Will.

"Too bad." said Craig. "I need a lift after school. This could have been your big chance to impress me."

"A staggering loss," Will murmured.

Craig simpered. "It's been a strange week. We both fell down the southeast staircase, but I got a fracture boot, and you got an attitude." He sniffed the air. "You smell like him."

"Who?"

"Ian."

"I stayed over at his place last night."

"And now you smell like him? Did you two take a bath together? Do you not love *me* anymore?"

"Don't be disgusting," said Will.

Craig chaffed, "are you homophobic?"

Rebekkah snorted. "Look who's talking."

"Shut it, Rebekkah," said Craig. "Homophobic means you're scared of queers. I'm not scared of them. I hate them. And I know them by the smell."

"I'm not like that!" said Will. "I'm Christian!"

Craig grinned. "Who do you think about when you jerk off?" He touched Will's shoulder.

Will pulled away, becoming red from the neck up. "Get off me."

"Seriously. Is it me changing in the field house? Or is Ian your type? Do you jerk off thinking about him?"

"I would never in a million years think of Ian like that!"

"You slept over at his house."

"I was beside him all night and nothing happened!"

They fell silent. Will's eyes grew wide. Craig broke the silence with laughter.

Will stuttered, "What I mean is—"

"You're kidding me. You were in bed with him?"

"Playing video games! I'm a guy! I like girls, like every other normal guy does! Why can't you get that through your skull?"

Craig went on, "The only reason your parents haven't noticed you're gay is because you're Asian, and they think it's normal to think of math instead of pussy."

"My parents think I'm dating Rebekkah."

Rebekkah's jaw dropped.

"They think you're Chinese," Will said to Rebekkah. "Sorry."

"That'll be a cold day in hell," said Craig.

"Do you want to go on a date?" Rebekkah asked.

Will froze. "Me?"

She nodded.

"What?" asked Craig.

"I need a homecoming date," Rebekkah looked at Craig, "now that I'm available."

"This is your way of getting back at me?" asked Craig. He pointed at Will. "It isn't funny. His face looks like he slept on a pizza! Plus, he's a fag! No matter what girl he says he likes or tries to date or takes to homecoming, he's a fag. He plays soccer like a fag, he fights like a fag, and when he's in trouble, he screams like a fag. He's always been a fag, and he'll always be a fag."

Wills fists tightened.

"It's no wonder you and Ian get along. He's the only person in this school who's an even bigger faggo—"

A dull hum filled Craig's ears. The room turned over, and his head cracked against the floor. Through one eye, he saw Will falling backward into a cafeteria table. Through the other, Ian threw fists that connected with the sound of heavy rocks breaking the surface of a frozen pond.

Ian picked Craig up by his hair and threw a blow to his eye. The bones beneath Craig's eye popped under his knuckles. A group of students pulled the two apart. Craig spit a tooth into a pool of blood.

"Jesus, Ian!" screamed Will, restraining him. "I had this under control! He was being a dick, but look at him! He looks like ground beef!"

Ian broke free. His knuckles bled.

Craig whimpered and moaned.

"I can handle Craig!" Will continued. "I don't always need you to do it for me! This wasn't your problem!"

Ian stared at Craig and glanced toward Rebekkah and Will. Matt and Nic stood paralyzed nearby. The cafeteria had fallen silent.

Ian backed away a few steps, then bolted off through a set of double doors into a quiet hallway. He tried knobs on classrooms and broom closets, all locked. His search for a place to be alone became frantic. Two hands grabbed him from behind, rushed him down the corridor, and threw him into the school's decommissioned library. He stumbled, fell beside a metal garbage can, wrapped his arms around it, and vomited.

When he finished, he spat acid and maple syrup and rolled alongside an overturned card catalog.

A stack of paper clips had long ago fallen to the floor nearby. The room smelled of mildew. Drapes covered shelves filled with yellowing encyclopedias, long out-of-date. Daequon Griggs stared down at him.

Tape wrapped his glasses.

Ian closed his eyes. "If you're going to kill me," he said, "make it hurt."

"Shut the hell up," said Daequon. He stared daggers. "I need you to do for me what you did for Will."

"Say what?" Ian moaned.

"I need you to do for me what you did for Will," Daequon repeated.

"I don't follow," said Ian.

"Craig threw me under the bus on Friday after his accident. Timmons and Principal Baxter met with his dad to make up a story about what happened, because the press wants to know. The official story is Craig lost his balance and fell, but if the media does any digging, Craig is going to tell everyone I beat up Will and it was all my idea."

"The media won't dig," said Ian. "You're ahead of yourself."

"That's not the problem," said Daequon. "To cover their asses, coach kicked me off the soccer team this morning. I need to be on that team or I'll lose my scholarship to college. You're clever. Fix it for me."

Ian straightened himself out. "Give me your glasses," he said.

Daequon handed them down, and Ian unwrapped the tape. His knuckles continued to drip blood. He took a paper clip from beside him and bent it until it snapped. "I'm sorry for what I said about your dad the other day. It was a means to a goal."

Daequon shrugged.

Ian continued, "You beat up Will. Why shouldn't I let you hang?"

"You don't get why things happened the way they did," said Daequon.

"Sure I do," said Ian. "I'm good with complex motives." He continued working on the glasses. "When Craig attacked Will, you were damned whether or not you helped him.

Looking back, given that choice, you should have been damned by the latter."

"I need to be back on the team," said Daequon. "I have no idea what I'll tell my mom. Yes, I deserve what's happening. But Craig does, too. I was going to beat him bloody this morning. I should be grateful you did the job for me."

Ian threaded the clip through a hinge in the temple. "I don't know if I can help."

"If you don't, I'll tell Will what I saw this morning," said Daequon.

"Will had a front-row seat," said Ian. "He missed nothing."

"He missed everything," Daequon replied. "You get clever when people mess with your friends, like last week when you embarrassed the hell out of me. Today, there was nothing clever. You were all fists. You were defending *you*, not Will."

Ian further bent the clip into place, but a growing discomfort made it more difficult to be precise with his hands.

"Which part got you swinging?" Daequon continued. "Craig calling you the three-letter F-bomb? Rebekkah inviting the guy you like to homecoming? Or was it Will, himself? *Disgusting*, he said. *I'm normal. Never in a million years. I'm a guy.* That had to sting."

Daequon's frames popped as the hinge snapped back into position.

Principal Baxter's voice thundered over the PA system. "Ian Racalmuto, report to the office now!"

"I've gotta go," said Ian. His heart pounded. He shoved

Daequon's glasses into the boy's hands and made for the exit. "Don't say a damn thing to anybody. I mean it."

"Sorry," said Daequon. "It's a means to a goal." He examined his frames. The repair held, and he put them back on his face.

38: KINTU'S TOOTH

On the night Deena and Ian left their house to meet the Secretary of State at the airport in Algiers, a bomb exploded and rolled their SUV. Deena studied the damage.

Erik called Ian's phone. "The embassy is under attack," he said. "Natalie McLauren is with me. I don't know how much longer the building will be secure. Stay away."

"No way," replied Ian. "I'll be there in fifteen minutes." There was a loud ping off of the side of the car. "Better make that twenty, Erik. Somebody's shooting at us."

"Don't forget to air down the tires."

"I know!" said Ian. "I'm not a child."

Erik continued, "CNN's interviewing the Secretary of State in Washington. She isn't coming. Nobody scheduled her to be here. Somebody set you up."

The connection severed. Ian pocketed his phone. He crawled over the gearshift and out the driver's side door, closing it behind him. Deena was already deflating the rear tire, and Ian deflated the front. A bullet grazed the passenger window.

"SecState isn't coming," said Ian. "Someone set us up."

"No surprise," said Deena.

"The embassy is under attack."

"Okay," she muttered. She worked in silence, then said, "let's talk about your friend, Kintu."

"Now?" asked Ian. "The embassy is falling. This isn't the time."

"It's never the time, so the time is now," said Deena. A rocket-propelled grenade landed wide of them, kicking up dirt.

"It's nothing," said Ian. "Kintu tried to throw a hook into my face. I ducked, and when I came back up my elbow connected with his tooth."

"It was over a girl?" asked Deena.

"I didn't find out about the girl until after I knocked his tooth out," Ian said. "They had been seeing each other for a month. I didn't know."

"Then why did he try to clobber you? Were you making moves on her? If you did not know they were dating, he should show a little more grace—"

"I tried to make out with him," said Ian.

She paused. "Why would you make out with Kintu, Ian!?" she asked.

"Why the hell do you think, Deena!?" replied Ian.

"Oh." She settled back. More distant gunfire. "There's a 9-millimeter magazine in the back seat next to a can of baby wipes. Grab it for me?" A fusillade of bullets struck the ground. Ian retrieved the ammo, and she loaded it. "So. Ian. Most boys don't want other boys to kiss them."

"You think that escapes me?" shouted Ian. "I misread everything. He was always drawing close or throwing an arm around me." He started again. "Sometimes people see what they want to see. I convinced myself he liked me. As soon as he pushed me away, I could tell the situation was in free fall."

Deena said, "So, you tried to make out with Kintu because of a misunderstanding. He tried to beat you up because you injured his manhood. You took out his tooth." She scanned the horizon. "I taught you well."

Ian replied, "It was an accident. I embarrassed him. I embarrassed me, too, but he blew some fuse and it was like we'd never been friends at all. He shoved me halfway across the room, called me a fag and said somebody should shoot me."

The machine gun fire grew closer, and they dodged flying debris.

"He may get his wish," Ian mused. "How was I supposed to know? How is anybody ever supposed to know? I'm in a Muslim nation. Nobody says anything! Nobody can!"

"Can you?" asked Deena. "You haven't been clear about yourself, so don't blame the Muslims." She fired three shots into the night. "Dammit, Ian! You gave me the magazine with the nine-millimeter metal-jackets. I'm not plinking here. I need hollow tips. Cup holder. In the back."

"But mom!"

"*Toute de suite*, son!" She clapped her hands. "Chop-chop! We're taking fire!"

Ian kept down, opened the back door, and retrieved the magazine of hollow-point ammo as a flare lit the sky and bullets sank into the frame of the SUV. He rejoined his mother, tossing the ammo toward her.

"Ian," she said, ejecting a round from the chamber before reloading, "There's nothing wrong with who you are, no matter what you are. I have two amazing, intelligent, compassionate sons who will make life better for themselves and for the people around them. They will make a difference in this world."

"I don't need affirmations!" Ian replied. "It's why I never talk. Our headmaster lectured that I needed to be more respectful. He said I can't expect the world to bend to my desires. Whatever. I'll deal with it."

"How dare your headmaster suggest you were culpable! He said nothing about Kintu's behavior? I'll talk to him first thing!" said Deena.

"First thing after the coup?" asked Ian.

"Don't be snarky." said Deena. Shielded by the engine block, she stood, took aim and pulled the trigger until the gun was out of battery. She ejected the magazine and handed it down to Ian. He reloaded it. Distant screams filled the night.

"Don't say anything," said Ian. "Please? It's embarrassing enough, and you'll make it worse. I need to keep low. I'll keep my distance from people who can't like me back. Whatever it takes to power through. I can brush off what Kintu said, but the worst part was watching him like a girl better than he liked me. It sucks."

"If it's any consolation, unrequited love happens to everyone. Do you remember how your brother behaved when Mayra Page rejected him? He bought that stupid accordion and played it under her window at three in the morning. She wasn't even home. Her dad hit him in the face with a shoe."

"Is that supposed to make me feel better?"

More bullets struck the ground. Ian handed her the magazine, and she fired again. "Does anybody else know about you?"

"Only my friend Mita, in India."

"Have you told your father or grandpop Racalmuto you're—?"

"I can't," interrupted Ian. "What if I'm not? What if Kintu was a one-time thing? What if it changes? What if I meet the right girl in a week? Once you say it, there's no going back."

"It's fine if you aren't sure," said Deena. "But once you're sure, don't be timid. Sometimes we need to say things because we can't move ahead until we do."

"I need time," said Ian. "We still have to air down the tires on the other side, and the shooters are heading this way." A pair of distant headlamps in the distance drew near, and the gunfire became rapid.

39: A BUFFOON

Tzvi milked scorpion venom into his poison ring. To his left, standing upright like a bust of Mozart, a styrofoam head sported an expensive toupee. To his right, a forged ID badge with his picture announced him as Winfred Vanhorn, an administrator from the Philadelphia School District. The lazy receptionist at Southeastern High would hand over Ian Racalmuto's class schedule. Tzvi would find the boy, kill him, and repose at his cabin in the mountains by day's end.

A knock at the door. Finzel sprang from the adjoining room to answer.

It was the ancient housekeeper, who held an envelope that had arrived via courier. Finzel thanked the man and dismissed him, then ran a blacklight over the seal to assure it was unbroken. Inside, Caleb Reid's expensive letterhead decorated paper that stank of cologne and cigarettes. Finzel read it aloud.

Ricky: Return to D.C. at once. Police have arrested your agent, Fant, in a diplomatic reception room at Main State. Against instruction, she detoured to Foggy Bottom to procure race-book advice from the negro custodian. The Racalmuto phone was not on her person. I believe it to be somewhere in the building. Do NOT-repeat-NOT go to Main State. Have your man Tzvi find the phone to-morrow morning and deliver it to me. That you trusted Fant will forever be a great sadness in my life. You are a buffoon. -Caleb Reid, Ambassador.

Finzel wadded the note. He clenched his fist and grew hot. "He blames *me* for Fant's capture? *I* didn't dispatch her to collect the phone! I thought her dead!" he shrieked. "Gather our belongings and put them in the car. We leave for Washington in twenty minutes. The phone is in the diplomatic receiving area, and I will find it."

Tzvi huffed in agitation. "The ambassador instructs you not to go near the Truman Building. Finding the phone is to be *my* affair. If I'm to have any hope of salvaging the remains of my holiday, we are best to follow his command."

"He refuses to grant me a moment of victory!" Finzel snapped. "He must acknowledge my success and his failure!"

"What of the boy?"

Finzel shook. "Never mind the boy! I will not be termed a buffoon by Caleb Reid!"

Tzvi replaced the scorpion in its terrarium.

Finzel sat on Tzvi's bed. "Tomorrow, you will resume your post at Main State. I will follow inside at 9:30, alongside a civilian tour. After retrieving the Racalmuto woman's phone, I'll break free. An elevator will carry me to a bank of computers in the basement." He unfolded the diagram of the computer mainframe Fant had given him in California and pointed to the red switch. "I'll disable the firewall here, then press a few buttons on the phone and go to Reid's bedside to watch Chinese rockets destroy our fleet and begin our war."

Tzvi took three sheets of paper and sketched simple diagrams of the basement, the ground level, and the 8th floor at Main State, labeling each accordingly. He marked cameras and guard points with letters X and gave Finzel advice to avoid detection. "Two of the east elevators near the reception rooms are not operating. It may be possible to activate them."

"Are they safe?"

"No, but they're operable in the short term. Sneak away from the tour group as soon as you're inside. I'll place a large fern in front of the elevator you are to use, and nobody will suspect you disappeared into it. Open the emergency call box in the elevator. I'll have a credential and a silenced firearm waiting."

"A credential and a silenced firearm?"

"If the former doesn't work to throw people off your scent, use the latter."

Finzel grew contemplative. "It's a peculiar grace the Lord has extended to Ian and his brother. I must pray on it and its meaning." He threw Tzvi's maps and Finzel's letter in the wastebasket.

Tzvi brought a luggage cart to their room and loaded their goods. He became winded lifting Finzel's Bible.

"Are you well, Tzvi?" asked Finzel. "You look peaked."

"Fine, Richard. Still recovering from yesterday." Tzvi belched.

They dropped their keys at the front desk. On their way out the front door, reporters and cameramen from local news outlets shined cameras and lights in their faces. A federal officer escorted the old housekeeper into a police car. Others carried Ziploc bags filled with gruesome mementos. An ear necklace. A bag filled with lockets of human hair. A mummified hand covered in rings and a stack of Polaroids with the faces of terrified young girls. A tow truck pulled a black conversion van from a secluded garage.

They brushed the reporters off, hurried into the Humvee, and made for Washington.

40: PRINCIPAL BAXTER

Mario Racalmuto sat next to Ian in Principal Corynthia Baxter's office. His fingertips made a steeple in front of his face. On the other side of the room, Craig and Paul Brooks mumbled to one another. Craig, swollen and blue, rubbed an eye red with blood. His tooth floated in a styrofoam cup filled with milk. Officer Timmons sat between the two families.

In the back corner, a white man of 65 wearing an expensive suit and Hugo Boss cologne flipped pages on a yellow legal pad and made notes with a black pen. His cell phone, tucked in an accordion briefcase, blinked and buzzed.

"Who is this?" Principal Baxter asked, pointing at the man.

"He's with me," said Mario. "What's happened here is serious."

"It's beyond serious. It's unforgivable," said Paul. "I'm taking my kid out of this school." He pointed to Ian with his bandaged hand. "This little shit broke Craig's leg last week and damn near killed him today. He's a terror. You can't control your school, Baxter. Find your own goddamn money."

"Before we continue, would you like legal representation,

Mr. Brooks?" asked Baxter. She caught her face in a reflection in glass and fluffed her hair. People said she looked like Angela Bassett, but her sister said Naomi Campbell.

Paul interrupted her thoughts. "I'm not hiding behind a lawyer or talking through one. When I went to this school, we didn't jump out of corners or push people down stairs if we had a beef, and we didn't phone lawyers."

The man in the suit grinned and began a fresh page of notes.

"We'll get to the bottom of things," Baxter assured him, "though we have no evidence Ian broke Craig's leg."

"He pushed me!" shouted Craig.

"What the hell's wrong with this country?" asked Paul. "When did we go from law and order to mollycoddling thugs? It isn't American."

"I spent time in Laos decades ago," said Mario. "America has a rich history of mollycoddling thugs and doing damage with impunity."

"Your kid's a spineless cunt," Paul harrumphed.

Baxter's eyes widened, and Timmons stood, anticipating trouble. Mario flicked his eyebrows, but didn't move his hands from his face.

"There was no exchange of words before the fight this morning?" asked Baxter.

"He called me a faggot," said Ian.

"Did you call him anything?" asked Baxter.

"I called him an ambulance," said Ian.

Baxter rubbed her forehead. "They're only words, Ian."

"Words have weight," Ian replied. "Craig and Daequon Griggs threw Will Xiang down a stairwell and stole hundreds of dollars from him. You and Officer Timmons refused to look into the matter. Forgive me if I'm unmoved by lectures on integrity."

"He's lying," Craig said through thick lips. "Daequon beat up Will. I had nothing to do with it. Why would I?" He looked at Ian. "Do you know what I do for this school? Do you understand who I am?" He coughed. "You aren't shit."

Ian muttered something to Mario.

"What was that?" asked Paul.

The man in the suit flipped through his notes. "Ian said, 'I'm about to add more teeth to that cup of milk.'"

Paul lifted his hands. "That's what I mean. That attitude. What are you going to do about it, Baxter?"

Baxter leaned against her desk. She spoke to the man in the suit. "What I'm about to say has little to do with the matter at hand, so please stop listening and don't take notes for the moment."

He nodded.

She continued, "Ian, you're new here, and grieving. I understand this is an adjustment. I've seen your transcripts. You've always attended well-resourced schools that never had to struggle to continue operating. Your old school didn't fill a critical role in the community like this one. We are a school, a hospital, a daycare, a language center, and to many of our children, a parent. Other schools long ago privatized and can opt to reject children. Those children end up here.

"Craig has unique gifts. Those gifts are helping us build an athletic team that will ensure financial stability and free up money for other programs. I cannot have students beating him up and breaking his legs." She shuffled some papers. "Just as there's no evidence Ian broke anybody's leg, there is no evidence Craig beat up Will or anybody else. I did, however, have 20 cameras recording what happened in my cafeteria today. That's an automatic three-day suspension."

"Three days?" asked Paul. "That's what he gets away with?"

"Also," continued Baxter, looking at Paul, "I will involve authorities. Officer Timmons will coordinate a police report. Ian, the district requires me to refer you for counseling."

"Counseling," scoffed Paul. "Pussification. Somebody needs to beat his ass. Give me a good reason to keep Craig here."

"He will continue to be safe here, Paul. We value Craig as a star member of our student body. He is an example of hard work and achievement to our students," said Baxter.

"I want the bike," said Craig. "The one on the chain above the door."

"Will has a good chance of winning it this year," said Ian.

Paul gave Baxter a contemptuous stare. "Give him the bike," he added.

Baxter nodded in the affirmative. "Is that everything? Have we overlooked anything? Ian?"

Ian stared into space. How could he explain *anything* that had happened to anyone? *Sorry, I took it personally when Craig called me a fag because I have a huge crush on Will even though I was hoping I'd never have a crush on a guy ever again after a similar one ended in disaster in Algiers.* His first intuition had been correct. They should never have become friends.

"Ian?" repeated Baxter. "We're good?"

Ian opened his mouth to speak, but Mario cut him off. "Ms. Baxter, you and officer Timmons erased the video of Craig and Daequon beating up Will Xiang."

"You're mistaken," said Timmons. "The camera in the

stairwell doesn't work."

Mario withdrew a thumb drive from his pocket. "The camera worked at the time of the attack. I have a copy of the video."

Baxter sat forward. Both Craig and Ian's eyes grew wide.

Timmons snatched the USB stick from Mario's fingers and stuffed it in his shirt.

Baxter exhaled and stared at Timmons. "We'll evaluate it."

"Please do," said Mario. He withdrew a second, identical USB stick from his pocket. Timmons dove for it, but Mario passed it behind him to the man in the suit. Baxter's face turned gray as the man put it in his briefcase.

"Here's what happens next," said Mario. "Paul will give Craig a bag of ice and take him to the dentist. You'll do nothing to Ian, and we'll consider this matter settled. Otherwise, I'll send the video on the thumbdrive to the local news. They'll have questions for Craig. They'll have questions for Timmons about why he erased the footage. And they'll have questions for you, Principal Baxter. You'll be here until one AM with microphones under your nose." He paused. "I don't know when this school became a shithouse without drains, but enough's enough."

Timmons chewed on his tongue. Baxter's underarms soaked through her shirt. Paul Brooks twitched.

"Anything else, Ian?" asked Mario.

"Daequon Griggs," said Ian. "Put him back on the soccer team. And the bike stays above the door. Craig can't pedal it right now, anyway."

Craig erupted. "What about the video of Ian? From today in the cafeteria? Nail his ass!"

"The news doesn't care about me," said Ian. "I'm not

shit." He shot Craig a penetrating stare that forced him to turn away.

"This meeting never happened," said Mario. "Craig stays away from Ian and his friends, and Ian stays away from Craig and his friends. I keep the video. It assures Ian's safe passage until graduation. Daequon gets reinstated on the soccer team, and the bike goes to whoever wins the competition."

"That's blackmail," whispered Baxter. She turned to the man in the suit. "Do you have anything to say about this?"

"I'm sorry," he said. "You asked me not to listen, and my mind was on other things. Is $120 too much to pay for an oil change on a BMW? It *is* synthetic."

The meeting adjourned. Paul Brooks got into his car and pummeled the dashboard until the plastic cracked. Fresh blood soaked the bandaging on his hand. Later, a dentist re-attached Craig's tooth. It would turn gray in his mouth and throb when it rained for the rest of his life.

Ian walked alongside Mario and the man in the suit. "Thanks, Grandpop," he said.

"Don't you dare think you're out of the woods," said Mario. "What the hell has gotten into you?" He turned to the man in the suit. "Jack, I can't thank you enough."

"It's nothing," said the man. "I'd love to stay, but I need to get back to the store and return the suit. Lunch ended fifteen minutes ago."

"Store?" asked Ian.

"Jack works with me in the men's department at Wanamakers," said Mario. "Re-attach the tags, and put it on the return rack. The cologne was a nice touch. Did you get that—"

"From the cosmetics counter." Jack pulled two dollars from his wallet and started down the stairs to the subway.

"Can't you get in trouble for pretending you're an attorney?" asked Ian.

"Did I ever say I was an attorney?" asked Jack. He returned Mario's USB drive and waved goodbye. "Do I send my bill to you, or to Lando Raab?"

Mario winked and nodded toward the subway. "Your BMW awaits on track number 2."

Jack disappeared.

"Where did you get the thumb drives?" Ian asked.

"Nic Delvecchio called me from school this morning. Matt Granados gave them to me on my way in. There's nothing on them."

"What if Timmons sees his is blank?"

"He'll still wonder if mine is." Mario sighed. "What's in your head, Ian?"

"I'm living a nightmare. Fenzel has mom's phone, and he'll start his war. I can't be friends with Will anymore. I'm at a standstill in the search for Erik, and by tomorrow night, the trail will be cold. I'm exhausted, and I need more time to figure things out."

"That's no excuse to beat the living daylights out of someone!"

When Ian got home, both Matt and Will had texted him. He did not reply. He closed the door to his bedroom, turned his phone off, settled between the sheets, jerked off, and fell asleep.

41: VOICEMAIL

On his walk home from school, Will dialed Ian. He'd been texting all day and, like the day before, Ian wasn't responding.

"Pick up, pick up," he muttered. The call went to voicemail. He disconnected and called Matt and Nic. "He's pissing me off!" he screamed. "This morning he was in my bed! This afternoon, he won't talk!"

"Weren't you in his bed?" asked Nic.

"He gave me his bed for the night," said Will. "It was my bed."

"Jilted," laughed Matt.

"Shut up!" said Will.

"He's probably still in Baxter's office," Matt replied.

"Ian's behavior makes no sense," said Nic. "He normally isn't volatile, and his response was disproportionate."

"I don't understand," said Will. "Craig was already holding the short straw. His foot was in a boot and his girlfriend asked me to homecoming."

"I heard," said Matt. "Congrats, buddy!"

"Whatever," said Will. "I need to talk to Ian."

He pocketed his phone.

At home, Li waited for him in the living room. Smoke wisps came from her cigarette. "Where were you last night?" she asked.

"With Benson." He removed his shoes.

She struck him across the cheek, and he fell back.

What the hell? He might have screamed had her dark stare not silenced him.

"Do not turn my house into a den of lies," she said. "Benson ran off to California last week. Failed out of school. Ruthie found out only today."

"What about his wedding?"

"His fiancée's family canceled it. She told nobody she was five months with child and flew to China for an abortion! We would have stopped her!" She took a drag on her cigarette. "Did you attend math club Saturday?"

Will said nothing.

"I talked to Mrs. Yang. I want to hear the answer from you."

He remained silent.

"Why are you behaving this way?" Li screamed. "You quit soccer, you befriend people I don't know, you find a girlfriend in the dead of night, and you lie to your parents. You turn against heavenly father! No wonder our family suffers!" She exhaled. "Your father and I only want what's best!"

"We're illegal," said Will. "We will never have what's best."

"We are in America and we trust God!" Li shot back. "A heart surgeon was on the news last week. Big surprise! He had no papers and still became a doctor."

"He was on the news because ICE deported him to

Honduras, even though he was a renowned surgeon," said Will.

"Better to be deported a heart surgeon than a garbageman! I'll enroll you in—"

"No!" Will slammed the palm of his hand flat against an end table. "No more enrolling!"

Li gasped.

Will continued, "I don't need people to tell me what to do and do everything for me! Why does nobody have faith in me to find my way?"

"You need guidance! You have no motivation like Benson!" said Li.

"You still use him as an example?"

"When he was in high school, he did not go about thinking he knew best. He listened to Ruthie. You nearly died placing an order for licorice tincture." She pointed to a small bottle on the table that had come in the mail that day. The label was Chinese. The handwriting was Matt Granados's.

Will smirked. "Benson wasn't obedient," he said. "He was better at keeping secrets."

"You're killing your father!" Li erupted. "You're killing me!" She grabbed Eddie's blood pressure cuff from the table, slapped it across her bicep, and inflated it. She nodded at the dial.

"That's not how you use it," said Will.

Li continued pumping the cuff until it was the size of a swimming pool float, and her hand turned blue. "Look at what you do to me! My pressure! So high!" she cried. "Go to your room. You're grounded until I sort this out."

His old, pink flip phone remained on the dining table. In a deft move, he pocketed it.

Will slammed his bedroom door. He put the pink phone on his dresser. The smartphone in his pocket buzzed, and he looked to see if it was Ian.

It was not.

He turned music on, then off, then leaned against the wall.

Maybe Li was right, and he wasn't ready to control his life. Over the past several days, had things gotten any better? His house never stopped being shit, his stepmother never stopped being a bitch, and he never stopped being poor and without options. He shook his snow globe with the coins that swirled around the Stardust hotel. He threw it in frustration against the wall. It bounced back and hit him hard in the balls.

He groaned and hobbled and tried to stand upright.

He would redouble his efforts at soccer once he was well enough. He'd say yes to Rebekkah's homecoming offer and see if romance bloomed. Screw Ian. He could sit in his basement alone with his phone silenced, doing his miserable hot-and-cold routine all he wanted.

The flip phone screeched like a hawk. The voicemail tone was from a lifetime ago. Whatever the message, it was days old. He dialed his passcode.

New message.

"Ian, it's Will. Shit. No. The other way. Where's the..."

Will thumbed to the next message. Ian again.

"...I'm just calling to say I'm thinking about you—wait. That sounds—that's not what I mean. This is a mess." Scratching of a rotary dial.

Click.

Will shook his head and chuckled. "It's a rotary phone, asshole."

New message. Ian, a third time.

"...Call me back. I really enjoyed sleeping with you last night—having you sleep over—Goddammit! No! No, no, no!!! Nothing's coming out right! Why won't my words work?" He dialed the rotary again. "Why doesn't this old man have a phone with buttons in the 21st century!"

"I'd replace it," Mario said in the background, "but I don't talk on the phone anymore. My friends and I all do the WhatsApp."

Will doubled over in laughter, and tears fell from his eyes.

"I'm in hell," Ian continued. "Call me back."

He stuffed the phone in the side pocket of his cargo pants. Without undressing, he pulled his blankets over him and turned out the lights.

Tears soaked his face, and he sniffled. He needed to go to Ian's—to tell him to eat shit and die, then drink wine and play video games with him for the rest of the night like normal people do.

A fitful, broken sleep consumed him until 3 AM, when a call from Nic Delvecchio jolted him awake.

42: STEVE BLASS

TUESDAY.

Alone in the basement, Ian threw a baseball against the wall, catching it as it bounced back. It was one in the morning. Mario slept upstairs. They hadn't spoken since the afternoon.

Earlier, Ian removed the map of Algeria from his bedroom and wadded it into a ball. He had run out of time to find Erik. If he hadn't met Will or bothered with the boy's affairs—if he had minded his own business as he promised himself he would—maybe things would be different.

Instead, he'd fallen in love.

Which was dumb. It was Will.

Will wasn't any more capable of falling in love with him than Kintu. If this kept happening, by age 45 he would find himself alone in a big Victorian house surrounded by tasteful antiques and lots of cats.

Video streamed on his phone. The news. Espinoza, again. China, again. He pitched his baseball sidearm at the wall. Plaster cracked, and it landed in the Professor's litter box.

Breaking news from Philadelphia. Police arrested a serial

killer at a hotel. The old man had been the housekeeper there for decades.

Ian would have ignored the story, but he recognized the round tower near him. Officers escorted the old man out in handcuffs. Behind him, two men shielded their eyes from the lights as they made their way with their luggage to a familiar Humvee.

Ian brought the phone closer. Fenzel? Impossible. A reporter shoved a microphone under the man's nose.

"I have nothing to say," said Fenzel. "He seemed a kindly old man, but so did the *Führer* to most Germans."

"Your name?"

"Finzel."

"F-e-n?"

"F-i-n," he corrected.

"And the gentleman with you?"

"Tzvi."

"Tzvi?"

"Tzvi."

"Does he have a last name?"

Ian ran outside, then west across Broad Street. Twenty minutes later, he was at the round hotel tower.

Mrs. Stuyvesant had asked the night manager, Mr. Moody, to find a new housekeeper, and the task consumed him. He searched job sites on the internet. Meanwhile, nobody serviced the rooms.

The handbell on his desk rang.

The manager looked up to find Ian staring back at him.

"My uncle sent me," said Ian. "He left his wedding band. If nobody has cleaned his room, it might still be there."

"It's 1:20 in the morning, kid," said the manager.

"How do you think I feel?" Ian fired back. "I have exams tomorrow."

"Name?" asked the manager.

"Fenz—" Ian cleared his throat. "Finzel. Checked out this morning. Might also be under Tzvi."

"Tzvi?"

"His lover."

The manager handed him a keycard. "403."

Ian ran upstairs and unlocked the door, reluctant to enter. Would Finzel return? Had he, already? He turned on a light.

Nothing remained. The room was quiet and cold and smelled of vinegar. A loud cricket chirped, and he followed the sound into the adjoining room. Somebody had ripped the safe from the closet. A hot water bottle and clyster pipes hung from the shower rod. The wastebasket beside the television overflowed, and he emptied it onto the floor.

He might have overlooked the note that informed Richard Finzel about Victoria Fant had the prominent letterhead not caught his eye. A large letter R. He withdrew his lighter from his pocket. The letters matched. Reid! Caleb Reid! Had the embassy bombing involved him?

He pocketed Tzvi's hand-drawn maps. On his way home, he read Reid's note twice more. Why was Victoria Fant involved? Where had she hidden the phone? If neither Reid nor Finzel had it, he might have time to stop their war.

By 1:45, he was back home. Erik's watch ticked beside Deena's ashes. He placed Reid's letter next to it, near the encrypted note from Erik. The Steve Blass baseball card fell face-down on the floor.

Blass collected Topps baseball cards, according to the back. He was also a cross-country runner. Kingsport '60,

Dubuque '60, Batavia '61. Ian rubbed his face where Finzel hit him. 1961. Bay of Pigs.

He squinted and examined the ciphertext, again. ESTONIA. 01961 93439 83630 43949 08449 30569 53304 01580. A string of numbers.

He compared it to the card. 1961 Batavia. 23 160 13 6 .684 227 117 3.32. A string of baseball statistics.

He rushed to the sofa and used a book on his lap as a hard surface. Beneath the numbers Erik sent, he wrote Steve Blass's stats from the year 1961, then subtracted them as he might numbers from a one-time pad. Using his Estonia checkerboard, he converted the difference to letters. 93439 became 70379. B-O-M...

B-O-M-B.... Bomb! He kept going. BOMB EDES... Bomb Edes? Had he done the math wrong? BOMB EDES K175 3XXE. The last two letters X meant *end of transmission*, and the E at the end was filler. BOMBEDESK1753. He typed the phrase into his web browser and called Nic and Matt three minutes later.

"My mom's phone!" he shouted. "It's in a 1753 bombe desk on the 8th floor of the State Department in Washington!"

"What the hell are you talking about?" groaned Matt.

"It's 2:15 in the morning," said Nic.

Ian explained the events of the night. "There's only one 1753 bombe desk that shows up on the internet. It's at Main State, in the entrance hall to the diplomatic reception rooms. They arrested Victoria Fant there today. It can't be a coincidence."

"Who's Victoria Fant?" asked Nic.

"A security agent who's supposed to be working for Caleb

Reid but dead-dropped mom's phone at Main State. I think she's working for Erik!"

"Who's Caleb Reid?" asked Nic.

"An ambassador!"

Matt remained monotone. "You intuited this from a bunch of numbers sent with a watch, stats on the back of a baseball card, and a note you found in a garbage can at a hotel?"

"You have to believe me!"

Matt yawned. "How could Erik have known where the phone would be when he sent his message weeks ago? Finzel didn't have the phone until this past weekend. If the wind had blown a different direction, you would have it now."

"I wasn't going to bother trying to get it, remember? They *assumed* Finzel would collect it. When he did, Fant must have executed her half of the plan—stealing it and dropping it in the bombe desk at Main State."

"And getting it from Foggy Bottom is your half of the plan?" asked Nic.

"The letter says come to this place!"

"Why wouldn't Fant give you the phone if she's working for Erik?" asked Matt. "Why take it all the way to D.C. and hide it in an antique desk? Does she not know where you live?"

"Talking to me would blow her cover. She may not even know I'm charged with retrieving it. Main State is a reasonable place for her to go, and they allow tourists and kids in the reception rooms," replied Ian.

"What will you do when you get the phone?"

"Destroy it," said Ian. "We have to put an end to this."

"Do you need a lift to D.C.?" asked Nic. "The Chrysler

I've been working on can make it."

"Can I go, too?" asked Matt.

"I was hoping you'd ask," Ian smiled. "Meet at 5 at the corner of my street. Also, don't tell Will about any of this. I don't want him along. It will only cause trouble."

They disconnected.

Nic made a private call to Matt. "What's up with Ian and Will? Ian's kicking him to the curb."

"Beats me," said Matt. "He was like that the other day, too. It's weird."

"Ian's about to do something stupid, and we have to be in this together," said Nic. "If Will isn't a part of this thing, it will cause lasting damage to their friendship."

"Better call him," Matt agreed.

43: REALITY'S A NUANCED THING

At 4:50 AM, Ian strapped Erik's Breitling to his wrist and snuck upstairs from the basement, unsure whether Mario was awake. He was—his coffee pot was on. The carafe was two-thirds full. Mario, however, was nowhere to be found.

Ian grabbed his barn coat and unlocked the front door. His coat was heavier than he had remembered. A toll transponder in the pocket weighed it down.

Nic's Chrysler rounded the corner and rolled to a stop like an enormous yacht coming into port. She had a cup of coffee in-hand and wore a gray NASA shirt. Matt ate a donut beside her and watched a video on his phone. Ian jumped into the back seat.

"I'm hoping to see the Peregrine Falcon on top of Main State today," said Matt. "Right now, it's off hunting." He turned the phone to reveal an empty nest. A street sweeper went by on the road below.

They drove a few blocks east, where Will waited on the sidewalk.

Ian sat straight. "I told you not to."

"Overruled," said Nic.

Will climbed in the back beside Ian. He turned on his phone.

They rode in awkward silence.

"What's the plan?" Matt asked at last.

"We'll park. I'll handle my business, finish by three, and we can all go home," said Ian.

"You can't just walk inside Main State," said Will. Matt rewound the film of the falcon and watched the street sweeper rumble past again. He changed the date and watched recorded video of the same street sweeper rumbling past on other days. "The falcon camera holds the answer."

He turned around and faced Ian and Will. "The street sweeper comes every Tuesday and Friday. If we scroll through the video throughout the week," he paused and made some mental notes, "the mail comes at 2 PM daily, and FedEx is there twice at 8 and 4.

"Compare that to the office supply lesbian. She delivers Thursdays at 3, but every other week. The copier guy was only there once in three weeks, so he's not routine. The old guard who arrives at nine AM drinks his coffee, then leaves to pinch a loaf at 9:30. He's back between 9:48 and 9:50. His bowels are like clockwork. There was only one day it didn't happen, and he didn't have his coffee that day." He zoomed in and out again.

Ian searched through the video on his phone. "Did you see the garbage truck that blocked the yellow catering van from making a delivery on Tuesday at 9:27? It happens every Tuesday at the same time. The catering guy and the woman who drives the garbage truck hate each other. They argue every time."

"They let catering trucks in under the bird's nest," Matt

offered.

Nic chimed in. "Do you know your way to the diplomatic reception rooms from the basement, if you can get into the delivery dock?"

Ian passed Tzvi's maps forward. "These are simple diagrams of the Truman Building. The first-floor diagram matches my recollection. He's labeled the other two B and 8."

Matt pointed to the letters *X*. "They mark something," he said.

Nic took the papers and held them to oncoming headlights, keeping one eye on the road. "If you look close enough, there are scribbles and scratches. Most of them are outside the sight-line of whatever X marks."

"Cameras," said Matt. "This is a plan to avoid detection by security." He grabbed his tablet. "If I can match a basic to-scale floor plan to GPS, I can guide you through the building with minimized risk." He handed Ian a USB stick. "Plug this into the first computer you see inside."

Ian contemplated the layout. "If the catering entrance is in the basement, there has to be an elevator to the Franklin Dining Room, where they hold state dinners. The bombe desk can't be far."

Will, who had been working on his phone, at last faced them. "They have tours of the Diplomatic Reception Rooms at the Harry S. Truman Building daily at 9:30 and 10:30. No need to break in. I just signed all of us up for the 10:30 tour. We can grab the phone while the guide is talking. We'll have time for pancakes when we arrive, now that I've saved us hours of plotting and planning a dramatic break-in."

Ian and Matt stared at him in silence. He continued, "I've

never been to Washington, D.C. I'm excited to get pictures. Harry S. Truman had an interesting post-presidency. I have David McCullough's book about him. He was the last president to live a normal life after the White House. He returned to Missouri and took walks around town with his cane."

Nic stifled a smile.

Ian shifted. "We are not going on a tour. I'll walk into the Truman building to get my phone, but there will be no pancakes and you're not coming with me."

"Yes, I am," said Will. "If there's a problem, we operate well together. Your chances of success multiply when I'm along. You like to impress me with your guile and you work harder. And there will be pancakes. And we'll stop in front of NPR news headquarters for a picture. And you will smile." Will grinned a happy little grin at Ian.

"Let me out of this car," Ian said to Nic. "He's insufferable. I'll take Amtrak."

Nic hit the gas. The transmission dropped into fourth gear with a clunk, and they merged onto Interstate 95.

The car rattled, cracked and popped.

"You're wearing the same thing you did yesterday," Matt said to Will.

"I dressed in the dark and grabbed whatever was close," said Will. He didn't mention how upset he had been, or that he had fallen asleep in a funk and slept in his clothes.

"Does anybody have toll money?" asked Nic.

Ian remembered the toll transponder in his pocket. He passed it forward.

"Where did this come from?" asked Nic.

"My mom might have been right about my grandpop,"

Ian replied. "I think he's an instigator."

Silence filled the car between Wilmington and Baltimore. The landscape passed in a blur. They crossed an endless bridge over a wide river.

"Hey," Will finally said to Ian, "can we talk?"

"I have to focus," replied Ian.

They continued on. Ian poured over the hand-drawn maps. Even when he did not concentrate on them, he would not talk to Will.

The car overheated as they approached a rest area. Will had to pee, so they pulled over.

Once Will was inside the service plaza, Matt said, "Hey Ian? Can I see your Zippo?"

They walked toward an embankment and sat in the grass. Ian gave his lighter to Matt, who flipped it open and shut. "Why are you being a dick to Will?"

"I'm not," said Ian. "I'm focusing."

"No, you aren't. You bite your knuckle when you're focused. You're pretending he isn't here."

Ian looked at his finger. "I can't be friends with him, Matt. His life is going in a good direction. I'll ruin it."

"What do you mean?"

"He's smitten with Rebekkah Batiste, and I hate her."

"You barely know Rebekkah Batiste."

"She was wearing my shoes yesterday!" Ian flapped his hands.

Matt raised an eyebrow, and Ian settled back.

"Days ago, nobody would talk to Will. In a few weeks, he'll be off to homecoming," said Ian. "What kind of friend am I if I'm not happy when girls like him?"

"Girls?" asked Matt. "Or Rebekkah?"

Ian muttered and turned away.

Matt giggled.

"What's so funny, Granados?"

"You have a crush on Will."

"Shut up."

"I didn't realize you were—I mean, Nic sort of thought, but—"

"Don't," Ian interrupted. "I don't know that I am, or if it's just a thing."

Matt continued laughing. "You survived a bomb in Algeria, and a fire. You threw a grown man from an intermodal cargo container, then chased him down on a motorcycle. You're about to raid a federal building. All that, but you don't have a clue what to do when you fall ass-over-teakettle for a pimply illegal Chinese kid in history class? That's funny!"

"Shut up!" said Ian, punching Matt hard in the arm.

"And your competition is Rebekkah Batiste!" Matt rolled sideways in the grass, laughing.

"I didn't sign up for this! Look, even if she weren't in the picture, Will's family is nutty Christian."

"Yeah," Matt said, "If he ever finds out you like him, he won't sleep over ever again."

"If you want to spell it out..." said Ian.

Matt stood up, reached down, and pulled Ian to his feet. "I wish I could say you're wrong—that we're in an enlightened time, when people don't care and accept differences. The truth is complicated. When you're honest about yourself, people you love might never talk to you again. Not everybody will accept you and not everybody will like you. You can't maneuver your way around it, but saying nothing is unsustainable."

Matt looked skyward. "Reality's a nuanced thing. People surprise you. If you have my luck, you'll find yourself in fun, interesting places with excellent people, even if you don't get exactly what you want. You don't think you can be friends with Will if he dates Rebekkah?"

"Every time I see them together, I'll want to choke her," Ian shrugged. "I think it might be better pulling the plug."

"So you think if you're a dick to Will, it will hurt less when he runs off with a girl?"

A miniature peanut butter cup hit Ian on the side of his head.

In the distance, Will laughed. He held five others in his hand.

"You could have taken my eye!" screamed Ian, though Will's goofy laugh made him, however briefly, laugh.

"Good luck," said Matt, handing the Zippo back. He reached into his sock. "Here," he said, giving Ian his plastic shank. "Take this. It'll get through a metal detector."

Ian examined it. "Is it wise to carry a blade if blood makes you dizzy?" he asked.

"I can take a bitch out before I faint," said Matt.

Nic added oil to her car's engine and tightened a bolt with a wrench. "I want candy!" she shouted from her car.

Ian placed his peanut butter cup atop her cast and walked away. "I'm not hungry," he said.

Will's face turned down.

When Ian was out of earshot, Nic said, "He'll come around."

"I'm not worried," said Will. "He's on the rag, but he can't dislike me forever. Let's keep moving."

They continued their journey to D.C., and arrived as the car banged, sputtered and overheated again.

44: SECURITY THEATER

The sky turned cherry-red behind the Washington Monument. The air was clammy and cool.

Nic parked her Chrysler against the curb on Virginia Avenue in Foggy Bottom. Sweet-smelling white smoke fizzed from under the hood and caught in her throat. The car backfired. Every light on the dashboard illuminated at once. A crash sounded, followed by the echo of a metallic disc spinning on its rim. Nic looked under the frame, using the light on her phone.

"Anybody have money for a bus ticket home?" she asked.

"I thought you said this car could make it to D.C.," said Ian.

"It did," replied Nic.

Edward J. Kelly Park separated Virginia Avenue from the imposing 1939 stripped-classical Harry S. Truman Building. On fair-weather days, government workers took their lunch in the triangular expanse of green beside a pair of tennis courts.

An armada of food trucks arrived and parked on either side of the broken-down car. A Turk with a thick mustache hung a sign that said "now serving breakfast." Will used the money his dad gave him for chocolate chip pancakes. When he returned, he offered one to Ian.

"I hate pancakes," said Ian.

"You love pancakes," said Will. "Especially with chocolate chips."

Ian fumed.

At 9:21, Ian examined the edifice with a pair of binoculars. "The 21st Street entrance is well-guarded," he said, handing the binoculars to Matt.

"So is the entrance with the underground driveway," said Matt, placing the binoculars to his eyes and swinging his head up and down. "Lots of cameras. Facial recognition is old technology. If social media can recognize a face from a picture, the government can." He paused. "The falcon's returned to her nest!"

Ian snatched the binoculars back.

Will imagined his stepmother telling him to stay beyond notice, and his knee shook.

Nic noticed. "If you don't want to involve yourself with this, it's fine," she said.

"You should listen to Nic," said Ian.

"Have a pancake," Will replied. "They're exceptional." He stuffed a bite into his mouth.

"I'm not eating it." said Ian, salivating.

Matt continued to scan the mounted cameras. "Most security is theater," he said. "A few years back, the secret service caught someone walking around the executive mansion in the White House."

Ian held his binoculars to his face again. "It was like that at the embassy in Algiers. The State Department hires private security contractors—an outfit called Nightwater. They're morons. Grocery stores have better security." He fell silent. Rick Finzel, dressed in his crimson tie, walked toward the front door with a group of tourists.

"No!" exclaimed Ian, dropping the binoculars. He read Erik's watch, put his earpiece in, kicked open the car door, and bolted across Kelly Park. Will followed, seconds behind.

"The tour's not for another hour!" Will shouted.

"Finzel's here! On an earlier tour! He'll get the phone before we do!"

"Let's stop him!" said Will.

"Stay with Matt and Nic!" replied Ian. "I don't want you along."

"Too bad," Will said, keeping up. "I know why you're mad at me. Yesterday—"

"I don't want to talk about yesterday! Not now! I have three minutes!"

"Why three minutes?" asked Will.

Ian tapped his earpiece. "Nic, are you there?"

"Yup."

"Steal a car," said Ian. "We need a reliable getaway vehicle."

"I'm not stealing a car!" replied Nic. "I'm supposed to go to Cornell in a few years. I can't go from prison!"

"Take online classes!"

"You can't be the David C. Duncan Professor of Astronomy at Cornell by taking online classes! I don't even have my pilot's license!" She disconnected.

Will and Ian neared the Truman building. Exactly three minutes after Ian leaped from Nic's car, the yellow catering van appeared, and a garbage truck rounded the corner. The vehicles stopped at the guard booth in front of the underground driveway, and the drivers screamed at each other in Spanish. Two guards—one old, the other young—stood from behind a desk.

"Here we go again," the older guard said to his subordinate. "Can you handle them? Coffee's caught up with me."

The younger guard nodded.

The old man pressed a button on his way to the toilet. A narrow garage door rattled and opened. The young officer examined the catering van with a mirror on a stick, waved the driver on, and walked out of sight. The driver folded his rearview mirrors inward to clear the opening.

"Go!" said Ian. They scurried and clung tight to the side of the van. The garage door frame brushed against their backs, and they disappeared inside.

45: AZEALIA

Tzvi, dressed in a fresh-pressed security uniform, arrived at Main State an hour and a half before his normal time. He would have been there two hours in advance, but his scorpion had died overnight, making venom extraction cumbersome.

He had planned to activate the east bank of elevators and mark the car Finzel was to use with a giant potted fern. When he could not find a fern—facilities had removed all indoor greenery in his absence—he rushed to a local garden center to buy one. The garden center had sold out of ferns, so he purchased a large Azealia.

He now walked along the sidewalk outside the Truman Building, holding the top-heavy shrub in his enormous arms. He brushed leaves from his nose and spat flowers from his mouth.

Through the branches in his face, he spied the garbage truck and the catering van—and Ian Racalmuto clinging to it and entering the building 100 yards away. He screamed to the guard booth, but the van blocked his view and noise from the garbage truck drowned his shouting.

He dropped the Azealia, removed his sidearm, attached a

silencer, and fired twice. The rounds stuck a concrete bollard and bounced into the sky. A loud squawk sounded from above him, and a fistful of feathers floated down from the sky.

The catering truck disappeared from view, and the garage door closed.

Acid rose in Tzvi's throat, and he burped to relieve chest pressure. He clutched a radio microphone on his lapel and dispatched a security detail to the 8th floor. "Watch for two boys, about twelve. One white, one Asian. Don't send the idiot brigade from the front of the house, either," he said. "This must end in tragedy. Send Nightwater."

He released his mic and dialed Finzel.

"You're certain it was them?" asked Finzel.

"I couldn't see through the Azealia at first, but I was certain once I put it down," replied Tzvi.

"Azealia?" asked Finzel.

He brushed dirt from his uniform shirt, but it only smudged. His armpits dripped. "I couldn't find a fern. Where are you?"

"Meeting my tour group," said Finzel. "The nicest couple from New Zealand is here."

"Go to the bathroom for five minutes," said Tzvi. "I'll place the Azealia in front of the elevator you'll take to the 8th floor. Meet me there." Lights again flashed and flickered in his vision, and he swallowed pink antacids.

A distant voice on Finzel's end asked, "Sir? Can you please put your phone away?"

46: PERSUASION

The narrow ramp leading into the parking garage widened underground. Ian and Will held tight to the side of the truck.

Matt followed the two on his tablet, marked by a pair of red dots. When the moment was right, he instructed them to jump. "There should be a service entrance to your left, linked to a long corridor."

The catering truck rolled on another fifteen meters. The red dots crept through the door Matt identified.

Will locked the corridor door behind them. Ian nodded at two pairs of coveralls and two gray hats on a nearby hook. In a rubbish bin, he found two empty coffee cups, lids attached, and a discarded paperboard cup carrier. He wiped a smudge of lipstick and placed the cups in the carrier.

"What are you doing?" asked Will.

He handed the carrier to Will. "Every prop tells a story. Nobody would break into a government building carrying coffee."

"Brilliant," said Will. "Dr. Robert Cialdini was on *Fresh Air* three weeks ago. He teaches methods of persuasion. He says people believe anything that looks official."

"I know who he is," Ian interrupted.

"The coffee cups just reminded me—"

"I don't care," Ian replied.

"You should," said Will. "He'll make you a better spy."

"I want to be a sommelier!" said Ian.

"Your nose is too small," Will muttered.

They started down the service corridor.

A security officer stepped from a doorway, and they collided, knocking her off-balance. She was Taiwanese, with a slight build.

Ian froze, and Will pretended to steady the empty coffee cups as she composed herself. "Catering staff?" she asked. "Kitchen's through this door." She pointed behind her and continued toward the parking garage.

The boys stepped into an enormous, vacant commercial kitchen. Will closed the door behind the guard and twisted a lock.

Matt's voice sounded through their earpieces. "Everything okay?"

"I forgot you were listening," said Will. "We have to work fast. I locked the caterers in the parking garage, and the guard in the hallway, but she has keys for both doors."

"No, she doesn't," said Ian, holding a keyring and ID badge he had lifted from her utility belt. An old computer flickered beside a wall of refrigerators and freezers. He plugged Matt's USB drive into the back.

"See anything?" Ian asked Matt.

"It's coming through now," Matt said. "Kitchen menus. They're serving cherries jubilee for a meeting of state attorneys general Thursday night." He paused. "I wonder if that's intentional?"

Will grinned. "Like bananas foster for senators elect?"

"Can you access other systems or just the kitchen?" asked Ian.

A pause while Matt typed. "Everything," he said at last, "including a floor plan."

"Excellent," said Ian. "This kitchen must access the Ben Franklin Dining Room at the top of the building, but I don't see an elevator."

"There's a service elevator ten meters ahead to the left," said Matt. "It leads to a prep kitchen off the Franklin Dining Room, close to where you need to be. Hug the wall to your left, and the kitchen cameras won't see you. When you reach the 8th floor, I'll disable the cameras floor-wide. That will give you a few minutes to operate unseen, but when an entire floor's worth of cameras go dark, people investigate."

Ten meters on, Will stared at the wall. "This isn't what I expected." He opened a door and pulled wire shelves from a large dumbwaiter. Two fresh loaves of crusty bread filled the car with an irresistible scent, and he put them under his arm.

"It isn't a passenger elevator, Matt," said Ian. "Is there another?"

The door leading to the hallway rattled. The guard beat on it from the other side.

"No time," said Will, waving Ian inside. "*Andiamo*!"

Ian rolled his eyes and climbed in. "Don't start talking Italian to me. You sound like my mother. Put the bread down."

"It's artisan bread!" said Will.

"Down!" shouted Ian.

Will placed it on a countertop. "There's a bottle of 2010 *Château Pontet-Canet* over here."

Ian jumped out of the dumbwaiter, snatched it, and studied the bottle. His eyes filled with lust.

"Put it down," said Will.

"This is a 100-point wine, aged over ten years!"

"Down!" shouted Will.

They crammed together in the dumbwaiter. Will reached outside, pressed an up arrow, and withdrew his arm before it caught as the lift shot skyward.

The guard burst through the door to the kitchen, too late to stop them.

47: OCCUPADO

"Has anybody seen Richard?" A svelte blond tour guide with a walkie talkie and a half-dozen tags on lanyards read his watch. It was 9:33.

"He went to the toilet," said a tourist in a thick New Zealand accent. "Want me to grab him?"

The guide brushed the offer aside, walked to the restroom, and opened the door. A putrid cloud swept forward, and he crinkled his nose. "Richard?" he gagged. "I need to begin our tour. Are you here?" He approached a stall and jiggled the door.

"*Occupado*," grunted the security officer from the outdoor booth.

The guide moved ahead two stalls and knocked again.

"I apologize," Finzel whimpered from the toilet. "Might I have help? I'm in crisis." The lock clicked open. "There's no time for an ambulance."

The tour guide blanched and pushed the door forward. Finzel threw his necktie around the man's neck and tightened the knot.

The guide's eyes bulged. He could neither scream nor

breathe and struggled for his radio. Finzel delivered a swift knee to his stomach, pushed his face into the toilet, and held his head in the water until the bubbles stopped.

A shadow darkened the wall. The old security officer stared down from the doorway, his mouth agape. Finzel lunged and strangled the officer bare-handed.

The man convulsed. His head flushed garnet under Finzel's grip. His fingers brushed the holster strap securing his revolver, but he lost consciousness and his arms fell limp before he could draw.

Finzel locked the man in an adjacent stall. He reattached his tie with a careful Windsor knot in a mirror above the sinks.

Outside, an azalea sat in front of a set of elevator doors—the rightmost in a bank of two on the east side of the lobby. Dirt lay on the surrounding floor.

"Our guide was looking for you," said the couple from New Zealand.

"Mmmm," Finzel acknowledged. He walked into the waiting elevator and pressed the button for the 8th floor. Before the doors closed, he pushed the loose soil into a small pile with his foot and fluffed the branches of the shrub.

48: ALONE IS ALL I'M GUARANTEED

Will and Ian fidgeted in the cramped dumbwaiter making its way to the 8th floor—the ornate Diplomatic Reception Rooms at Main State, where high-level administrators hosted foreign leaders.

Will was nearest the opening, hunched over and facing Ian. Their shoulders touched and their heads were inches apart. The fusty odor of Will's shirt—a combination of cigarette smoke, kerosene fumes, and traces of residual lemon soap—filled the car.

To kids at school, Will stank. To Ian, it was a vital smell that tore through his blood, at once unpleasant and electric. He did not want Rebekkah Batiste or anyone else to have it. He looked away.

After a few moments, Will broke the silence between them. "How much of my conversation with Craig did you hear yesterday before you came out swinging?"

Ian watched the blank wall pass in front of him. "All of it."

Will sighed. "I'm sorry I told Craig we were in bed together. I'm used to everyone calling me gay, but I didn't mean to make it sound like you were, if that's why you're pissed off."

Ian tensed.

"I can fix it," Will continued. "We could keep a chair between us like Daequon and Craig. Rebekkah asked me to homecoming. If she and I can hit it off, that will put down rumors."

"Shut up," said Ian. "Please?"

"I want to make things right."

"Well, you're doing a terrible job!" Ian exploded. "We're trespassing in a federal building, and you want to talk about dating Rebekkah because we might look gay at school? Where's your head?" He turned away. "Date her. Don't date her. Make out. I don't care. Can we just get the phone and go?"

Will fell silent.

The dumbwaiter stopped. A bell chimed. Will opened the door, and the boys exited into a prep kitchen filled with heating cabinets and refrigerators. The red lights on the security cameras went dark.

Muffled voices in the next room paused.

A swinging kitchen door with a square window led to the enormous Benjamin Franklin Dining room. Ian peeked through. A gilded plaster sculpture of The Great Seal of the United States decorated the center of the ceiling above cut-glass chandeliers, scagliola columns, and Savonnerie carpet. A portrait of Franklin from 1767 hung above a fireplace, and bunting from a recent state dinner draped a podium.

Two men walked through the ballroom toward him. One had a suppressed M4 rifle, and the other a handgun—a Beretta M9 with a colossal laser sight. The men wore tactical armor and helmets with visors, and had belts with riot batons, tasers, and handcuffs.

"The guy on the left has a carpal tunnel glove," Ian said to Will, "and I bet you anything the guy on the right smells like Murray's pomade. Winter and Kitteridge. I know them."

Will ground his heel into the floor and frowned.

Ian closed his eyes and sighed. "I was harsh, back in the elevator. There's a lot going on in my head, Will. I'm sorting through it, but I can't do two things at once. I need more time. Let's keep moving. I promise, I'll let you talk when we finish."

Will snapped. "You'll let me talk? Who the hell do you think you are? You can refuse to listen, like you've done all morning, but I don't need permission to talk. You want to control everything, including our friendship, which you turn on and off depending on your mood. One minute I can stay over with you whenever I want, the next minute you don't answer the phone. With Craig, I knew where I stood. He would never listen. He told me I suck outright, instead of all this back-and-forth. You're an asshole." He left for the dumbwaiter. "I'm done."

A warning shot from the M4 splintered the kitchen door and struck the wall over Ian's head.

"Hands up!" shouted Kitteridge from the dining room.

Ian lifted his hands and crept outside, where the man held him at the point of his rifle.

Will, still out of sight, stared into the dumbwaiter.

"Go!" Ian whispered.

"I remember you," said Winter. "Damn near killed us all in Algeria. Who are you talking to?"

Ian ignored the question. "I remember you," he said.

"You don't know how to zero your laser sight."

Winter clenched his teeth.

"I was outside your office in Algiers when your C.O. wrote you up for incompetence," Ian continued. "Did the instruction manual lack pictures?"

"Shut your mouth," said Winter.

"He called you an illiterate, mouth-breathing fuckknuckle," Ian added.

Winter's breathing grew heavy, and he pressed his gun to Ian's forehead.

Ian's eyes rolled up. "Did you ever fix it?"

Kitteridge said, "He asked who's with you."

"There's no one else," said Ian.

Dishes smashed in the kitchen. "Bullshit!" Will screamed. "That's the problem." He entered the dining room with his hands overhead.

Winter swung his Beretta and centered a laser dot on Will.

Will continued, "Ian likes to pretend he isn't with anybody and doesn't need anybody and can do everything just fine all alone. I'm sick of it." He turned to Ian. "You can go to hell."

Kitteridge's crosshairs remained on Ian's skull. "Tie them up," he said to Winter. "I'll cover."

Winter holstered his Beretta and readied a fistful of zip ties.

Ian faced Will. "I'm sorry, okay?" He nudged his head toward Winter. "Let's handle the illiterate, mouth-breathing fuckknuckle, then we'll talk."

"Stop saying that!" Winter screeched. He drew his riot baton, bludgeoned Ian in the stomach, and smashed the club against the boy's back until he was on the floor.

Will scowled.

"Don't be like that," Ian groaned.

"Don't be like what?" screamed Will. "Don't stand here and let you treat me like crap? I feel bad enough about my life, and sure as hell don't need your help to feel unwanted."

"Quiet!" Kitteridge yelled. "Both of you."

Will pointed at Ian. "He acts like he's interested in what I say until he isn't, and thinks he can predict what I will say when he can't. He thinks I'll put up with his horseshit, like I have no other choice. He's a dick. You should hit him again."

Winter brought Ian to his feet by his hair.

Will said, "If you weren't in over your head, Ian, I'd let you handle these Kevlar dudes by yourself in this oh-so-sweet mess you've created."

Kitteridge trained his rifle on Will. "No more talking." He turned to Winter. "Cuff the white kid. I'll get the Chinese."

Ian spat. "I'm in over my head? I can handle this fine. I don't need you or anybody else! I didn't want you here. This isn't the time to dissect feelings! Why can't I just get things done and make right what few things I can?"

Will stabbed a finger. "Fuck you!"

Kitteridge drew near. His eyes moved from the long end of his rifle to his belt, where he kept his zip ties. Will noticed the shift of focus and grabbed a nearby fire extinguisher.

"Don't move!" Kitteridge barked. He clamored for his gun, but fumbled. His zip ties fell to the floor. Will pummeled him with the extinguisher.

Winter drew his Beretta, but Kitteridge stood in the way of a clear shot.

Will parried Kitteridge's attempts to level his rifle, hitting him back and forth with the metal canister. He screamed at Ian, "You pretend you're without feelings, but you brood worse than anybody I've ever met. I can tell you about feelings. I can't get anything in my life right. You keep saying I shouldn't be here? Of *course* I shouldn't be here, Ian! I have no papers! We're almost at war with China, and I'm breaking into a federal building! They'll send me straight to a prison in Shenzhen if this doesn't work!"

Kitteridge backed away. Winter aimed his laser at Will's chest and fired.

Kitteridge's nose evaporated in a cloud of misty blood. He recoiled and howled in pain. His rifle thundered, and a round clipped the base of Will's fire extinguisher. Foam spewed, and the extinguisher took off like a rocket. Will swung it by the hose into Kitteridge's neck, and the man fell to the ground, unconscious.

Winter fired twice more. Bullets fragmented the podium and chipped the plaster columns. Gunsmoke rose, triggering shrill alarms. Before he could fire again, two sharp barbs sank into his ass. Ian had swiped the taser from his belt. Agonizing current stiffened his muscles, and he fell on his stomach.

Ian struck him in the back of his head with his riot baton.

The boys gathered the weapons, threw them in the dumbwaiter, and sent it down.

"We'll be in a lot of trouble for this," said Ian.

"Don't talk to me," replied Will. "I can't stand you right now."

Matt laughed through the earpieces. "Get used to each other. You'll share a cell together and have plenty of time to talk about your feelings."

"Shut up, Matt," said Will.

"I forgot you were there," said Ian. "Can you shut off the alarms?"

"No use," said Matt. "Officers are on the way."

They raced from the Jefferson Room into an elevator lobby, unlocking doors with the ID Ian had stolen. Across the Tabriz rug of the entrance hall, a stately mahogany bombe desk stood beside an antique mirror. Ian pulled away a velvet cordon. Will tugged at the cabinets and drawers. Someone had locked the lowest one.

Ian removed Matt's shiv from his sock and used it to force a clasp. The mahogany splintered, the shiv broke, and the drawer opened, weighed down by the hotel safe.

Will lifted it free and held his phone over the keypad. "Hey Matt!" he screamed over the sirens. "I have a Newlin safe, model 34457. Can you open it with the RF chip in my phone?"

"I think so," said Matt. "You have about two minutes before guards reach."

Ian looked at his watch.

"How long will it take to open the safe?"

"Longer if you keep asking questions," said Matt.

They waited.

"Hey Will," Ian shouted, "I owe you an explanation."

"I don't care anymore," said Will.

"But—"

"Now's not the time, Ian. Maybe I'll let you talk later. The alarms are too loud." He waved his phone over the safe, but it did not unlock.

"Why are you even helping me?" asked Ian.

"Helping you?" asked Will. "I'm doing all the work. Get it through your head! You can't do everything alone!"

"Alone is all I'm guaranteed, so I'm going to have to learn! I can't, with you here!" bellowed Ian. "Besides, you would have died if I hadn't tazed officer Winter!"

"No, I wouldn't have!" Will replied. "His sights were off by a mile! You would have died if I hadn't entered the dining room!"

"I want my shoes back!" said Ian.

"Sambas suit me better than you," said Will. "Why can't you see that?"

"Wear Rebekkah's Sambas, now that you're in love!" said Ian.

"I want yours!" said Will.

The alarms fell quiet. The resulting silence startled both boys.

A gun hammer clicked.

"Hello, Ian," croaked a voice from behind them.

Finzel.

Will darted next door into a long gallery. Seconds later, he ambled back, guided by Tzvi at knifepoint. The scent of heavy aftershave filled the room.

"New Sambas will give me blisters," said Will. "Yours are comfy."

49: CARDIAC EVENT

Finzel pulled the hotel safe from Will's hands and glared at Ian. "I'm sorry I don't have time for one of our talks," he said.

"Next time," Ian replied.

"There won't be a next time," said Finzel. He stuffed his gun in his coat pocket, turned to Tzvi and muttered, "Kill them once I'm gone."

Tzvi squinted his eyes. A stabbing pain that had moved from his gold plate through his skull and into the back of his neck would not ease.

Finzel examined the safe. "We still have no code?"

Tzvi clutched his gold plate. "What?"

"No code?" repeated Finzel, "To open the safe?"

Tzvi waved Finzel off. "There's a drill in the maintenance room downstairs, next to the central computer server. You'll be in place to disable the firewall as soon as you cut through." He inflated his cheek with a soft belch and blew it forward.

"You look terrible," said Finzel.

"I have reflux and my goddamn head is killing me, Richard."

Finzel struck Tzvi's cheek and pointed at the man's nose. "Don't take the Lord's name. I'll pray for relief of your symptoms once I'm in the elevator." A bell rang. The elevator doors opened—the car to the left of the one Finzel had taken earlier. "It's safe?" he asked.

"Go!" said Tzvi.

Finzel hurried in. "Kill them. Now," he said, and disappeared behind the closing doors.

Tzvi faced the boys, clutched his knife, and yawned as though he were trying to pop his ears.

"Work fast," said Ian. "You won't be able to justify killing us in front of other guards. They're almost here."

"I need no justification," said Tzvi. He closed one eye and then the other.

Ian cocked his head. "What's with the blinking? Are you seeing double? From your headache?" He took a step forward. Could he move fast enough if the big man attacked?

Tzvi extended his knife, rattled his head, and belched.

"You're gray," Will said, "and I think your eyes are moving in different directions. Maybe put the knife away and have a seat?"

Tzvi aimed his knife at Will and belched again, winking his eyes back and forth. Sweat beaded on his brow. He moved his knife to his left hand and squeezed his right eye closed.

"Your one pupil's really big and the other's really little," Will continued. "Tell you what. Put your knife down and let's get you a glass of water."

Tzvi pumped his right fist. His knife fell to the floor, and he used his empty hand to grab his wrist.

Ian and Will continued standing on guard.

Tzvi flipped open his poison ring and threw himself

forward from his left leg. The boys stepped from his path, and the big man crashed into the bombe desk. When he turned, they were on the other side of the room. He lunged again.

Ian snatched an antique chair and raised it over his shoulder, but Tzvi fell face-first on the floor. His gold head bounced and became still.

Ian and Will looked down at Tzvi.

Ian looked at Will, then back at Tzvi.

Will looked at Ian, then back at Tzvi.

They looked at Tzvi, then at each other.

Will collected Tzvi's knife and tapped the gold plate on his skull with the blade. There was a pleasant metal ring, but no movement. Ian nudged Tzvi's arm with his foot.

"He's dead," said Ian.

"He isn't dead," replied Will.

"Yes, he is!" argued Ian.

"He has gas!" said Will, before resigning himself to the fact Ian was correct. "Perhaps he had a heart attack. He was clenching his fist."

"It wasn't a heart attack," said Ian. "It was an aneurysm of some sort. He has bolts in his head, and a metal plate."

"It was a heart attack," Will said, pointing to the cadaver. "His lips are pink from antacids. People often mistake heartburn for the symptoms of a heart attack. I wonder if he's on aspirin?"

Ian threw his hands up in frustration. "You can't assume. Before saying it was a heart attack, any medical provider would do a headache history and work out from there. Either way, he was medically fragile. I wonder if his doctor ever talked to him about limiting his activities secondary to head trauma?"

"It was a heart attack," muttered Will.

"Aneurysm," Ian muttered back.

Will screamed again. "Doctor Ian is so damn sure of his diagnosis, isn't he?"

Ian said, "You're a dick, Will!" He pointed at an emergency defibrillator on the wall. "Why don't you jump start him with the cardiac paddles and ask him when he gets up?"

"Hey guys," said Matt through their earpieces. "Security's in the Franklin Dining Room, headed your way. Finzel is getting away. I'm sending an elevator."

"I forgot you were there," said Ian.

A bell sounded. The elevator beside Finzel's arrived.

Guards in the Jefferson Room spotted them and screamed out. Alarms again pierced the air. A helicopter passed low overhead.

The sudden clangor set the hair on Ian's neck on end. His heart jumped, and he took off running in the wrong direction.

Will did not bother calling to him. He tackled Ian in a full embrace, shoved him into the elevator on the right side of the bank, and body-checked him against the wall. The doors closed, and the elevator started down.

50: THE SHAFT

The decommissioned elevator was filthy and smelled of damp, rotting wood. A cockroach scuttled across the floor and into a crack between the walls. Recessed fluorescent bulbs hummed and flickered overhead.

Will continued holding Ian upright.

"Let go," said Ian.

"You're shaking like a dog shitting a peach seed," said Will.

"I'm fine," said Ian, batting him away.

"You'll fall to the floor if I let go."

"I won't."

Will let go, and Ian fell to the floor.

Will threw his hands up. "What the hell's wrong with you?"

"Shellshock," Ian replied, burying his head in his knees.

"I don't mean the helicopter. You're arguing with everything I say!"

Ian looked up. "No, I'm not!" he screamed.

Will raised an eyebrow.

"Sorry," Ian muttered.

"Don't apologize if you plan to keep being an asshole," Will said. He sat down beside Ian. "You pissed me off yesterday when you beat up Craig. Nobody ever thinks I can decide for myself or act on my own. He's been a jerkoff to me for years. You already beat him up once. It was my turn to knock out his teeth, and I could have done it in front of Rebekkah. You robbed me of opportunity."

"I'm sorry if I robbed you of a chance to impress Rebekkah by beating up Craig in front of her."

"Impress Rebekkah? I wanted to embarrass Craig by beating him up in front of her. Impressing her didn't cross my mind." Will exhaled and stared at the corner of the ceiling. "It should have, right? What's wrong with me? Had she asked me to homecoming two weeks ago, I'd have screamed *yes* and run through the streets. I said nothing. Shouldn't I be over the moon? Or feel something? It excites everyone else."

"I'm the wrong person to ask," Ian shrugged. "Anyway, I had selfish reasons for beating up Craig. It wasn't about you."

"Explain," said Will.

An ear-splitting crack interrupted them. The elevator stopped in place. Seconds later, a crash below made the floor tremor. They jumped up.

"Hey guys," said Matt. "Sorry to interrupt another of your moments."

"Hi Matt," said Ian. "I forgot you were there."

"I have your elevator on my display. You're stuck between levels six and seven. That noise was the main cable snapping, and the counterweight hitting the floor below."

"So, we won't move soon?" asked Ian. The car shook and dropped a foot.

"I wouldn't be so sure. The safety brakes have fired, but it doesn't seem like they're holding. Somebody will have to extend a ladder from the floor above you and get you out of the trapdoor in the ceiling."

"Have you heard from Nic?" asked Will.

"Not a peep," said Matt.

The elevator crashed six inches more, taking their balance. It tilted to the right.

Ian looked up at the trapdoor. "Give me a boost."

"You shouldn't," said Will. "The safest place in a stuck elevator is inside it."

The elevator dropped again and leaned left. Will fell into the wall and regained his footing. "Let's go," he said. He laced his fingers and pushed Ian up and through the hole in the roof.

Ian pulled himself out, cutting the palm of his right hand. He reached toward Will. "Grab my wrist. Mind the blood."

Will did as instructed, and Ian pulled him to the roof. The car fell again.

The boys studied their situation. Grease and oil and the scent of damp concrete filled their noses. As Matt surmised, all cables had disconnected from their car. A creaking, corroded safety system held them in place. To the left, six stories down, the car that Finzel had taken earlier sat at basement level. Above it, cables stretched around a pulley in the ceiling. If Finzel's elevator moved up, the cables would move down.

Will viewed the pit far below. "So, why did you beat up Craig, if not on my behalf?"

"This isn't the time," said Ian, evaluating the perilous drop.

"It's never the time," said Will, "so the time is now."

An electric motor whined to a start. The car next to them moved up.

"I'm sending the adjacent car to you," said Matt. "Climb on the roof when it gets there."

"Tell me," Will said to Ian.

"I need more time to figure things out," said Ian. "Anyway, I'm sorry for shutting you out. I won't do it again. I'll always answer the phone when you call from now on, and you can always come over, no matter what mood overtakes me. But, when I get pissed, you have to sleep on the sofa in the basement."

"I'm the guest," said Will. "I get the bed. "

"I get to sleep in my bed if I want," said Ian.

"You can take half," said Will.

Ian looked away.

Will's phone vibrated. Rebekkah.

Are we on for homecoming? You never answered. LOL.

He typed a few words and pocketed his phone.

The elevator creaked and jolted and dropped almost two feet. Will stumbled toward the shaft, planted a hard foot to regain his balance, and caught his breath. Ian extended his arms as though on a tightrope. The opposite elevator continued its slow climb, but was nowhere close.

"We won't make it if we stay here," said Will. "C'mon!" he said, tugging at Ian's sleeve. He ignored the chasm and jumped, catching the steel counterweight cable of the opposite car. He wrapped himself around it like a fire pole. When he did, he cut his hand, and blood ran to his wrist. He held tight through the pain.

Will descended with the counterweight. He secured his ankle through a small loop in the cable. "Be careful when you jump," he said, now several feet below Ian.

The floor popped. The elevator tremored. Ian jumped and grabbed at the steel cable above Will, but missed. In a spasm, he locked his leg and foot around the cable and flipped upside down. Hanging face-to-face with Will, his Zippo fell from under his coveralls. Will caught it one-handed and pocketed it. His phone fell next, and Will repeated the move.

"Can you grab the cable between us?" Will asked.

"I'm trying," Ian replied, his fingertips brushing the steel.

A metallic crack filled the shaftway. The 500-pound motor above the damaged elevator broke free and crashed onto the roof where Ian and Will stood moments before. The safety brakes failed, and the car screamed past them. It slammed into the pit in the basement with the roaring echo of crumpling steel and breaking glass. Displaced air and dust rushed into their faces.

Ian's leg slipped. Weightless and unrestrained, his limbs thrashed. Gravity took hold, and he plummeted.

His shoulder pulled. Pain shot through his palm. Will had grabbed his hand and flipped upside down, tethered by the loop around his ankle. Ian dangled in space, saved by Will's reflexes. Their blood flowed together and down Ian's forearm.

I need more time, Ian had said, again and again. Until the night he lost his mother in Algeria, time was guaranteed. He recalled Deena's blowing hair, her quiet smile, the smell of Shalimar and vodka, and the silence of things left unsaid, and by the time the first tear had streaked along his dusty cheek to his chin and into the void past his sneakers, he was convulsed in sorrow.

"*Cosa facciamo ora, Deena?*" he sobbed.

Will gritted his teeth. "Hang on to my hand," he said, "like we're arm wrestling." An eternity passed as they descended and the adjacent car to rose to meet them. Will's grip remained constant. When it was at last safe, he released Ian onto the roof of the second elevator, then untethered himself.

He touched his earpiece. "Send us back down, Matt," he said. The car stopped and reversed into a slow descent. "Are you okay?" he asked Ian.

Ian sat with a hand over his brow and continued sobbing.

Will stood over him. "You could use a glass of wine."

Ian said, "I'll never see my mom again. I'll not know her when she's little and old and has white hair. I couldn't save her when she died, or my brother when he disappeared. I couldn't stop Finzel like I promised. I botched everything today, and I can't even be nice to you like you deserve. Mom always said I'd make a difference in the world, but I nearly killed us both."

Will remained silent.

"I'm a total screwup. Why catch me?" asked Ian.

"Today, you; tomorrow, me," said Will. "You're no screwup. Not like me. Remember the night you were fighting with your cheesesteak? I nearly blew the soccer game in front of hundreds of people. When it was over, nobody even noticed I was standing on the field. Don't be so hard on yourself. At least you have courage."

"I don't have courage!" Ian replied. "It isn't brave to do things that don't scare you. What we're doing now is nothing." He paused. "Who cares about a government building or an elevator shaft? My mom wanted me to be honest with her the last time we were together. I had no confidence. She raised me to be brave, but she died before I could show her I was."

"Confidence has never been your problem," said Will. "If Rebekkah had asked *you* to homecoming, you wouldn't wobble with doubt."

"It's easy to be confident when the outcome doesn't matter," said Ian.

"Okay, so maybe not Rebekkah, but another girl. One you like."

"I don't like *girls*," Ian shot back. Electrical cables crackled and sparked above them. Bits of plaster fell. He took a deep breath. "I have spent five years waiting. With each passing grade, while all of my friends fell in love and coupled off, I kept saying *I need more time*. It's bullshit. It will never happen." Ian sniffed. "I don't like girls. I never will."

Will tilted his head. "Maybe the right one hasn't come along. Things change."

"This won't."

"How are you so sure?"

Ian shot his hands toward Will. "Because, asshole, when I'm with *you*, my brain goes into overdrive. When we're together, I can climb walls and storm battlements and turn the world into embers. Little, stupid people are insignificant, and all the broken, missing parts of my life I can't piece together stop hurting. You think nobody noticed you on the soccer field? *I* did. You were the *only* person I noticed."

A steel cable popped and flew toward them. Ian pulled Will's foot from under him, and he fell to the roof as the sharp rope zipped past the tops of their heads. They continued down.

Ian continued, "Hanging out with you has been my favorite part about moving to the States, but the better I like you, the faster things circle the drain. You're trying to find a girl. Church is important to you, and Craig already gives you hell about whether you're gay. People will find out about me. Do you want to be in bed with me after all that? Even in the best circumstances, your stepmom would never let you come over. My choice is between being honest and having a friend who catches me when I fall. Do you know how bad that sucks?"

They passed the third floor.

Will continued to look at Ian. "I'm not sure what to say."

"What can you?" Ian interrupted.

"Wait," said Will, interrupting back. "Let me finish for once, would you? I'm not sure what to say without making a mess, so I'm going to ramble. Let me do it. Please? I was hanging upside down over an elevator pit a few seconds ago, and nearly had a steel cable take out an eye. That may be normal for you, but I can't be fluent. Let me talk.

"Li always controlled who my friends are. The friends I wanted never liked me. Church is hopeless. So is soccer, so is math. Before you arrived, I only wanted to make it through to the next day. Sometimes, I didn't even want to do that." He spat dust into the shaft. "You didn't fix my problems. You had my back. It's all I needed. You can have the world when someone has your back."

The wrecked elevator at the bottom of the pit settled with gravity, and more glass shattered.

Will continued, "I have a snow globe at home. Little coins fly around a casino. I used to dream of catching the money and never having to worry. What would it buy that's worth anything? It can't buy eggplant parm when my dad is sick or a motorcycle chase. It doesn't buy a used pair of Sambas, an old pair of jeans, a huge bed in a tiny room or a night of video games. It can't make me feel useful, or buy the fun we're having now. And, it can't buy a medicine bottle—not one that breaks through the tape on my busted-out window and makes me feel like somebody in my rotten life thinks I'm worth a damn. You think you make no difference, but when we're together, a billion dollars doesn't matter. So chill, okay? If a billion dollars doesn't matter, neither does whatever has you so uptight."

Ian sniffed again.

"You guys are sweet!" said Matt through their earpieces. "I can't wait to tell Nic."

"Shut up," said Ian and Will, together.

"I forgot you were there," said Ian. "Anyway, tell her before the Chinese launch their rockets. There's little chance we can stop Finzel."

Will reached into his pocket and handed Ian his Zippo and his phone. Then he grinned and handed over something else entirely. Ian's eyes widened and his heart raced.

51: SAY IT.

In the basement of the Truman Building, Evens Pierre sat on a three-legged stool in front of the maintenance room door. Beside him, a mop stood upright in a bucket of soapy water. He scrolled his phone and made notes on a pad on his knee. Oddsmakers favored Velvet Roller to win at the Big Sandy at Belmont, but she always did better on turf than dirt and forecasters predicted rain.

A distant elevator bell chimed. Footsteps grew loud on the terrazzo floor—a bizarre clicking that resonated through the corridor. A blond man appeared. He wore a credential on a lanyard draped over a crimson tie and carried a hotel safe under his arm. Pierre returned to his phone.

"Forgive me," asked Finzel, "do you have a drill in your closet?"

Pierre pointed deep into the maintenance room. He spoke in a Haitian Creole accent. "Bottom shelf. Lightbulb's out."

Finzel fumbled in the dark. The drill was the size and length of a jackhammer, with a bit the diameter of a soda can. Finzel called out, "What do you do with a drill this big?"

"Dental work," Pierre said from outside.

Finzel tongued a space between missing teeth and did not laugh. Using what light he could from the hallway, he placed the safe on the floor and bore a hole through the door. His fingers found the phone inside, and he transferred it to his pocket.

The Haitian had disappeared by the time he left the maintenance room.

Finzel rushed across the hall to the central computer mainframe—a room as dark as Pierre's closet. He withdrew his gun and extended it into the shadows. Tiny LED lights from dozens of processors illuminated a hand-held cordless vacuum cleaner in the corner.

He recalled his diagram. A red switch beside a bank of CPUs would disable the network firewall. Before redundancies kicked in, he would launch his cyberattack using Deena's phone.

The switch was easy to find, and he threw it. The room illuminated. A lone figure emerged from the shadows beside the vacuum cleaner, and Finzel brought his gun around.

"Hullo, Richard," said Erik Racalmuto.

"My goodness," said Finzel, grinning. "Home at last." He pointed his gun at Erik's head, drew the hammer, and searched him for a weapon. Erik was unarmed.

"What happened to your teeth?" Erik asked, pointing at Finzel's mouth.

"Your brother," said Finzel.

"People who cross him sometimes walk away minus a useful number," said Erik.

"I'm glad you're here," said Finzel. "You are in time to witness the consummation of months of planning. The *coup de grâce*, if you will, to globalist free trade policy."

"Why are you attacking free trade?" asked Erik.

"Sorghum," said Finzel. "Our sorghum trade is off balance."

"Sorghum?" asked Erik.

"The world's fifth most precious cereal grain. Soon, I will begin a war with China. In the conflict's aftermath, we will negotiate export terms favorable to our sorghum farmers."

"How will you start your war?"

Finzel withdrew the phone in his pocket and shook it toward Erik. "With your mother's phone."

Erik erupted into laughter. He attempted to speak, but could not get a word out. Instead, he gasped and laughed again.

Finzel's eyes moved sideways. He held a pink flip phone, bedazzled in rhinestones. His eyes went wide, and he gritted his teeth. He aimed his gun at Erik's head and yanked the trigger.

The hammer fell into an empty chamber with a lifeless *click*.

Erik thrust his fist into his pocket and threw fifteen bullets at Finzel's feet. "Your body man was belching really loud when he put your roscoe in the elevator this morning. I've never heard such a racket. He needs to be under medical care. Anyway, I unloaded it. I hate guns."

Finzel's lips turned down. He threw his pistol into Erik's face, and it connected with a magnificent crack of bone.

Erik recoiled. "*Porca Madonna!*" he cried.

Finzel smiled, but only until the sharp crack of splintering wood sent his eyes to the top of his head. He collapsed forward onto the floor. Victoria Fant stood behind him, Evens Pierre's mop handle broken in her hand. Pierre handed her a zip tie and flashed a credential at Erik.

"Pierre," he said, "Section V, AIT, Taipei."

Erik stanched blood pouring from his nostrils. "Erik Racalmuto. Algiers." His eyes watered, and pain radiated through his face.

Fant bound Finzel's hands and returned the switch on the wall to its original position.

"What's the switch?" asked Erik.

"It's for the outlet that charges the Dustbuster," said Fant from the side of her mouth. "I gave Finzel a diagram that suggested it disabled the IT firewall."

"You don't disable a firewall with a switch," said Erik.

"People believe anything that looks official," said Fant. "Didn't you ever read Robert Cialdini?"

In the basement hallway, Ian and Will forced the stainless elevator lobby doors open and crawled from the shaft.

Ian gripped Deena's smartphone and gazed at it in disbelief. "Matt helped you unlock the safe?"

"It didn't take long," said Will. "I made the swap before goldilocks intercepted me."

Ian searched for words.

"Admit it," said Will. "You needed me along. It was brilliant legerdemain."

"I probably would have been fine," Ian said, at last.

"You're an idiot. I did all the heavy lifting. You'd be dead, and I'd be in the car eating pancakes. Frankly, that doesn't sound like a bad outcome right now, seeing as how you've been an asshole all day."

Ian's mouth hung open. He started a few sentences, but stalled. Finally, he asked, "Do you want to go on a date sometime? It's okay if it isn't your thing, but I'll buy dinner. Pancakes, even. With chocolate chips."

Will turned red. "My stepmom panics at the thought of me dating a white girl. She would toss me on the street if I dated a guy."

Ian's eyes turned down.

Will continued, "You can still buy me pancakes, though. And I need another round of video games. I'm not busy tonight, if you're free."

"Your stepmom won't lock you in?"

"I snuck to Washington before sunrise, broke into a federal building and nearly died in an elevator shaft," said Will. "I think I can make it past Li."

Ian gave Will a middle finger, and they walked toward the computer server.

"You still haven't said it," said Will.

"Said what?"

"*It!*" said Will. "The thing you never told your mom. The thing nobody in your family knows. The great unspeakable that had you sobbing in the elevator."

"I wasn't sobbing," said Ian.

"Totally sobbing."

"I *wasn't!*"

"Say it."

"Haven't I said what you need to know? Do I need to be so formal about it?"

"If you don't say it, I can always convince myself otherwise. I have to hear it so I can decide if we're still friends. Do you need more time?"

Ian laughed, "Fine. I'm gay."

"Was that so hard?"

"Breaking in here was easier," said Ian.

Will rolled his eyes.

"Seriously," said Ian. "It's still the number-one thing no kid wants to be called, and no parent wants their child to be."

"Change is slow," said Will. "Look at how long it took them to get rid of pancake syrup with a minstrel character on the bottle." He brushed dust from his clothes and continued forward, but Ian had stopped and now stood in the hallway with wide eyes.

"Erik?!" shouted Ian.

52: ERIK RACALMUTO

Richard Finzel stirred from unconsciousness and rubbed the back of his head. His fingers found a long, painful knot. An acrid flavor on the left side of his mouth replaced the love of Christ in his heart. He spat and wiggled his tongue away from his cheek, but found no relief. Evens Pierre brought him to his feet and walked him to a security office.

Erik followed them into the hallway. He hung his head at his knees to protect his $600 Saint Laurent shirt.

"Erik?!"

His head snapped up, and on recognizing his brother, the shirt no longer mattered. They rushed and embraced and shouted over one another.

Ian reached for Erik's nose and reset it with a twist of his hands.

Erik screamed. When the pain subsided, he said, "you've gotten good at that."

"It's how he says hello," said Will, introducing himself.

"A pleasure," said Erik. He examined Will and spoke to Ian in Italian. "You found a boyfriend?"

"He isn't my boyfriend," Ian replied. "He isn't gay."

Erik raised a brow.

"What makes you assume I am?" Ian asked, now in English.

"Oh, please!" shouted Erik. "You're wearing each other's shoes. Although, Chucks are more your style, Ian."

"I keep telling him," said Will.

"Shut up, both of you," said Ian. "How did you get here, Erik?"

"Yeah," added Will. "What was all this about?"

Erik continued to pinch his nose and explained everything in a nasal voice. "Our mom was a CIA operative, posing as a consular in the diplomatic corps."

"I only ever knew about the diplomatic post," Ian said. "I only discovered her CIA dealings recently."

"Didn't you ever wonder why she had a new secretary every two months? It's also why she had a different health plan," said Erik. "She couldn't get to a doctor and had to use a sitz bath for—"

"Skip that part," said Ian.

Erik continued. "Last summer, mom picked up intelligence from a source in Thailand. Caleb Reid wanted to start a war with China to bolster President Espinoza's re-election chances and drive up stock he held in Nightwater, the security firm.

"Mom posed as an agent for Caleb Reid in Bangkok and met a Chinese source eager to unload secrets. He gave her access codes to penetrate the PRC internet firewall, then drowned in the Chao Phraya River before Reid's *real* agent could make contact. When Reid found out someone had stolen the codes from under him, he was furious. He suspected mom. He ransacked her office. He searched her computer and went through her desk, but found nothing."

"Reid did it himself?" asked Ian.

"He helped himself to her gin and left his lighter by accident. The entire office smelled like cigarettes for a week."

Ian produced the lighter from his pocket, and Erik nodded.

Erik said, "To measure how deep the rot, mom used Fant as a dangle."

"A what?" asked Will.

"Fant pretended to be a traitor to infiltrate Reid's inner circle," said Ian. "It was the perfect setup. Deena and Fant hated each other. But how does Finzel and his sorghum come into play?"

Erik said, "While Reid was talking to China, Fenzel attended the Global Grain Conference in Stuttgart. At some point, he had a psychotic collapse and became paranoid that the American government no longer existed to serve Americans. Reid sent him to Tenerife for six days, hoping the sea air would help him re-focus, but his nervous breakdown only worsened. He strangled a cocktail waitress with his tie and returned to Algeria obsessed with sorghum. Reid used Fenzel's obsession to further his goals. Both hated China, but for different reasons."

"Finzel, not Fenzel," Ian corrected. "He changed his identity. So how did you escape from the embassy the night of the raid?"

Erik said, "After leaving you, I found Natalie's body." He drew a finger across his throat and whistled. "I moved Finzel's bomb into the computer room and got the hell out before you triggered it. I watched medics pull you from the rubble, then met Fant at a fallback in Tablat. You set Reid's operation back when you blew up the embassy, but by the time we learned mom's phone was in Aunt Judy's urn, it was on a boat to Philly. Reid and Finzel would want it. So, Fant and I hatched a plan. She'd get the phone to Main State, and you'd collect it."

"It makes no sense!" said Will. "Once Fant had the phone, the game was over. Why bring it here?"

"To bait Finzel. We needed to catch him red-handed and smoke out his operatives—Winter and Kitteridge and his body man with the gold head. We were hoping Caleb Reid would be here, too, but bees attacked him yesterday and he was in traction."

"He shouldn't be too difficult to catch if he's in hospital," said Ian.

Erik replied, "I got word this morning that he escaped when detectives came to question him. He stole a medivac chopper and disappeared."

Ian scratched his head. "You could have lured Finzel here without me."

"Yeah," said Erik. "But it's fun watching you scheme. You need practice, and I need a lift home."

"*A fanabla!*" Ian lifted his hands into the sky. "*Sono assente da scuola, quasi morto, e perché?* Will could be in real trouble for being here. We all could."

"Fant's going to erase the video trail and fix everything," said Erik. "She has her man."

"Anyway," said Ian, "We don't have a way home."

"Yes, we do," said Nic Delvecchio, through their earpieces.

"Nic!" said Will. "You're alive! Where did you find a car?"

"I'll explain later," said Nic. "Head back through the kitchen into the loading dock. Matt will direct you."

On his way out, Will grabbed the loaves of bread he had left behind. Ian snatched the bottle of wine.

53: FOR IMPORTUNATE EXIGENCIES AND ENTANGLEMENTS UNFORESEEN

A green Humvee with an enormous American flag flying from the back sped north on Interstate 95 toward Philadelphia. Matt sat in the front with Nic. Ian sat between Will and Erik in the back. They stopped only once, so Ian and Will could get a selfie in front of NPR headquarters. They thought they saw Louise Schiavone, but it wasn't her.

"Whose car is this?" asked Matt, bouncing and shaking with every imperfection in the road beneath them. He removed the registration certificate from the glove box. It read *Tzvi.*

"Tzvi?" asked Erik.

"Tzvi," said Ian. "He's dead."

"Heart attack," said Will.

"Aneurysm," said Ian.

"Does he have a last name?" asked Erik.

"We think he only has one name," said Will. "Like Beyoncé. How did you find his car?"

"It's a long story," said Nic. "It took some time because

of my wrist. I'll tell you the story over dinner."

For the next several minutes, Matt and Nic murmured back and forth. Matt sent Ian a text. Ian laughed and shouted, "Are you serious? Absolutely!"

"What's going on?" asked Will.

Matt took the blue pouch from the glove box and threw it into Will's lap. "$99,000 cash, as I eyeball it. It should pay the rent if Li can't, but I'd save it for college."

Will's eyes grew enormous. "Can we split it?"

"You can buy us dinner," said Ian.

"Take Rebekkah to a proper homecoming," said Nic.

Will blushed. "She texted when we were in the elevator shaft," he said. "It was a weird time to answer her invite."

Ian's stomach turned, but he forced a smile. "Rent a decent tux. Don't go cheap. Erik can help."

"I turned her down," said Will.

Ian's forced smile faded. "Are you an idiot?" he asked.

"Oh, now you're mad he's *not* going out with Rebekkah?" asked Matt.

"It's what he always wanted," said Ian.

"She was never interested in me until I had a motorcycle," said Will.

"So you'll sit at home?" asked Nic.

Will slapped Ian with the back of his hand. "Terry Gross is hosting a fundraiser at WHYY homecoming night. A dinner with sea bass. I was thinking we could sneak in and steal dessert, but now that I have money, maybe we can go?"

"Yes!" screamed Ian.

Erik throttled a laugh. Ian scowled at him.

"Gay," Erik mouthed.

Ian said, "let's break in, anyway, and steal dessert for fun."

The temperature dropped as a cold front brought early snow to Philadelphia. The city came into view. Planes landed at the airport.

Will ripped pieces of bread for everybody from the loaf he had stolen. "This is quality grain," he said, his mouth full, "but it isn't wheat or rye or oat. I'm not sure what it is."

Matt checked email on his phone.

"A note from Coach Osbourne. Craig's out for the season. He wants me to join the soccer team. *You might like to prove yourself to the world,* he writes."

"You'd save their season," said Nic.

Matt sat back. "He can suck my dick. I don't have to prove anything to him or anybody else." He shifted in his seat. "Talk to your brother. I want him to teach me how to fly airplanes."

The enormous Humvee barely fit on Tree Street. Nic parked it half-on-the-sidewalk so other cars could pass.

Daequon Griggs sat on the steps under Mario's awning, shivering. The Professor watched him from inside.

"I wonder why *he's* here?" asked Matt.

Ian opened his door.

"I'll stay in the car until he's gone," said Will. "I want nothing to do with him."

"We talked the other day," said Ian, brushing crumbs. "He won't come at you, again."

"Why entertain him at all?" asked Nic.

"It's an opportunity," said Ian.

Will grabbed Ian's arm. "Promise me something."

"What?"

"I'm your best friend. Not Daequon. If you're friends, he doesn't get the other side of your bed, and he doesn't get to play Xbox."

"I don't think we'll have that kind of relationship," said Ian.

"Or wine," continued Will. "He doesn't drink wine with you, unless I'm there, too."

Erik bit a knuckle, his eyes watering from suppressed laughter. "Not even bi," he muttered.

"Should I play an accordion under his window?" Ian mumbled.

Erik's smile faded. "That was low," he said.

Ian crawled over him to exit and elbowed him in the stomach.

Daequon stood and approached when the car door opened.

"How long have you been waiting?" asked Ian.

"Two hours."

"Does my grandpop know you've been freezing on his steps?"

"No."

"He would have let you in."

Daequon shrugged. "I'm back on the team," he said.

"Good," Ian replied.

Daequon handed him a $5 bill.

"What's this?" asked Ian.

Daequon said, "You gave me $50. I don't have $50 to pay you at once, so you'll have to take it in pieces."

Ian smiled and pocketed it. "$45 more and we're even."

By then, Matt, Nic, Will and Erik formed a loose semicircle around the two. Nic tore a piece of Will's bread and handed the loaf to Matt.

"Anyway," said Ian, "You were right. Everything you said in the library the other day was right."

"I don't need you to tell me." His eyes met Will's. "I'm sorry about what I did to you. I've got no excuse."

Will stared at the ground. Dry snow drifted from the sky.

"I should go," said Daequon.

"Hanging out with Molly Yang?" asked Will.

"She dumped me. Her mom's racist and she doesn't want to push back. Craig wants to meet up. I don't feel like talking to him, but it's something to do." Daequon walked away.

"Hey," Will called. "Talk to him some other night. We're about to open a bottle of wine."

Daequon paused and scoffed. "I don't need pity-friends and I don't like wine."

"I can pardon the first of those sins," said Ian.

"We don't care what you need," said Matt.

Nic said, "You may not need friends. We do."

"For what?" asked Daequon.

Ian took the bread from Matt and threw it to Daequon. "For importunate exigencies and entanglements unforeseen."

The snow became heavy. Daequon wasn't sure what to make of the people surrounding him. He tore at the bread, examined the crust, and stuffed it in his mouth.

54: CODA

A bomb in a baby carriage had exploded on the road to the airport. Deena's SUV had rolled, but she and Ian were okay.

"Don't forget to air down the tires," said Erik.

"I know!" said Ian. "I'm not a child."

Ian and Deena finished with the passenger-side tires as headlights on the horizon drew near. A fierce torrent of automatic weapons fire followed. Deena reached through the broken passenger window, unlocked the door, and opened it. "Get in. You're driving."

Ian crawled through to the driver's seat. Shots pockmarked the car. Deena climbed in and closed the door. He put the car in gear, swung it about, and drove through a barbed wire fence into an olive grove.

"Why am I driving?" asked Ian. Deena gripped her side. Blood pulsed through her fingers. "You're shot?"

"Not in a good place. I'm losing vodka at an alarming rate."

"I'll get you to a hospital."

"No!" she shouted, turning gray. "Get to the embassy.

Find your brother."

"You need him?"

"He needs *you*."

He opened his mouth to argue.

"Ian!" said Deena. "*Con il tuoi anni, dovresti avere più senno.* You know what's happening. Point the front of this car to the embassy, hit the gas, and find your brother." She shifted and nudged the steering wheel. Her speech weakened. "I love you. Be brave. You're a Racalmuto. You need not be anybody other than who you are."

"*Che cazzo!*" screamed Ian, glimpsing Deena's blood as it soaked the floor. They picked up speed as the suspension creaked. "You want me to say goodbye to you here in an olive field, then drive to the embassy like nothing happened?"

"No good about goodbye," Deena replied. "How did you see the IED?"

"What?"

"The IED. In the baby carriage."

Ian sat confused for a moment, then answered, "I thought the woman by the side of the road might have needed help. Who has a baby carriage out at 3 AM? She didn't move. Our headlights hit her, and she didn't flinch. She didn't do a thing to protect her child. She wasn't human."

Deena lost consciousness, and her eyes fluttered.

"Why is it important?"

"Your first instinct was that she needed help," Deena said. A wispy smile crossed her lips. "I have two amazing, intelligent, compassionate sons who will make life better for people around them. They will make a difference in this world."

She became still, and the hand that had been gripping her

stomach dropped to her side. The morning air blew through her window and caught her hair. She leaned against the door frame and her eyes closed. Between them, near the gearshift, was her SIG Sauer P226. Ian eyed it and pressed the decocker, fearful that the bouncing of the vehicle might cause the gun to discharge.

"*Cosa facciamo ora, Deena*?" asked the boy, filled with uncertainty. "What now?"

Erik had been teaching him how to drive stickshift, and he dropped the SUV into fourth gear. He pointed it through the grove, toward the highway ahead and the embassy, beyond.

WANT A SEQUEL? RATE THIS BOOK!

Ratings drive sales. Sales drive sequels. If you enjoyed this book - even if you don't normally rate books - please take a moment to review this one on Amazon.

I read my reviews. Leave some kind words if you're so inclined. I want to know you're reading, and I want to know if you want more.

ACKNOWLEDGEMENTS

A book is only as good as its editors, and I'd like to thank Erin O'Connor and Minda Briley for their contributions and their patience.

Huge thanks to my beta readers: Amy Trout, Chris McCloskey, Inigo Drake, Matt Harry, Rebecca Webber Gaudiosi and Johnathan Kemmerer-Scovner. In whole or in part, you helped me chew over what worked and what didn't, and that was huge.

Rosa Schofield & Ralph Aurora: Thanks for your encouragement as I batted around stupid ideas. I miss laughing with you two.

Uwe Stender: I can't thank you enough for spending time reading this, and for your notes and encouragement.

Curt, Corliss, Malinda and the crew at Rot Gut Pulp: I owe you dinner and beer the next time I'm in Hanoi. It was wonderful reconnecting.

No thanks would be complete without smiling at my husband Ardi Hermawan, who wishes I'd pry myself away from my computer but continues to be a good sport about my writing.

ABOUT THE AUTHOR

CT Liotta was born and raised in West Virginia before moving to Ohio for college. He now uses Philadelphia as his base of operations. You can find him the world over.

Liotta takes interest in writing, travel, personal finance, and sociology. He likes vintage airlines and aircraft, politics, news, foreign affairs, the scientific method, evidence-based decisions, '40s pulp and film noir.

Connect on Twitter @CTLiotta
or at www.CTLiotta.com

—

A portion of the proceeds of this book will go to Mighty Writers, a non-profit that teaches kids in Philly to "think clearly and write with clarity." Groups like Mighty Writers help bring diverse kids who may not otherwise have access to tools and training into writing and publishing.

Please consider donating: www.mightywriters.org

OTHER STORIES BY CT LIOTTA

The Ian Racalmuto Prequels:

Relic of the Damned!

Death in the City of Dreams

An age-of-sail yarn:

Treason on the Barbary Coast!

CPSIA information can be obtained
at www.ICGtesting.com
Printed in the USA
FSHW010753101121
86114FS